Greyladies

SUMMER TERM

"As the wife of a headmaster of a public school, and as one who herself taught for some years, Susan Pleydell has a wide knowledge of schools and human nature.

"Of this, her first novel, Susan Pleydell says: '*Summer Term* was actually written almost entirely during the summer term and though Ledenham is an imaginary place, peopled by imaginary characters, I have used my intimate knowledge of some schools and acquaintance with many others to give an authentic picture of life in a school community.

" 'If I have a purpose in writing novels it is two-fold. First, to contribute something to a class of fiction of which there seems at present to be a shortage; that of civilised entertainments. Second, to write about the kind of people among whom I have lived. I believe in the 'nice people' who are still to be found in great numbers in all walks of life; who though they are aware of the dangers and horrors of our time, manage to maintain the standards of morals and manners which belong to civilisation'."

From the original 1959 dustwrapper

GW00535729

SUMMER TERM

SUSAN PLEYDELL

Greyladies

Published by
Greyladies
an imprint of The Old Children's Bookshelf
175 Canongate, Edinburgh EH8 8BN

© Susan Pleydell 1959

This edition first published 2010
Design and layout © Shirley Neilson 2010
Preface © Claire Smerdon 2010

ISBN   978-1-907503-03-0

Set in Sylfaen / Perpetua
Printed and bound by the MPG Books Group.
Bodmin and Kings Lynn,

Susan Pleydell

Susan Pleydell was the *nom de plume* of Isabel Senior, née Syme – my mother. She was born in 1907 into a well-to-do farming family at Milnathort, near Kinross. They moved to Dollar when she was in her teens, and later to another farm near Rumbling Bridge. She had great musical ability, inherited from her mother, and after a local education was sent to the Royal College of Music to study the piano. She lived in the 'club', a students' residence run by one of her numerous cousins – she had over forty first cousins and seems to have known them all well.

Later she taught at a girls' school in Bexhill at which time she was introduced to Murray Senior, then head of History at Shrewsbury School. They married in 1935. He had two headmasterships in the 1950s, one of a grammar school near Manchester until 1956, the other in South Wales. She taught the piano at Shrewsbury and for some years afterwards.

She had always been well read and having long had an urge to write began in earnest in the mid 1950s. It took a lot of effort to reach publication, but the first novel, *Summer Term,* eventually appeared in 1959. It makes full use of her experience in schools, as does its sequel, *A Young Man's Fancy* (1962). Her other eight novels, the last published in 1977, benefit from her experience in music, her Scottish background – and, of course her own imagination, sympathy and powers of observation.

She died in 1986.

Alan Senior
Sevenoaks, Kent. 2009.

Preface

"It *is* a school story, isn't it?" I asked cautiously. I had wandered into *The Old Children's Bookshelf* in Edinburgh's Royal Mile just as Shirley Neilson, the shop's proprietor and publisher of *Greyladies* books was putting together the prelims for *Summer Term.* My crass suggestion of filling some of the blank pages with sponsored advertising fell upon very deaf ears; Shirley retaliated by asking if I'd attempt to write an introduction.

"It's a *sort of* school story," she replied. "At least — it's set in a boys' school." She assured me that the fact that I'd never heard of Susan Pleydell was not an impediment as somebody else was taking care of the biographical bit. Even so, I accepted the assignment with some trepidation as I don't usually read fiction responsibly, that is, knowing I'm going to have to find something to *say* about the book, preferably (in this case) something good.

My flight back to Canada was delayed for three days, so I read the book on my laptop in one great gulp, pausing only for cups of tea — and it's saying a great deal about the captivating quality of the story that I *could* enjoy reading it on-screen.

Any adult story set in a boys' school will inevitably invite comparisons to R. F. Delderfield's epic novel, *To Serve Them All My Days* (1972) and there *are* a few similarities. Both schools are set in remote locations: Pleydell informs us that Ledenham School is "very difficult to get to," with the nearest railway station five miles distant. Both stories unfold from an adult perspective, the view from the Masters' Common Room rather than the Prefects' Study. In both books we meet young men in their first teaching jobs, but their only commonality is their inexperience; for Delderfield's David Powlett-Jones, teaching is suggested as a cure for his traumatic experiences in the trenches of the Great War, while Angus Cameron is a recent graduate of the University of Edinburgh and a Rugger International. Culturally they are worlds apart – David's father was a Welsh coalminer, while Angus is a clergyman's son – but both share uncertainties about their suitability as teachers and require considerable bolstering from senior members of staff. There are far greater similarities between Algernon Herries, the maverick head of Bamfylde School and Hugh Fielding, Headmaster of Ledenham, known affectionately to both the School and his family as "the Beak."

I can see why Shirley described *Summer Term* as "sort of" a school story – while the school setting is vital to the plot and interactions of the characters, and the Fielding family are entirely preoccupied with school activities, Pleydell barely visits the classroom long enough for us to witness Angus in action as a teacher. Delderfield takes a great interest in individual boys, particularly their interaction with and influence upon the adult characters, but Pleydell's boys are interchangeable and almost featureless, part of the buzzing hive that forms the physical presence of the School, rather than individuals.

The story opens with the Beak and his assistant discussing the impending arrival of Angus, the new maths master. We learn that his predecessor left under mysterious circumstances and our curiosity is piqued by veiled references to a mysterious and difficult "Henry" with whom the new master is to board. Upon returning home, Fielding is met with the unwelcome news that his niece Frances, a "very pretty, spoilt little thing" is coming to stay, fresh from her Paris finishing school. How will this pampered London sophisticate view sleepy Ledenham, with its single cinema? Further complicating matters, Fielding's wife Hester is off to Italy to convalesce following an operation, leaving Clare, the eldest of family, to run the house. We have a fleeting glimpse of the younger members of the family who soon disappear off-stage to their respective schools, only to reappear at the end of term.

So – the stage is set. Three young adults, Angus, Clare and Frances, all finished their formal education and undecided about their futures, are plunged into circumstances beyond their experience. Angus spends much of the drive from Edinburgh to Ledenham wracked with insecurities: "Rather late in the day he was now considering whether he would be able to teach; whether he wanted to teach." We first see the devastatingly beautiful Frances in her first-class carriage: "She was going to Ledenham because she had been sent there and she looked forward to it with unmitigated gloom." While Clare, a newly-trained nurse, has spent most of her life at School House, she finds the prospect of filling the social role of "hostess," a role her mother occupies so effortlessly, plus the additional responsibility of her glamorous cousin, rather daunting.

While Clare, Angus and Frances may be considered the principal actors, from a theatrical perspective *Summer Term* might be seen as a true ensemble piece. Pleydell has created a rich cast of characters, not only strong "character parts," including the Beak and the self-centred Henry (who illustrates the dangers of never leaving the school he attended as a youth), but also "featured players" in the form of the younger masters, and memorable "extras." The more notable "walk-ons" include Miss Perry, older sister of the highly likeable Chaplain; Delia, provider of lavish feasts for famished young people; and Hacket the all-knowing school porter. All these characters have lives "off-stage" and are far more interesting individuals than the schoolboys.

The community of Ledenham School is populated by (mainly) likeable characters, secure in their world. But all is not sweetness and light and the introduction of two "outsiders" plunges the closed society into an emotional turmoil which requires all the skills of its senior members to repair. And yet, even after causing the entire community considerable grief through his elaborate scheming, the black sheep is not cast out but viewed with sympathetic tolerance.

Pleydell presents the school through an outsider's eyes. Frances, although mystified by the traditions and rituals of the tight-knit community, demonstrates considerable maturity in her sincere efforts to adapt to the established customs – and dress! Her apparent confidence contrasts with Angus' lack of security and anxiety to do the right thing, although both are particularly concerned about wearing the right clothes and behaving appropriately at

Lady Courtney's dinner table. Clare, although confident in Ledenham traditions, works hard to emulate her mother's skill in welcoming visitors and putting them at ease and, as Frances astutely observes, "There's quite a bit of technique involved."

Today's readers may be amused at the extensive use of cigarettes as "props," both to cover socially awkward moments, and to signal peace and relaxation. Smoking is also a symbol of maturity; while forbidden to the pupils, cigarettes and pipes are seen as "reasonable grown-up indulgences." Cars are also significant markers of adulthood. For Pleydell's young people, their cars are not only status symbols, but also represent independence and freedom. Clare's two-seater "Tishy," is described as "a much loved and cherished vehicle" and Angus drives a "very ancient but well-cared-for Morris" whereas Henry's car is "a shining monster." The possession of a car is also, as Pleydell informs us in her second sentence, the *only* means of escaping from the school, and cars play a significant role in the young peoples' social lives, not only providing a means of escape, but also to explore the countryside. I was surprised to find that the River Ledd and village of Ledenham are not "real" places though they obviously represent familiar countryside for the author who has a great affection for the fishing spots and peaks.

I seem to have described my impressions of *Summer Term* largely in theatrical terms: the players, settings, props, even costumes, and yet I would not have described it as a "theatrical" book. While the book certainly contains dramatic moments and intrigue, my overall impression is of a highly satisfactory comfort read, a leisurely stroll through a summer landscape populated by quirky but kindly individuals.

"Is there a sequel?" I asked hopefully. Pleydell's ending certainly suggests this possibility.

"Well, yes," Shirley replied. "But it's really about some of the minor characters. The younger brother . . ." While I await its arrival, I look forward to rereading *Summer Term* properly "between covers," rather than on-screen, preferably in a garden, amid the scent of ripening raspberries and the hum of bees.

Claire Smerdon
Edinburgh 2010

SUMMER TERM

CHAPTER 1

LEDENHAM SCHOOL basked in the sunshine of a fine morning towards the end of April, its holiday peace rather deepened than disturbed by the sound of the groundsman's distant tractor and the hammering, clanking and whistling of those tradesmen who invade schools whenever boys leave them.

It was an ancient school in the north of England standing in a great curve of the river Ledd and almost surrounded by hills. Its buildings were of grey stone, its grounds and playing fields, green and ample, were set about with fine old trees and it was very difficult to get to it, or get away from it, unless one had a car. The town of Ledenham at its gates served a large agricultural district, but the School was its main industry and interest, apart from a small but steady supply of knowledgeable summer visitors, and was the reason for its two or three unexpectedly good hotels and shops. The manager of the one small cinema regretted always that his "Regal" was out of bounds for the boys except on the rare occasions when a Coronation film or a *Henry V* stimulated the Headmaster to order a special run-through for the School, but he chose his programmes with one eye on the common room and its ladies, and had his reward in a fairly regular custom from what was, after all, an important proportion of the town's population.

The School House, where the Headmaster lived, housed some eighty boys, but it had been arranged with such tact and skill that the private side of the house and the large garden which sloped down to the river were comfortably secluded, and the Headmaster and his family could play tennis, sunbathe or otherwise disport themselves without being observed by inquisitive or critical eyes.

On this April morning the Headmaster, Hugh Fielding, and his senior assistant master, Mr. Clayton, were at work in the study, surrounded by time-tables, form lists and calendars in an atmosphere of smoky concentration.

"Yes—well, I think that's the lot," said the Headmaster at last, getting up and knocking out his pipe. "You've been away, haven't you? Good time?"

Mr. Clayton was collecting papers with a practised hand. "We had a fortnight," he replied, "London mostly. What about Mrs. Fielding?"

"Oh, doing very well I think, thank you. They kept her in longer than we expected after the operation, but she's been home for about ten days."

"She'll have to take things easily," said Mr. Clayton.

"Yes—she's taking the term off. Going to Italy. Clare is home. Oh—by the way—I nearly forgot. This maths chap—Cameron. Have you fixed up somewhere for him to live?"

Mr. Clayton paused with his hand on the door. "Yes," he said slowly. "It wasn't easy at the last minute, of course. He's going to Courtney."

The Headmaster looked up quickly and met his senior assistant's understanding eye.

"H'm," he said. "I'm afraid that will be rather—expensive for him."

"Yes, sir. It isn't ideal, I know. But there doesn't seem to

2

be a hole anywhere for him this term except these rooms Tomlinson had with Courtney."

"Yes," said the Headmaster thoughtfully. "It was a bit of a crisis Tomlinson going off suddenly like that in a bye-term. Cameron was the only possible substitute. I think he's a good boy. He's got a very good degree. But this is his first job and he's a Scot born and bred—Edinburgh educated."

"Is he the Cameron who was in the Scottish fifteen?" asked Clayton.

"Yes—he did very well. I'd like to staff him, but we'll see how he fits in. It will be unfamiliar ground for him."

The two gentlemen parted and went thoughtfully towards their wives and lunch.

"The Beak's a bit shaken about young Cameron digging with Henry," remarked Mr. Clayton to his wife.

"I'm not surprised," she replied. "Was there really nowhere else?"

"Nowhere obvious enough to refuse Henry's rooms without being offensive. It's not good though. Cameron's a Scot with no experience of English public schools, either as they are or as Henry sees them."

"Golly!" said Mrs. Clayton. "Henry will chew him up. Should we give him the spare bedroom?"

"It may come to that. He's a rugger international. That might help, but I trust it won't have to."

Mr. Fielding went through to his drawing-room and found his wife resting on a sofa by the large, sunny window. "Hullo," she said. "Are you organized?"

"Pretty well. I say, though, Hester—that young maths chap is going in with Henry."

3

"Henry!" exclaimed Mrs. Fielding, "Oh how tiresome."

"Clayton couldn't find anything else, and of course Henry does want somebody to take Tomlinson's place. I don't like it much though. Cameron is promising but very green. I'd have liked him to have an easier start."

"Yes—well, you'll have to keep an eye on it," said Mrs. Fielding firmly. "We don't want another Tomlinson. You'll have to take young Cameron in here for a bit if it isn't working. Now, here's something else you won't like much. A letter from Caroline by the second post."

Mr. Fielding sat down, pipe in mouth, and read the letter she handed to him.

"Park Street.

"Darling Hester," it ran,

"I was so glad to hear from Mother that you are recovering well from your operation and as Clare is at home I hope that you will be able to have an easy and peaceful convalescence. How fortunate that Clare has finished her training so that you can have the benefit of her nursing for a while.

"I am writing in some haste as Geoffrey is rather suddenly going to the States for three months and I am going with him. The social side of the business is very important and he needs my help—but we are in some difficulty about Frances. She, as you know, has been at home since returning from Paris, but she has not yet decided what she is going to do and will be at a loose end. Could she possibly come to you? I suggest it with less hesitation because she will be a companion for Clare. We are flying to the U.S. on

4

Monday. Could Frances come to you on that day?

    All love to Hugh and yourself,

Caroline."

Mr. Fielding sighed heavily.

"How I dislike my sister Caroline!" he said irritably.

"I know," said his wife. "But we'll have to have the child, Hugh. We've got plenty of room as everybody knows."

"How old is Frances? I hardly remember her."

"She'll be about twenty. It's seven or eight years since we saw her and she was a very pretty, spoilt little thing then. Quite bright though."

"What does Clare think about it?"

Mrs. Fielding laughed. "Clare is bored, but willing to cope as usual. Here she is."

Clare Fielding was twenty-two and was the eldest of the Headmaster's four children. She was a thin, brown girl with short dark hair and beautiful grey eyes, and she resembled her mother in her expression of faintly amused calm—a look which is not uncommon in ladies who spend their lives in the liveliness and recurring crises of schools.

"Lunch," she announced. "Have you broken Cousin Frances to the Beak?" She held out a hand to help her mother up from the sofa and grinned at her father.

"He has taken it quite calmly," said Mrs. Fielding. "He's chiefly concerned for you."

"As well he may be," said Clare. "I'll be the one to hold the baby."

The family round the lunch table was complete except for the elder son, Richard, who was abroad on National

Service. Alison, who was seventeen, and Michael, the youngest, discussed the impending visit of their unknown cousin with the detachment of those who would not be present.

"We'll just see her," said Michael. "It'll be interesting, and something to think about for the end of the holidays and not long enough to be boring."

Alison said, "I'd forgotten we'd got a cousin Frances. Why haven't we seen her more?"

"They never come North and we hardly ever go South," replied her mother.

"And we don't like Aunt Caroline much, do we?" went on Alison cheerfully. "Or Uncle Geoffrey. I remember him a bit. Very rich and patronizing. I bet Frances will stir Ledenham up."

"Why?" asked her father.

"Oh well—London and a Paris finishing school. She's sure to be gloriously glam. I wish I could be here to see it. Poor old Clare!" and she grinned at her sister.

Clare raised her eyebrows.

"This coarse phase is nauseating," she said. "I suppose you'll grow out of it."

"I trust so," agreed the Headmaster. " 'Gloriously glam!' Really, Alison!"

Alison giggled.

"All the boys' necks will be permanently twisted peering round at her," she said gleefully, "and the common room will be full of new ties and dirty looks."

"Huh!" said Michael with all the authority of two terms' experience of another public school. "If you think the chaps

6

will take that much notice of a girl you're very far wrong. I don't know so much about the masters," he added darkly, "they might. But then they're all old."

His parents exchanged a look of rather rueful amusement, thinking of their youthful junior masters, and Clare said,

"She may have adenoids and thick ankles."

"Not b. likely!" said Alison decidedly. "Uncle Geoffrey and Aunt Caroline wouldn't have a daughter like that. They'd have drowned her when she was a kitten."

Term was to begin on the following Wednesday and on Monday Ledenham was astir with preparations. The tractor and mowing machines went faster, painters and carpenters hurried to finish their jobs and load their equipment on to lorries. Cleaners clanked mops and buckets in the class-rooms, and in the boarding-houses windows were thrown open and vast quantities of bedding were shaken and aired. Hacket, the School porter, was never off his feet, the station bus brought matrons, and cars of mature years and varying decrepitude brought the bachelor masters.

One very ancient but well-cared-for Morris journeyed from a manse near Edinburgh bearing Angus Cameron, B.A.(Edin.), to begin his career as a schoolmaster, while the other newcomer to Ledenham, Miss Frances Cheriton, travelled towards it by train from London. When the Morris had crossed the Border and was drawing near to its destination, its pace grew slower as Angus Cameron, B.A., grew more and more thoughtful.

He was a very large young man with flaming red hair and spectacles which enhanced his natural look of caution, and as he drove he was wondering what on earth had made him accept a job in a school—and an English public school at that.

He had, as Mr. Fielding said, taken a very good degree in mathematics, but he had taken it without any clear idea as to what he would do with it and when the Ledenham job presented itself, he took it since he wanted a job. Rather late in the day he was now considering whether he would be able to teach; whether he wanted to teach; what boys are really like and how different Ledenham would be from the great Edinburgh day school where he had been educated himself.

Angus's appointment was an emergency one made necessary by the abrupt departure of his predecessor, and it had been a very hurried and rather confusing business. He had gone to the School earlier in the holidays and when, after a gruelling interview, the Headmaster offered him the post on a temporary basis, with the possibility of its becoming permanent, it had never occurred to Angus to do anything but accept with the grateful relief of one who has survived a trying ordeal.

And now here he was, almost into the thing and feeling sorely unprepared. He was cheered as he drew near to Ledenham by the country. Hills were good wherever they were, and he saw some promising fishing water. There should be some nice trout in these burns—only of course they wouldn't call them burns. "Streams" sounded affected and soft. Becks, perhaps, in these parts. He remembered the geography of Ledenham better than he expected and drove slowly but without hesitation to the school gates.

Here he was greeted by Hacket, whom he also remembered having seen before.

"Mr. Cameron? You're staying with Mr. Courtney, sir, but the Headmaster would like to see you. Will you go to the School House? Door at this end, sir."

The School House door stood wide open and Angus rang the bell and stood peering nervously in at the big square hall with its polished floor and vases of flowers. Running feet were heard and a tall girl in shorts came racing down the stairs.

"Hullo," she said. "You're Mr. Cameron, aren't you? I'm Alison Fielding."

"I remember seeing you when I came before," said Angus. "How do you do."

"My father wants you, I believe. And you're to come in for tea afterwards. Oh—here's Miss Wills."

A rather severe middle-aged lady came forward across the hall.

"Good afternoon, Mr. Cameron," she said in an efficient voice. "I am the Headmaster's secretary, Miss Wills. You have come to the wrong door."

Angus started nervously.

"Oh—I'm sorry," he said, "I didn't know—I—Good afternoon—I—"

"It's all right," cried Alison, "come through this way."

"Thank you, Alison," said Miss Wills. "It will be better if I show Mr. Cameron the proper door and then he will know another time."

Frances Cheriton, gazing at the flying landscape from her first-class carriage was, like Angus, filled with apprehension about the future, but her emotions were simpler. Angus suffered from doubts as to whether going to Ledenham was a good idea or not. Frances had no doubts. She was going to Ledenham because she had been sent there and she looked forward to it with unmitigated gloom.

She was an extraordinarily pretty girl. Really golden hair is rare outside the covers of romantic novels; so are violet eyes and rose-leaf complexions, but Frances had them all. The eyes were large and the eye-lashes phenomenal, she was slim and graceful and, since she was the only child of rich and fashionable parents, her natural loveliness was so polished and dressed by the most expensive arts of London and Paris that it was breath-taking.

As Angus followed Miss Wills and learned from her that the Headmaster's Private Residence was one thing and he himself was School Business and quite another, Clare Fielding drove her car down a long and winding hill and drew up smoothly in the station yard. The station was five miles from Ledenham and nobody now knew why it had been placed where it was. There was no town or village near it and not unnaturally it was not at all busy. A few trains carried passengers and goods from the main line ten miles away, meandering slowly among the hills till they came to another more important line thirty miles further on and the rush days were those on which Ledenham School's trunks and a certain number of its boys arrived or departed. Clare was in good time to meet her cousin's train and the sight of an advance guard of trunks reminded her

10

that she did not know what Frances' idea of luggage for such a long visit might be and that her own little car might well prove inadequate.

"Hullo, George," she said to the station staff. "Are these trunks going up tonight?"

"Hullo, Miss Clare. Aye—Willie said he'd get this lot up tonight, and whatever comes off this train."

"We've got a cousin coming from London and I've just thought she'll probably have too much stuff for my car. I should have brought the big one."

"Oh, Willie'll take it. Never worry. She's running late—eight minutes."

Clare went slowly on to the platform and sitting down lit a cigarette, glad to have a few moments of peace. She had spent a busy day among luggage and preparations for the departure of her mother and Alison and Michael, who were all setting out together next morning and she was a good deal oppressed by the thought of running the School House in her mother's absence. It was not, she knew, going to be an easy job for anyone as young and inexperienced as herself but after three years of nursing training in Edinburgh she had been delighted that she was to have a summer at home. The School was always fun, full of companionable people and there were the hills and the fishing and golf. But now there was also Frances. Clare moved uneasily and frowned. Any visitor must add to the burden of the job and an unknown London girl might so easily ruin the pleasure.

The train came into sight and she threw away her cigarette and stood up. The station bus had rattled into the yard, but there were very few passengers and none of them could be Frances except the girl at the end of the train. A dazzling girl, startlingly beautiful in her sophisticated London clothes and almost blatantly out of place in this windswept, hill-country station. Clare's heart sank. This was worse than anything she had imagined. This girl in Ledenham could be nothing but sheer hell. She managed a smile and went forward to meet her cousin.

"Hullo, Frances," she said as cordially as she could. "Do you remember me? I'm Clare."

Frances had looked fleetingly but, Clare felt, piercingly surprised but she smiled a beautiful, radiant smile.

"But of course!" she cried. "I remember you now quite well. How nice of you to meet me. What do we do now? I've got some luggage somewhere."

"In the van, is it?" said Clare. "We'd better see that it comes out. Have you got Miss Cheriton's luggage there, George?"

"Two trunks, suitcase, hat-box. Is that all, Miss?"

"That's all," said Frances.

"Well, now—we can't take it all with us, Frances," Clare said. "We can take what you want immediately and the rest will come with the boys' trunks tonight."

There was not much choice in the matter. The suitcase alone could be stowed with some difficulty in the back of Clare's little car, and the girls got in and drove off.

Clare's car was her greatest treasure. She had a great love for cars and was knowledgeable about them and she handled them lovingly, as a born horseman handles a horse. Her Tishy, a Morris eight and the same age as herself, had been bought with a small legacy from a godmother and was a much loved and cherished vehicle. She had again been pierced by a momentary look of surprise from Frances, and Tishy went humming out of the station yard and up the long hill at speed.

"I should have brought the big car," said Clare. "But I forgot you'd have a lot of stuff. I don't think we'd have got it all in even if I had, though."

"It's quite all right," said Frances politely. "I suppose it will come sometime today."

"Oh, it'll do that," said Clare. "They—or rather he, because there's only one man on the job—is always in a hurry about the trunks. He likes to clear them as they arrive or the situation gets out of hand." She waved a hand towards the hills. "Do you like this sort of country?"

There was a short pause and then Frances said, "It was very nice of Uncle Hugh and Aunt Hester to have me—and you too, Clare. I didn't want to come, of course, and I'm sure none of you wanted me. The country doesn't mean a thing to me."

Her voice sounded rather forlorn and Clare glanced round, but Frances was staring straight ahead and the perfect profile gave no clue to her expression.

Clare said carefully, "I'm sorry you didn't want to come, but I hope you won't feel that we don't want you. Cousins ought to know each other. You know Mummy's going away? You can help me to housekeep and I'll introduce you to country life."

"Well," said Frances doubtfully, "we'll have a bash. Don't think I'm ungrateful. I'm not. But this kind of thing just isn't me."

"Try anything once," said Clare cheerfully. "You may get quite keen on it."

Frances laughed. "I wouldn't bet on it."

"I won't," Clare said, grinning. "We're nearly there. This is the town of Ledenham."

Frances glanced round and then closed her eyes.

"My God!" she said.

Tishy whisked in at the gates and drew up at the School House door. Frances could not remember her last visit to Ledenham and looked round at what was a very beautiful house and setting with a slight rise of interest, while Clare said, "Here we are. I'll tell Mummy." Getting quickly out of the car she ran into the house in time to meet Alison and Michael coming out. Both wore expressions of stunned astonishment and Clare jogged her sister sharply with her elbow and simultaneously achieved a side-long kick on Michael's ankle.

"Hitch your chins up for Pete's sake," she hissed at them. "You look like half-wits. Think of Grace Kelly. Oh, Mummy—here's Frances."

Even Mrs. Fielding's disciplined features displayed surprise for a fleeting moment, but she greeted Frances with easy kindness and led her into the house, while her children turned to relieve Tishy of the large suitcase.

"Gosh, Clare!" gasped Alison. "Honestly!"

"All right, all right, I know," said Clare and went round to Tishy's off side where Michael had disappeared behind the suitcase in convulsions of laughter. "Brace up, idiot! You're not bowled over, are you?"

"It's the heels!" giggled Michael. "Last summer term a

chap's mother walked right over the wicket with heels like that. About six inches high and as thin as spikes, only hers had diamonds on them. You should have seen old Beefy's face!"

"Well," said Alison, laying hold of the suitcase, "if you ask me Frances could walk all over our wicket and Nick and Patsy would do nothing but watch with goggling devotion."

Clare was inclined to agree, but Michael was outraged.

"Alison," he said angrily, "you're an absolute clot. You're so dashed romantic. Patsy's a Test Player and nobody would be so dam-silly."

"Heave," said Clare, "and mind the paint. There are two trunks and a hat-box to follow. Is tea on?"

"Nearly," said Alison. "The new Mr. Cameron's coming and Nick. Cameron's going to live with Henry."

"With Henry!" cried Clare, "Good Lord!"

CHAPTER 2

By the time Clare had shown Frances her room and gone to her own to get tidy, she decided that there was no time to change into more civilized garments. She was not usually seen about the School in slacks except in holidays, having an in-bred and almost unconscious feeling that since the boys were forced into uniform and tidiness, other people ought also to be properly dressed. This was a border-line case with term still two days off; but a new young master coming to tea. Also there was Frances in her high heels and elegant London clothes. Clare shrugged her shoulders and ran downstairs, shouting as she passed Frances' door that Alison would pilot her down. Her thin young figure wore slacks well and hers, though old, were well cut and becoming and her equally old shirt was of a blue which had an interesting effect on her grey eyes. As she went into the drawing-room the two young men who were there with her parents looked appreciative.

Nick Vincent had been a tutor in School House for some years and the young Fieldings knew him well and regarded him as a particular friend. He was a square young man with curly yellow hair and a red face which broke into a wide and friendly grin of welcome as Clare came in.

"Hullo, Clare," he said, shaking hands warmly. "Good news that you're here for the term. We'll get up the Pyke and haul some trout out of Benenbeck."

"We will," said Clare, "and I'm going to take my golf in hand." She turned smiling to Angus and held out her hand.

"How do you do, Mr. Cameron. What's your line? Fishing or golf? Or are you a full-time cricketer?"

Angus cleared his throat.

"How do you do, Miss Fielding," he said. "I'm not that keen on cricket. I like fishing and golf, but—" uneasily, "I don't know if I'll have much time."

Clare and Nick laughed and were assuring him that time could usually be found, "In strict moderation of course," added Nick with a grin at his Headmaster, when the door opened and Frances was ushered in by an unnaturally subdued Alison.

Frances' heels were high, her legs in sheer nylons were exquisite. Her suit was unbelievably smart, her hair shone and her eyes, as she came into a room full of strangers, held a touching look of appeal. There was a tiny silence in which Clare heard her mother give a small exasperated sigh and saw Nick transformed into flushed uneasiness and Angus looking as though he had been stunned, while Mr. Fielding went calmly forward to greet his niece.

"Frances my dear, I'm glad to see you," he said kindly. "Did you have a pleasant journey?"

His wife saw with amusement that he was wearing the New Boy look, a bland geniality which concealed a rapid and devastating summing up. He had a wide experience of inch-long silken eye-lashes and petal-like skins since they are not uncommon in small boys, and he was not easily moved.

Mrs. Fielding introduced the silent and embarrassed young men and led her party hastily into the dining-room where the long table was laid for ordinary tea, with the addition at Mr. Fielding's left hand of a loaf on a wooden platter, a large plate of butter and a jar of fish-paste. To this place came Michael with clean, rather damp hands and his hair showing clearly where the perfunctory dab with the brush had landed.

"Beak," he said in loud, cheerful tones. "Do you want to cut this bread or shall I do it myself?"

"I don't in the least want to," replied his father mildly, and Nick Vincent, who seemed to have recovered some of his self-possession, grinned across at Angus.

"You'll find, Cameron," he said, "that the Headmaster, whom you will always address as Headmaster, is occasionally referred to elsewhere as the Beak. His children are less respectful than we are and use the title direct."

Angus was in no condition to reply, but was saved from any necessity to do so by Michael, who, having spread a thick slice of bread lavishly with butter and fish-paste, turned his cheerful, freckled countenance to his cousin saying:

"Frances—do you know anything about cricket?"

His sisters looked at him, Alison with dismay, but Clare with a certain faith in his common sense.

"Nothing," said Frances. "I've been to Lords. Why?"

"Well," said Michael, chewing firmly, "there's one thing you must know. You must never walk across the squares—specially in heels like these."

Enquiring eyes were turned upon him from all round the table.

"What on earth are squares?" asked Frances, and the Headmaster added, "What made you think of that, Mike?"

18

Mike grinned at his mother, "Remember, Mum? Last year at Beecroft, Fenwick-Smith's ma tramping across the wicket in diamond-studded spikes?"

Mrs. Fielding leant back in her chair and laughed.

"Of course I do," she cried. "What a scene! I'll never forget it. Everybody holding their breath, Hugh, and this woman perfectly unaware."

"Yes—well, Frances' heels reminded me," said Mike.

Frances was looking apprehensive and the Headmaster said kindly,

"Don't worry, Frances. Somebody will soon shoo you off if they see you heading for the sacred turf."

"They'll yell like blue murder," added Michael cheerfully.

"No, no," said Nick, "we'll be more polite than that. We'll educate Miss Cheriton."

Frances turned appealing eyes to Angus.

"You're a newcomer too, aren't you?" she said. "Do you get all this?"

"H'm, h'm!" Angus, blushing again, made his preliminary throat-clearing noise and Clare glanced at him, amused and slightly exasperated, but Michael allowed him to get no further.

"Of course he knows all about it. He's a Rugger International," he cried, and leaning across Clare he addressed Angus in tones of respect.

"I saw the Calcutta Cup match. Our housemaster's beastly stingy with the telly, but I did see that. That kick in the second half—that was you! By golly!"

Everybody except Frances joined in with interest and the conversation was at last flowing happily when the door opened and a melodious voice said, "May I come in? I'm in search of my lodger," and Henry Courtney was in their midst.

Henry was not a young man, but he was exquisite. He was an old Ledenhamian, the only son of wealthy parents, and immediately after a creditable university career he had come back to his old school as a master. The Fieldings, on their arrival, had found him comfortably established in the pleasantest house in Ledenham with his widowed mother and a domestic staff which was unique in its time. Lately the inflation had made it desirable, even for Henry, to have some help with the expenses of his house, though he made it clear that having a bachelor master as a paying guest was just one of the ways in which he helped the School.

The Fielding children had early decided that he belonged to the cat tribe, and they received his purring pleasantries coldly and kept well out of reach of claws. Even Michael was now immediately silent and devoted all his attention to the loaf. Henry had a small up-turned moustache and very white teeth, and he was a picture of casual elegance in a shirt of dove-grey silk and an old Ledenham scarf. The Old Boy colours which looked so ordinary on thousands of worthy Englishmen looked exotic on Henry, mysteriously suggesting past deeds of valour, and Frances lit up a little, rather like a bored traveller in the desert who spots an oasis.

Mrs. Fielding said, "Henry, let me introduce you to our niece Miss Cheriton. Frances—Mr. Courtney. Have you had tea?"

There was another fractional silence in which the

Fieldings watched the impact of Frances, but Henry was a man of the world and his wits did not desert him. He bowed impressively and straightening said, "Thank you—yes. We expected Cameron and waited, but in the end we had it."

"H'm, h'm," said Angus anxiously, preparing uneasily to leap to his feet and follow Henry home without further delay, but this time it was the Headmaster who came to his rescue.

"I wanted Cameron," he said pleasantly, "and since it was tea-time he had it with us. I know that Lady Courtney knows better than to postpone her tea for any school-master."

"Of course, sir," agreed Henry, "since you wanted Cameron—my mother will quite understand. Clare, my dear, how very nice to see you. And how long are we to have Miss Cheriton with us?"

Mrs. Fielding rose and in the general movement Angus was faintly comforted to see Michael look at Alison and make the gesture of one about to be sick, while Mr. Courtney's voice was heard explaining to Frances that though she was, of course, the Headmaster's guest, all the Ledenham community expected to share each other's exciting visitors. Presently, leaving her looking pleased and amused, he collected the unhappy Angus and went away, followed by pitying and slightly anxious looks from the Fielding family and Nick Vincent, who gave a brief sigh and announced that he'd better go and unpack. Frances, hearing that her trunks had arrived, also went to unpack, accompanied by Alison as a sight-seer, and followed by

21

Michael bound for an unknown destination. Clare and her parents relaxed rather wearily in the drawing-room.

"Some explosive material about," remarked Mrs. Fielding, settling herself on her sofa.

"Damn Henry," said the Headmaster. "That's quite a good boy but I don't know if he'll survive Little Campion."

"It's not only Henry," put in Clare. "There is also Frances."

"Frances?" said her father surprised. "What's wrong with her? Quite a pretty girl, I thought."

"Oh, Beak—what an understatement! She's a—a riot," cried Clare.

"Think so? Bit chocolate-boxy."

"Oh no, Hugh," said his wife, "she is devastating."

"I don't know how we're going to manage, Mummy," said Clare. "Without you—and Mike." she added laughing.

"I should have thought Mike would be a liability rather than an asset if things are tricky," said the Headmaster, grinning, but Mrs. Fielding laughed and said, "Mike's invaluable. I never know how conscious it is, but he flows on and never quite puts his foot in it. He had the party thawing nicely when Henry arrived and froze it again."

"Yes," Clare agreed, "even Mike can't cope with Henry."

Angus, following his host to the door, saw a shining monster parked in front of his Morris and Henry, turning to him, said,

"That your car, Cameron? Just follow me then," and drove off so fast that Angus had difficulty in keeping him in sight. They went across the School grounds and out by a side gate, and immediately turned into a short drive which led them to a very charming grey house. For the second time that day Angus was led into a wide hall, not quite so spacious as that of the School House, but even more highly polished.

"If you leave your things," said Henry, "Rogers will take them up. You can put your car away later—or he'll do it— but come and meet my mother now before she goes up to dress."

He opened a door and Angus followed him into a drawing-room with a wide window looking out over a colourful garden to the river. A tall old lady turned to meet them.

"Here is Cameron at last, Mother," said Henry. "Cameron—my mother, Lady Courtney."

She was a formidable old lady with white hair and diamonds and an expression of haughty disapproval and she might well have proved to be the last straw for Angus; but she reminded him of the great lady of his father's parish whose bark, he well knew, was worse than her bite, and he felt unexpectedly at home and met her cool greeting with a hearty hand-shake and a broad smile.

"I hope you had a pleasant journey, Mr. Cameron?"

"Yes, thank you," replied Angus easily. "It's not very far after all, though it's a different country."

"Cameron was detained by the Headmaster," said Henry. "He ought to unpack now. Dinner at seven-thirty?"

"Perhaps Mr. Cameron will join us for sherry as it is his first evening," said Lady Courtney. "A quarter past seven, Mr. Cameron please."

Henry rang a bell and when a neat manservant appeared

he said, "Show Mr. Cameron to his rooms, Rogers. It's notalways possible for us to dress during term, Cameron, but my mother likes us to do so when we can."

"Certainly," said Angus, and bowed himself out.

"This way, sir," said the servant.

Henry's lodgers were accommodated in a very small bedroom and a sitting-room only slightly larger in a part of the house which did not overlook the river, but had a pleasant view to the North. Their meagre furniture and wilting decoration were in surprising contrast to the luxury and elegance downstairs, and Rogers cocked a grimly amused eye at Angus as he opened the doors.

"Your things are here, sir—all that were in the car. I'd have put out your evening things, but I didn't have the keys."

"Thanks," said Angus, surveying his belongings without enthusiasm. "Nothing's locked, but I'll do it. I'd like a bath, please."

"Oh, certainly, sir. I don't know if Mr. Courtney made any mention of arrangements for baths. He has his at this time and generally expects the other gentleman to have his in the morning or at night. But I think there will be enough hot water."

"I hope so," said Angus. "I've had a good long journey and I want it."

Angus knew very little about English public schools, but from books he had read and from what his father had told him of dimly recollected experiences of his own youth, he had gathered that they were dressy, and that "late dinner" in a dinner jacket would be a daily occurrence. He had therefore added to his stock of starched shirts and packed tails and white ties for special occasions, and as he dressed for his first dinner in Ledenham he was mildly gratified that in this matter anyway he had known what to expect.

He went downstairs at a quarter past seven looking very large and very correct, and saw with surprise and austere disapproval his host's soft shirt and velvet jacket.

"Ah, Cameron!" said Henry. "Sherry?"

Angus accepted a glass of sherry and went politely to stand beside Lady Courtney.

"A fine view you have here," he remarked. "It seems to be a very pleasant place, Ledenham. Are you able to get about much, Lady Courtney?" Lady Patterson at home was not, but she was always pleased to be asked about it.

"Do sit down, Mr. Cameron," said Lady Courtney, looking up with an expression of irritation at his towering height. "Not that chair—it's rather fragile and very precious. That one is stronger. Get about?" she went on as Angus lowered himself carefully to the strong chair. "Oh yes, I am out every day."

"My mother is a very busy woman," said Henry. "So much in demand for committees and as a speaker that I am always afraid she will over-tire herself. She doesn't think of that of course, do you, darling?"

"One likes to do what one can," said Lady Courtney graciously. "And so few people nowadays seem to have any public spirit or willingness to help and advise the less fortunate."

The Courtneys' standards were high and the dinner was well served and delicious, but like all their meals it was

25

planned for an elderly lady and a gentleman growing dangerously near the forties and a little anxious about his figure. Poor Angus when he had dispatched the clear soup, the cutlet and the crème brûlé felt almost as hungry as when he began. He was large and young, he had driven a long way and he had plunged into a new and somewhat formidable world. A world, moreover, which contained Miss Frances Cheriton whose appearance had greatly shaken him and added to his need for sustenance and comfort.

After dinner Henry led him into his study for what he called a little chat.

"Finance," he said, amused but rueful. "So boring but necessary, I'm afraid. And then I'll just give you an idea of how we arrange things."

The Headmaster had told Angus the sum which he would pay for his board and lodging with Courtney and it had seemed to him to be a good deal more than he could reasonably afford, but the little chat made it plain that without extra expenditure life would hardly be tolerable and even with it was not likely to be comfortable or enjoyable.

Courtney was surprised to hear that Angus liked a cooked breakfast. He and his mother, he said, had toast and coffee and a little fruit, but no doubt Mrs. Rogers could send in an egg. Porridge was not mentioned, indeed it would hardly have seemed suitable to speak of such a coarse food in Henry's presence. Angus learned that fires would be extra, but that he would not want them in the summer term. Afternoon tea, if he wanted it, would be served in his own room and would be extra. The servants must always be considered. Punctuality at meals and quietness about the house were essential. Angus must not smoke in his bedroom, must be economical in the use of electricity, and baths must fit in with the Courtneys' habits and be moderate in size and number.

"We do our best," said Henry, "but one can't have unlimited hot water."

At nine o'clock Angus said good night to Courtney and went upstairs feeling hungry, angry and depressed. He had been rather grudgingly presented with a latch key and it was in his hand as he looked round the sitting-room which was to be his home for the next three months. His fishing rod, golf clubs and tennis racket stood in one corner. Half a dozen books, mostly mathematical, stood on the writing-table. There was no fire and the two arm-chairs held no welcome or promise of comfort. Angus threw on a burberry and went downstairs.

"Going out?" asked Henry, looking out of the drawing-room door in surprise.

"Going to walk around a bit."

"Oh—well, come in quietly, won't you? My mother is so easily disturbed."

"Right," said Angus and shutting the front door carefully behind him he strode down the drive and turned in to the School grounds, the angriest and most forlorn young man in the North of England.

As he passed School House Nick Vincent emerged from the School Business door and hailed him.

"Hullo, Cameron. Are you going anywhere or are you just exploring?"

"Just walking," said Angus.

"Well, come and call on Patsy Henderson with me," said Nick. "He lives in the Zoo—which is the bachelor house. I eat there, but I've got rooms in School House because of being tutor. Patsy's got some beer in—it's always the first thing he does. Come and help to drink it."

"Thank you," said Angus doubtfully. "If I wouldn't be intruding."

They were walking on together and as they went through the gates he added in desperation,

"Look here, Vincent, before I go to see anybody or drink anything, I've got to see if I can find some food."

Nick looked quickly at him.

"Gawd!" he said, "of course. We were always feeding Tomlinson. O.K., we can do you. Come on."

He led the way into a tall, rather bare looking house near the gates and with a careless bang on a door at the back of the hall, opened it and put his head in.

"Delia," he said, "got any bread and cheese for a hungry man?"

Angus over his shoulder saw a comfortable, rather untidy kitchen, and a very fat, cheerful woman came into view.

"Och away wi' ye, Mr. Vincent," she cried, "you're no' telling me you're hungry again after that steak and kidney pudding?"

"Not me," said Nick. "Here's Mr. Cameron—a fellow countryman of your own—and he had no steak and kidney pudding, I'll bet."

"Oh I've heard about Mr. Cameron," said Delia. "Where are ye from, sir?"

28

They exchanged geographical information while she bustled about and then, handing him a large plateful of substantial sandwiches, she remarked with contempt, "I ken fine what like a denner ye got. Bits o' fish and wee creams! Just mind ye can aye come to me, sir."

"Beef, by gum!" said Nick. "Ye'll no fickle Tammas Yownie. We're going up to Mr. Henderson, Delia."

"Ah well, he's in," said Delia encouragingly, "and the beer came and it's had time to settle."

Patsy Henderson's room was large and shabby and very comfortable with a cheerful fire burning, and Patsy Henderson himself was large and faintly shabby too. He was a little older than Nick Vincent and had a blunt, rather frowning face and very blue eyes.

"Hullo, Nick. This isn't bad beer," he said, and then seeing Angus in his dinner jacket carrying the plate of sandwiches. "Good lord! Who's our dressy friend?"

"Cameron," said Nick. "Billeted on Henry," he added, indicating the sandwiches.

"Ah," said Patsy comprehending. "Sit down, Cameron, and stoke up. Take no notice of Henry."

Angus sat down.

"I would be very pleased to take no notice of him," he said, "but living in his house it isn't easy."

"True," agreed Nick, "we'll have to work out a modus for you. Clare's here for the term, Patsy—while Mrs. Beak goes away to convalesce."

"I know," said Patsy, "I saw her. Delia says they've got some glamorous female staying with them. Cousin or something."

Nick rolled his eyes and threw up his hands.

"Honestly, Patsy—you wouldn't believe it if we told you! Cameron and I drank tea with them today and I have never seen such a dazzler in all my puff. Don't you agree, Cameron?"

"That's so," said Angus cautiously. "She's—very beautiful. I liked Miss Fielding too, though."

"Oh Clare's a poppet," agreed Nick. "She's in a class by herself. But it would embarrass her no end if she found herself sending up the blood pressures all around as this one does. Wait till you see her, Patsy."

"O.K.," said Patsy calmly, "I can wait."

Angus spent two comfortable and enlightening hours with his new colleagues. Hours in which the talk ranged through games and army, schoolmastering and schools, and partly for his benefit but largely because it was their habit, finally settled down to Ledenham School itself and all that concerned it. It was not far short of midnight when Angus let himself quietly and guiltily into Little Campion and went noiselessly to bed. He was warm, he was full of food and beer and the future looked almost hopeful.

CHAPTER 3

FOR the next few days Angus was the innocent and unconscious centre of a campaign which, though hardly seen and little heard, was of considerable magnitude. The passing of Tomlinson was not greatly regretted by his late colleagues because, though mathematicians are scarce and he was quite a good one, he was, as Nick Vincent said, essentially a rabbit. Nevertheless, it was fairly generally felt that rabbit or no Ledenham had given Tomlinson a raw deal, and that Cameron must not be allowed to suffer a similar fate.

A great many matters which were normally submerged came near to the surface in the Cameron campaign. Henry Courtney, rich, sufficiently clever and with a genuine love for the School, had a unique position in Ledenham. He knew everybody. Governors, Old Boys, Dons and the "county", anybody who had any interest in Ledenham School was an acquaintance of Courtney, entertained by Courtney and talked to by Courtney, and he had acquired a degree of influence which, if dangerous is too strong a word, had at least a powerful nuisance-value. He was not a popular member of the common room, but he had his followers there, though they did not perhaps altogether love him, and since he was an able and stimulating school-master, most of the boys whom he taught fell more or less under his spell for a time. Like many other Old Boys, he felt that his school had been at the height of its glory in his own school-days and he looked back to old Dr. Thornely who retired in the nineteen-thirties, to the days of man-servants and maids, of gentlemanly masters in well-ordered houses, and fought against every change, however inevitable or desirable, with all the weapons he could command.

Nobody knew whether Henry set himself deliberately to get rid of masters whom he considered "the wrong type for Ledenham", but he was adept in the use of the raised eye-brow, the amused smile and the murmured joke, and those he did not altogether confine to his colleagues, but used with effect among a few of the senior boys. Tomlinson, young and unhappily conscious of his midland accent and grammar school background, had been an easy victim, living as he did in Courtney's house, and it was an hysterical young man on the verge of a break-down who finally went to the Headmaster and threw up his job.

The first steps in the Cameron campaign were taken by Vincent and Henderson, who decided that Angus, though green and somewhat comic, would, if properly handled, be a valuable colleague; and they were unobtrusively assisted, though they did not know it, by the Headmaster and to some small extent by Clare.

The news flew round quickly that the new maths bloke was the Scottish forward. Scotland had not, it was true, had a very successful season, but that was because there was only one Cameron. Henderson, who had played cricket for England and his university, and was a rugger blue as well, had Ledenham's final word concerning these matters and he spoke of the new-comer with respect. The first point was scored when Courtney arrived in the common room for the beginning of term masters' meeting.

"Where the hell is my cub?" he said in tones of exasperation. "Has he forgotten this meeting? Or is he just too shy?"

Vincent looked up. Most of the masters were already in the room and he spoke clearly.

"Cameron, d'you mean? Patsy took him down to look at the remains of the pitch. They'll be back."

Courtney laughed.

"Kind of Patsy!" he remarked.

"Patsy?" said a comfortable voice across the room. "He was never kind in his life. Not about rugby football. I'll be proud to meet the man he thinks worthy to share his mourning over the first fifteen pitch."

The speaker was the School Chaplain Mr. Perry, a small, ruddy, rotund gentleman of middle-age, with an expansive geniality and a pair of extremely shrewd eyes twinkling behind his spectacles. He went forward to meet Angus when he presently entered the room with Henderson, and in his company Angus found his first masters' meeting a much less confusing and a much more comfortable occasion than he had expected.

Angus had never been so busy in his life as he was for his first week in Ledenham. He spent strenuous and somewhat alarming hours being briefed by Stevens the senior mathematician, a hard-bitten, unsympathetic, but extremely efficient schoolmaster, and a good many other hours being less obviously coached by Vincent, Henderson and the Chaplain. He was so absorbed that it was a surprise to him to see, late on Wednesday afternoon, that the place was suddenly swarming with boys, but it happened, luckily

Angus felt, that he spent half an hour walking about the grounds with Henderson, in the course of which he learned how to acknowledge salutes and lost his self-consciousness. One way and another he met the sets he had to teach with reasonable confidence and his reputation and his size and, to a lesser extent his undoubted ability earned him a respectful reception.

"His rugger will carry him over the first bit," remarked Nick to Patsy, "and by the time that wears off they'll have got used to him and he won't be funny any more."

The Courtney ménage was no more comfortable than the first evening had promised. Angus was in a chronic state of apology to Lady Courtney for the disturbance he caused by going out or coming in or running his bath, and every day Henry pointed out to him in a patient, humorous manner all the things he had done wrong. He managed to keep body and soul together by laying in supplies of biscuits and chocolate and a bottle of whisky, and was resigned to the fact that, loathsome though the set-up was, he had no time to do anything about it for the present. Altogether the Cameron-boosting party considered that it had got away to a good start and was going nicely, and they were hardly to be blamed for leaving out of account the disruptive effect of Miss Frances Cheriton.

Frances spent a few very quiet days in the midst of other peoples' intense activity at the beginning of her visit. To the Fieldings it was very much like the beginning of any other term. They expected to be too busy and absorbed to think of anything or anybody outside School, but to Frances it was something altogether new. The Headmaster was in his study coping with streams of people and piles of paper from morning till night, and Clare, in the absence of her mother, had tradesmen, telephones, matrons and cleaners pressing upon her ceaselessly from all sides. The weather was wet and cold and Frances stayed indoors, observing all that went on, reading a good many detective novels and doing some surprisingly beautiful sewing.

On Saturday afternoon Clare came into the drawing-room at tea time and throwing herself wearily into an arm-chair beside the fire said to Frances,

"Well—I think we're off all right."

"Off?"

"I mean term is really started."

"It seems to take a bit of starting," said Frances looking critically at her sewing. "Shall I pour out?"

"Oh do," said Clare and then went on remorsefully, "Frances, I feel I've hardly seen you since the day you came."

"You haven't much," agreed Frances. "When present you've usually been looking through me at some distant matron or something!"

"Oh poor Frances! This is a deadly time to visit a school. Have you been desperately bored?"

"Not very," said Frances, "hardly at all really. I must admit I wouldn't mind if things livened up a bit, but it's been quite interesting. I never guessed how complicated schools are. From the receiving end you don't see it."

"Well you've been a marvel of patience," Clare said, and looked at her cousin with something approaching affection. She was so exquisitely pretty that it was a pleasure to look

35

at her, and she really had been very good about being left so much to herself.

"Is it always like this?" asked Frances when she had poured out their tea.

"Like what?"

"Oh—streams of people and visitors at nearly every meal and general bustle."

"More or less. But I shouldn't be so busy now that everybody's got back to routine. Also I think the weather's clearing. We'll get around a bit."

Frances said nothing and Clare looked at her thoughtfully. "What do you usually do with yourself?" she asked.

"Do?" said Frances looking up. "Difficult to say. I just do what one does in London. I know a lot of people and I'm out with somebody or other or at parties most of the time. Why?"

"I'm afraid," said Clare, "that we can't lay on that high-pressure kind of entertainment for you here."

Frances looked at her with an amused and unexpectedly friendly smile.

"Sez you!" she remarked. "Don't worry, Clare. It's not so dull as I thought it would be. And I can spend ages fooling about with my clothes and hair when there's nothing else to do."

Clare burst out laughing.

"That's obvious! Your clothes are pretty well a life-work, I should think."

"An interest anyway," agreed Frances.

There was a loud thump on the door and Nick's head

36

appeared.

"Hullo," said Clare. "Tea?"

"Had it thanks. Are you drawing breath yet, Clare?"

"Just about. Why?"

"Patsy and I wondered if you and Miss Cheriton would like to go to the Regal."

"Oh yes!" said Clare. "I remember thinking it was quite a good film. Would you like to, Frances?"

Frances had seen the film before, but didn't mind seeing it again.

"Come in for a sandwich afterwards, Nick," said Clare.

"Well—we want you to come to the Zoo," he replied, and added with a grin, "Delia's feeling cheated because she hasn't seen Miss Cheriton yet."

Both the girls were pleased by the prospect of this mild entertainment and after dinner put on macintoshes and sallied forth cheerfully.

"We usually meet them outside the gates if it isn't evening frocks or car journeys," explained Clare. "There are so many windows, and boys have such vivid imaginations."

"I dare say they're glad of any colour in their drab lives. I was when I was at school," said Frances. She was striding along briskly, her hands in the pockets of her strawberry-pink mac and its hood over her head, and Clare laughed and said:

"Well you'll provide some colour for them this term."

The film was much like other films and was largely an excuse for the coffee and sandwiches and talk in Patsy's study afterwards. The imperturbable Patsy showed to Clare's interested eye none of the symptoms of concussion displayed by Nick, Angus and Henry on first beholding Frances—possibly because he was forewarned; and she gave her cousin credit for appearing to be unconscious of her own devastating prettiness and for demanding no particular attention. Frances ate a great many sandwiches and pleased Delia by her appreciation of the excellent coffee, and conversation flowed easily and entertainingly.

"I gather that Mr. Cameron has got going all right," said Clare when the talk had drifted round as usual to School.

"Is he the red-haired young man?" asked Frances.

"He is," said Nick, "and yes, he's got going. He suffers a good bit at Little Campion I'm afraid, but he's putting up with it."

"He looked fairly meek, I thought," said Clare. "He may not mind being bossed about by Henry."

Patsy looked thoughtfully at his pipe and said,

"I wouldn't say that. He's nervous, but there's six foot four of hefty Scot, and I don't think he'll be very meek if he decides to deal with Henry."

Clare laughed, "Gracious, Patsy! That sounds sinister. Is Henry going to get what's coming to him at last?"

"I don't get all this Henry stuff," remarked Frances. "He keeps popping in and out of conversations in a sinister sort of way, but he seemed quite ordinary when I saw him. Nice, if anything and rather appealing."

Clare and Nick shouted with laughter, and Patsy who very rarely laughed aloud, grinned.

"Frances," said Nick, "we will now tell you about Henry."

"Remembering, of course, Nick," put in Patsy, "that we have the Beak's little girl with us."

38

"I dare say the Beak's little girl could tell us a thing or two we don't know," said Nick. "But she's always so dashed discreet."

"Cagey," agreed Patsy, smiling at her. Clare laughed, but was not to be drawn.

"Do go on, though, about this intriguing Henry," insisted Frances.

"Well you must know," began Nick, "that Henry has very, very high ideals. He feels that the school which he attended as a boy, and now serves with such grace and distinction, has its work cut out if it's to be worthy of him. He also disapproves of the social revolution and most of us are the social revolution."

"Let the show down," put in Patsy. "We don't dress properly and we drink far too much beer."

"So you see," Nick went on, "when Henry gets a chance to raise the tone of the school he takes it."

"What has the poor red-haired young man got to do with the tone?" asked Frances.

"Henry doesn't think he's up to it. He thinks that nobody who wasn't at one of our Great Public Schools and one of the major Universities is worthy. Tomlinson wasn't, poor chap, and now here's Cameron."

"He's all right though," said Clare. "Edinburgh should pass."

"How does Henry do it?" asked Frances with interest.

"Grandeur," said Patsy. "And his mother."

"Likewise he starves them," added Nick cheerfully.

"Now that is nonsense," Clare protested.

"Not altogether," said Nick. "However we don't intend

him to sink Cameron. He's a good chap."

"We're dealing with it," added Patsy.

"Oh lord!" exclaimed Clare. "What are you up to?"

"Now, Clare," said Nick warmly, "come off that school-marm line or go home. We're not 'up to' anything. We're just gently and unobtrusively boosting Cameron."

"I must cultivate Henry," remarked Frances. "He sounds right up my street."

Patsy rose slowly to his feet and offered her a cigarette. "Have another look at him," he said.

Frances smiled up at him. "I intend to."

"He's the gigolo type," said Nick gloomily.

"And so oily," added Clare with distaste.

Frances laughed, "I bet he knows all the answers though."

"He bites," said Patsy mildly.

"Oh well," said Frances, "I can bite too—and scratch."

Clare got up and looked around for her coat.

"Time to go home," she said. "It'll be a great trial if you bring Henry into our midst, Frances, but if you think he's a twin soul go ahead of course."

When the girls reached home Clare found a note waiting for her, and she grinned as she read it and passed it to Frances.

"Dinner at Little Campion on Tuesday! Henry must be intrigued too, Frances. We aren't nearly due for a Courtney dinner."

"How thrilling!" said Frances. "Now we'll get the whole picture—unless Angus is sent to bed before dinner."

Frances made her first public appearance on the Ledenham stage at Chapel on Sunday morning.

"Chapel," said Clare. "Ten forty-five and nice and short. Do as you like of course."

"O.K." said Frances, laconically. "Hat?"

"Customary, but not essential. Not too dressy."

"Oke," said Frances again and disappeared to her room with a faintly mocking smile.

Clare as she ran downstairs in her trim suit wondered with some amusement and some slight trepidation what Frances would consider suitable attire for a service in a school chapel. She had enjoyed Frances' clothes a good deal in the last few days but they were undeniably dramatic, whether in expensive simplicity or the almost grotesque hilarity of what she called her "casuals".

"Tweeds," said Frances complacently, as she made a leisurely descent of the stairs, "right?"

Clare looked at her.

"Pretty glamorous tweeds," she remarked, "but heavenly of course. Come on." They went out into the sunshine and she went on. "You'll look like an orchid in a bundle of hay. Lady Courtney does too."

"Lady Courtney?"

Clare laughed. "Oh yes. Not the same kind of orchid, you know. She's one of the dark, important kind—but just as exotic. You'll see."

"Hell," said Frances. "You've unnerved me."

Five hundred boys attended chapel having no choice in the matter. The masters and their families, who were under no compulsion, attended with fair regularity, and on this first Sunday of term the ladies' pews were well filled. Everybody had heard of the Headmaster's beautiful visitor,

41

and, though it was too well-bred and certainly too well-disciplined a company to stir, far less to stare, there was an air of unusual alertness. Frances, perfectly composed, looked around with interest. Rows and rows of boys in blue suits. The dignity and colour of the masters' gowns and hoods; their wives and children sitting together. The ladies certainly looked as though they were thoroughly familiar with their own and each other's clothes, but they were far from dull and there were some very attractive young women among them. Like Clare, thought Frances, attractive without thinking much about it. She heard a slight disturbance and looked round. A tall old lady, white-haired and important, had come in and was waiting with a slight air of offence while several ladies and children made way for her to pass to the inner end of the pew. She was reminiscent of past Royalty and her clothes could only be described as sumptuous. Frances rolled an enquiring eye at her cousin and received a gleam of amused confirmation as the congregation stood up and she turned to watch the choir and clergy come in, with her uncle, tall, stooping and distinguished, bringing up the rear. The service was short and business-like, the Headmaster preached for seven instructive minutes, and they all streamed out and stood about sociably in the sunshine.

Everybody wanted to speak to Clare, to hear about her mother and to meet the beautiful cousin, but when presently Lady Courtney approached, the crowd round the two girls melted before her. Clare accepted the invitation to dinner and was excused from accepting it again in writing, and then she introduced Frances.

"I have heard of your pretty cousin," said Lady Courtney patronizingly, and putting up her lorgnette looked Frances up and down. Her emotions were perhaps mixed. To a mother who is comfortably established with a bachelor son a pretty girl is apt to appear as a potential danger or disturber of the peace, but when the pretty girl is also clearly a rich girl the prudent mother may well hesitate to be altogether hostile. Lady Courtney's expression certainly mellowed as she priced Miss Cheriton's misty blue tweeds and she spoke graciously of the coming dinner-party.

Clare, who had nothing of affectation about her and who was never anything but her natural self whoever she talked to, now observed with astonishment a display of varied and accomplished manners on the part of her cousin. Frances returned Lady Courtney's stare coolly and spoke to her with a polite indifference in contrast to the friendly interest she had shown in her other meetings, and when Henry, whose gown and hood contrived to look richer and more silken than those of his colleagues, joined them accompanied by his cub, his impressive and significant greeting was met by Frances with an air of one accustomed to receiving homage, and with a slight suggestion of challenge which actually heightened his colour a little. Then she turned to Angus, her smile direct and friendly again.

"As one newcomer to another," she said gaily, "how are you getting on?"

"H'm, h'm," said Angus, whose colour was higher than Henry's, "Quite well thank you, Miss Cheriton. So far," he added cautiously.

43

"Mr. Cameron," said Clare, "I believe my father has asked you to come in for supper this evening. I hope you can? We always have boys in on Sundays after chapel."

"Thank you very much Miss Fielding. I'll be delighted," said Angus.

Henry raised his eyebrows and remarked, "I didn't know you were to be out this evening, Cameron."

"H'm, h'm," began Angus apologetically, but Clare cut in cheerfully. "He didn't know himself. My father only thought this morning that it would be a good chance for him to meet the boys," and she took Frances away.

Prefects to supper, with or without other guests was a regular feature of Sundays at School House, and the invitations were less casual than they appeared. When Angus emerged from Chapel after Evensong, he was firmly collected by the Chaplain, who said,

"We're both going to School House supper and if we're quick we'll get some sherry. If not, not. It isn't offered to boys, but the custom is for them to appear first in the dining-room, so that the grown-ups have a snifter in the drawing-room if they're in time. That's Mrs. Beak—she's a fine organizer."

They had their sherry, and in the ten minutes they spent over it Angus fell completely, blindingly in love. He had gone over the edge of the precipice when Frances entered the room on the day they both arrived in Ledenham, but the business and pre-occupations of the intervening days had held him poised, as it were, in space. Now he plunged down into the abyss.

If a boys' supper-party with their Headmaster is to be a

success, if silences are to be avoided and conversation sufficiently easy and general, a good deal of skilful work on someone's part is required. Boys are usually ready and willing to put their backs into it themselves but they are easily thrown out, and the presence at one party of a dazzlingly pretty girl, who was a stranger to them and to schoolboy life, and of a new master similarly inexperienced and dazed by a sudden descent into love, was a challenge to the experts and was the reason for the Chaplain's invitation.

For the duration of the soup course the Headmaster, Mr. Perry and Clare divided the conversation between them. By the time Clare mobilized the boys to help in removing the soup and substituting the cold chicken and ham, thus carrying out the well-known principle that it eases things to let them move about a bit, Frances had found her feet and assisted by airing her ignorance. She told them of the fright she had been given about heels on the wicket and demanded instruction as to what she must, and must not, do in a school. This line, with hilarious co-operation from the Chaplain, brought in the Head of the School and the captains of rugger, cricket and athletics who were all present, and by the time the fruit salad was on the table the party was ripe, and Angus as ready as he was likely to be for the Headmaster to make the neat switch which brought the new master into the centre as a distinguished athlete. The boys were warmed and genuinely interested, the Headmaster, the Chaplain, Clare and Frances all helped, and Angus found his wits and grew easy and interested himself and did well.

"That was rather fun," remarked Frances to Clare when the guests had departed and the Headmaster had gone to his study.

"Not bad. A bit wearing," said Clare. "I haven't got Mummy's technique."

Frances looked at her thoughtfully. "There's quite a bit of technique involved," she agreed. "It's quite a job, this. But you're very good at it. I don't see how Aunt Hester could have been better."

Clare laughed. "She'd have managed without the Chaplain. I couldn't. You were very good Frances. You came out strong. What kind of job are you thinking of doing eventually?"

"Well—not a matron if that's the way your mind's working," said Frances drily.

"It wasn't," said Clare grinning and offering her a cigarette.

"I don't think I want a job," Frances said when the cigarettes were lit. "I don't need to earn any money and I've no missionary spirit at all. At least not often," she added darkly.

"But you'd get so bored with nothing to do."

"Oh I don't think so—not for a long time anyhow. And I dare say I'll get married presently."

"I dare say you will. But it seems a bit dull just to hang about waiting for it."

"Not necessarily," said Frances.

There was a short silence while they both stared at the fire and Clare tried to summon the necessary energy to get up from her chair and go to bed, and then Frances said,

"Clare—tell me, what made you do nursing?"

"Oh I don't know. I'm not particularly clever and I'd no special line. I like people and I'm interested in medicine."

"I should have thought you'd have plenty to do and rather a good life here."

"No. I wouldn't like to stay here being the Headmaster's daughter for very long," said Clare decidedly. "Anyhow we couldn't afford it. There are three of us still being educated. Richard's university's to come when he's out of the army. I'd got to get myself off the parents' hands."

Frances looked surprised. "Well, you do amaze me!" she exclaimed. "From the way Mummy and Daddy talk about 'my brother the Headmaster of Ledenham' I thought you were way up beside the millionaires."

"Academic eminence hasn't much to do with wealth," said Clare. "There are no rich schoolmasters—except people like Henry with private means. And even Henry's feeling the draught—that is why he has Angus living with him."

Frances looked at her curiously. "What are your ideas about getting married?"

"Me? Oh—it'll happen or not. I hope it does, but I could have a good enough life without it."

"I think you could," agreed Frances soberly. "But I don't suppose you'll have a chance to try. You're very— marriageable."

Clare laughed. "Sez you! Thanks for the compliment—if it is one."

"Oh it is one. Anyway you're surrounded by eligible bachelors."

47

Clare suddenly thought that Frances was trying to get some information, but she did not know what. She got to her feet and said grinning. "Heaven preserve me from marrying one of the Beak's assistant masters. It's just too obvious. And the resulting situation would be fraught with difficulties."

"You wouldn't think that if you fell for one of them," said Frances.

"Maybe not," replied Clare firmly, "but it's what I think now. Bed, Frances."

CHAPTER 4

THE second week of term began with a slight but definite worsening in the Little Campion situation.

There were guests at Sunday luncheon from the Courtneys' County circles, who, following their host and hostess's lead, looked at Angus as though he were some remote foreigner who could speak no English, and conversed steadily across him. Angus went to tea with Stevens, the senior mathematician and played croquet with his children, and his evening has already been described. He went straight to bed on his return from School House, but he spent a restless and miserable night; the satisfaction which he might have felt at having made a reasonable start in his school-mastering and in the friendliness and admiration of the boys at supper, having been swept out of his mind by love. He saw nothing, he thought of nothing except Frances, her eyes, her smile, her lovely slimness, the turn of her shining head. He groaned aloud as he thought of himself beside her, crimson, speechless and clumsy, with red hair and spectacles and nothing whatever about him for a girl to admire; and after a sleep which began about three o'clock in the morning and lasted uneasily till seven, he went down to join the Courtneys for breakfast in a frame of mind which did not promise well for the day he was beginning.

While Rogers the manservant was still in the room Henry looked up from his letters and said,

"By the way, Cameron, I must ask you to be more

considerate in the matter of your engagements. It is difficult for the servants if they don't know in good time whether you will be in or out for meals. There is also of course the courtesy due to my mother. Possibly also to me in some small degree."

Angus made his mouthful last until Rogers had rather unwillingly withdrawn and then said coldly,

"You refer, I presume, to the Headmaster's invitation to supper last night?"

"That was the particular instance," agreed Henry.

"There has been no other. The Headmaster gave me the invitation just before Chapel, you heard of it immediately after."

"From Miss Fielding," put in Lady Courtney.

"From Miss Fielding certainly, but only because she had the opportunity before I did. Would you have expected me to refuse the invitation because I could only give you about eight hours' notice, Courtney? Or wait till I had your permission before accepting it?"

"Really, Mr. Cameron!" exclaimed Lady Courtney, shocked.

"That sounds rather unpleasant, Cameron," said her son. "It is never altogether easy to take a stranger into one's private house, and I am sorry that when I give you a hint as to how you could help us by adapting yourself, you take it in this way. Rather rudely, if I may say so."

"I beg your pardon, Lady Courtney, and yours too, Courtney, if I was rude," said Angus, "but—"

"It is only," interrupted Lady Courtney, in tones of patient suffering, "that as one grows older one does so depend on courtesy and consideration from those who are near one."

"Darling—I'm so sorry," said Henry. "I know how even the slightest tone of anger upsets you. I grovel—and so I'm sure does Cameron."

Cameron got up from his chair.

"Certainly I'm very sorry if I have upset you, Lady Courtney," he said. "If you'll excuse me I'll get along now."

He faced his first set that morning with a mind over-loaded with a mixture of love and resentment, and he made a slip as he demonstrated the working of a problem. He became aware that it was going wrong at the moment when he noticed a ripple in the docile ranks of the lower Vth B set, and simultaneously a hand went up and a spectacled youth in the front row said,

"Sir, should that x not be xy?"

Angus looked at the board, feeling his ears grow hot, and for a panic-stricken moment could not see where the mistake had come. There was a very slight sound of a stifled giggle as he spotted it, and clearing the board with a majestic sweep which did not betray any unsteadiness, he worked the problem quickly and correctly. He kept the set hard at work and held their attention for the rest of the period, but he was much shaken and went through the remainder of the day's work grimly determined not to be caught out again.

"That Cameron chap was bloody unpleasant this morning," said Benson of the VIth to Bates of the Remove. "What was he like with you?"

"Snapped my head off. I asked a civil question—genuine I

51

may add—and he whirled round and tore a strip off me. I half thought he was going to clout my head."

"Pity. He seemed quite reasonable at first."

"Digestive trouble," suggested Bates.

Benson who was in School House laughed coarsely.

"Heart trouble more like. Haven't you seen our lovely?"

The rest of Monday passed for Angus in a chill cloud of depression and Tuesday, which was the day when the School House party was to dine at Little Campion, alternated between hopeless gloom and delirious anticipation.

"White tie I suppose this evening," he remarked to Henry as they rose from lunch.

"White tie? What for?"

"Isn't this the day the Headmaster and—and the young ladies are coming to dinner?"

Lady Courtney said,

"A dinner jacket with black tie is the proper dress, Mr. Cameron."

"Oh," said Angus, "I thought that as there were to be ladies present—lady guests I mean," he floundered, "you would want us in tails."

Henry Courtney laughed in a manner which was almost uproarious.

"What a surprise it would have been for the Beak, and the 'young ladies'," he spluttered. "Never mind, Cameron—we won't give you away. You did your best!"

As the hour drew near—seven forty-five for eight o'clock Angus's fever grew. At six o'clock he began to correct a pile of papers. At six fifteen he realized that if he wanted a bath he must have it now or there would be trouble with Henry, and at six thirty-five he was dressed and waiting. At seven thirty-five, after an hour of deliberation he decided that it would be easier to be in the drawing-room when the party arrived than to enter it after they had assembled, and went downstairs. He stood by the fire alone for a few minutes and then Henry bustled in and, raising surprised eyebrows, glanced suspiciously at the tray of drinks which had been placed in readiness. Lady Courtney joined them, and remarking,

"You are in good time, Mr. Cameron," exchanged amused glances with her son which placed Angus neatly, as he was well aware, in the position of a lout who did not know what was expected of him.

The party arrived. Lady Courtney, regal and important in black lace, greeted her ladies who looked very slim and young beside her magnificent bulk, and turned to the Headmaster with a gracious air of giving deference generously.

Mr. Fielding shook her hand heartily and commented favourably on the weather, and then greeted the two younger men together with friendly informality. The girls shook hands with everybody, Henry bowing elegantly over Clare's hand and then with a flashing smile bending lower before Frances, and Angus in his turn causing them some pain with his vigorous and, it must be confessed, slightly moist grip. They forgave him, however, and while Clare answered Lady Courtney's inquiries about her mother and the Headmaster engaged his host, Frances turned her warm, radiant smile on the dizzy Angus and addressed him in confidential tones.

"Are you finding your way about yet?" was what she said, and seeing him speechless kindly answered the question herself.

"I dare say you still find it pretty muddling. I do. There are such a lot of people to meet all at once and you've got the boys to teach as well. I've only met the four at supper on Sunday. Do you think you'll like schoolmastering, Mr. Cameron?"

"H'm, h'm," said Angus. "I don't know yet. I liked it all right the first few days, and then yesterday I made an awful hash in one set and I've been scared ever since."

He was astonished to hear this being said and blushed hotly, but Frances was sympathetic.

"Oh how grim!" she said. "What happened?"

Angus describing the crisis was able to laugh at it with genuine amusement and Frances joined in.

"It's all very well to laugh now," she said, "but it must have been quite ghastly at the time. I think you coped jolly well. Uncle Hugh," she went on, raising her voice, "Mr. Cameron has been telling me about a near-crisis."

The Headmaster turned, smiling, and Angus found himself telling his story again and, with Frances' assistance, making quite a good joke of it.

"Yes," said the Headmaster, "it isn't funny at the time as I very well know. So does Courtney, I'll wager."

"Indeed I do, sir," replied Henry pleasantly. "It's one of the worst of the schoolmaster's nightmares."

"I remember a story your old Headmaster told of himself," went on Mr. Fielding. "He was in full flow one day

54

and suddenly went absolutely blank—couldn't remember what he'd been talking about. So he turned to the nearest boy and ticked him off for not attending and then said to the class—'Where was I when this imbecile interrupted me?' They told him and he went on from there."

In the laughter which followed he smiled at Angus. "Technique, Cameron. It soon comes."

The dinner, which was the most ample that Angus had eaten in Little Campion was very good. So was the wine, and Angus himself was happily placed between Lady Courtney, who ignored him and devoted all her attention to Mr. Fielding, and Clare, who was in her turn largely ignored by her host, who talked to Frances in significant, low tones with a good deal of laughter. Mr. Courtney and his lovely guest were enjoying each other, and Clare, turning her skill and friendliness to Angus, found him pleasant company and made him as happy as circumstances and his condition allowed.

It was hardly likely that an experienced man of forty would fall in love with the same overwhelming thorough- ness as the twenty-three-year-old Angus and whatever his feelings he should have had greater powers of concealing them. Henry Courtney, however, was, by the end of dinner, so caught by Miss Cheriton that whether his emotions were those of genuine love or not, his jealousy was aroused and his judgement impaired. He should, after twelve years of service under the Headmaster, have remembered the observant mind behind the bland social manner, and he had known Clare from her childhood and might have realized the power of her honest intelligence.

But his thoughts were all on Frances, and when she smiled across the table at Angus and made some friendly little remark about him, Angus was transformed from a lout to a menace.

"A handsome young animal," said Henry's mind and went on nastily to repeat—"young", and it egged him on when conversation became general to be rather unpleasantly funny at his "cub's" expense, even to the point of being compelled to tell them the joke about the white tie.

Angus' face was stony and Mr. Fielding said:

"Your home must be in one of these admirable places which are behind the times, Cameron. It's a long time since I put on a white tie for a private dinner-party, but my father always insisted on it except for the most informal parties. I must say I regret the present-day carelessness about proper clothes."

"I think my home is rather up to date, sir," said Angus. "They're far too busy and short of help to sit down to dinner in the evening. My people have an early supper or even high tea and hurry on to the next job." He realized as he spoke that his tone was too solemn, and was saying "inverted snobbery" furiously to himself as Lady Courtney turned to the Headmaster and, smiling at him with a charm that she did not often use, said,

"Mr. Cameron does not understand us very well yet. He will know presently that there is no need to defend himself or his home from us, and that we laugh at him to help him over the difficulties of being new to Ledenham. But that was naughty of you, Henry," shaking her head at her son.

"I know," said he with charming penitence, "but,"

laughing again, "I couldn't resist it, Cameron. You put me down so neatly." A description of the episode which astonished Angus.

The ladies withdrew and the gentlemen settled down to port, cigars and shop.

"I have two delightfully pretty guests," purred Lady Courtney in the drawing-room. "You cannot imagine, my dears, what pleasure it gives to an old woman just to look at you both."

"Oh, Lady Courtney," said Clare laughing, "my brown and homely countenance shouldn't be coupled with Frances."

"Nonsense, child. You are of opposite types, but don't underestimate your own loveliness!"

"She needn't," agreed Frances unexpectedly. "I'm pretty in the most obvious dumb-blonde sort of way, but Clare gets better and better the more you look at her."

Clare was taken aback and blushed, and Lady Courtney with a laughing pretence of immense secrecy said,

"Now I want you to help me, both of you, with my rather difficult and so touchy young man."

"Angus?" said Clare surprised.

"Of course—Angus Cameron. But I think, dear, that your wise mother would tell you to wait for a time before calling him by his Christian name."

"I haven't called him by it as a matter of fact."

"No—better not. It is different of course with Henry and others who knew you as a child, but Mrs. Fielding is so clever in her management of the young men, and I am sure she would agree with me that it is necessary to handle this one carefully."

"In what way, Lady Courtney?" Clare asked anxiously and a little defensively.

"He comes from so different a background," said Lady Courtney solemnly. "Not, of course, from a lower class as his father is a clergyman. But a day-school and a provincial university. It makes Ledenham difficult for him. It may prove impossible—still we must hope not. Meanwhile he is uneasy and it makes him a little, shall we say, ungracious."

"The other young ones seem to like him," said Clare, "and Be—Daddy thinks he's started quite well I believe."

Lady Courtney smiled.

"That is good hearing! I am so glad. I do want to help him to fit in if it is at all possible."

"And how do you think Clare and I could help?" asked Frances. Clare glanced up sharply, but her cousin's eyes were fixed on her hostess with an expression of mild helpfulness.

"Well really, dears," said Lady Courtney laughing candidly, "I think I am simply going to warn you. Think of the effect of either of you, or both of you, on this very young, inexperienced man with his flaming hair and quick temper and don't, I beseech you, distract him when it is so important for his future that he should give all his mind to doing as well as he can here."

Frances sighed gently.

"You must have thought so much about Mr. Cameron," she said reverently, "I do hope he appreciates all you are doing for him."

"Ah well," said Lady Courtney, smiling a little sadly, "we

don't expect young people to see these things."

"Must we snub him?" asked Frances.

"Oh no, dear! Certainly not. Just a little reserve. And I think I should not invite him to School House again, Clare, till your mother is home."

"My father usually decides who is to come," said Clare bluntly.

"But we could warn Uncle Hugh," added Frances earnestly.

"No, no!" said Lady Courtney rather quickly. "On no account do that. The last thing I want is that my influence should cause the Headmaster to think less well of the poor young man. It would make too much of it. But," she finished gaily, "I know I can leave it to you both to be— discreet."

The men came in and after half an hour of general conversation which was cheerfully dominated by the Headmaster, he rose to his feet and said,

"Lady Courtney, it is time I took these children home. Run and get your mantles, girls," and in five minutes they were in the car, their good-byes politely said, and in ten minutes he had vanished to his study. He liked a pot of tea at this time and Clare went to the kitchen to make it followed by Frances looking highly amused.

"Tea for you?"

"Please," said Frances. "Uncle Hugh has a very quick getaway hasn't he?"

"Very," agreed Clare. "He goes to all the dinner parties and gives good value, but he hardly ever stays after ten o'clock and he loathes hanging about."

She carried the tray through to the study and her father, taking off his spectacles, looked up at her and remarked,

"Rather an uncomfortable party I thought."

"Very uncomfortable," agreed Clare. She hesitated and then went on. "Lady C. would be very angry if she knew I told you, but I didn't say I wouldn't. She put on an impressive woman to woman act about Mr. Cameron after dinner."

"Did she? What was her line?"

"Uneasy, hot-tempered young man, not exactly from the lower classes, but not quite the type. Frances and I were warned to keep from shaking our curls at him, thereby distracting him and adding to his troubles."

"Humph!" said Mr. Fielding stirring his tea. "Very thoughtful of her."

Clare laughed.

"That's what Frances said. She did hope that Mr. Cameron appreciated it."

Mr. Fielding smiled rather grimly and Clare went on,

"I think the poor young man is probably having a fairly bad time. But do you think he is touchy? And perhaps a bit of a goop?"

"He isn't a goop and I shouldn't have thought him unduly touchy. He's on unfamiliar ground, but it's up to him to cope with his living problems."

"I suppose so," said Clare doubtfully.

"Certainly," said her father decidedly.

Clare returned to the kitchen where Frances was sitting on the table drinking tea.

"Her ladyship's a queen b. isn't she?" remarked Frances.

"I've been warned to lay off before in my time but never with such a ham fist. I can't understand why she bothered."

Clare picked up her tea-cup.

"General interferingness I should say. Unless she thinks you'd do for Henry."

Frances grinned widely. "That idea is not without its appeal for dear Henry himself, I fancy, but I shouldn't think it would fit in with mamma's plans. I'm not quite sure what to do about Angus."

"Angus?" cried Clare. "You're not interested in Angus are you?"

"Well—no—not as you mean. Not my style. But he's rather sweet and I don't want him to be crushed to death by Lady C. and Henry."

"There's nothing you can do about that," said Clare firmly. Frances raised her eyebrows and said politely,

"You think not? I can think of two things."

"What?"

Frances got down from the table and collected her handbag and coat.

"Broadly speaking one might A, boost Angus into standing up for himself or B, haul off Henry. C would be a combination of both—rather more tricky."

Clare said solemnly, "Frances, have you ever heard of the danger of playing with fire?"

Frances looked up and smiled. "Yes—grandmamma!"

"Well this is it," said Clare. "You keep out of it. If Angus can't cope for himself he isn't up to much and Henry's one of those best left alone."

"You do intrigue me," replied Frances.

CHAPTER 5

A FEW days after the dinner-party at Little Campion, Angus said at lunch-time,

"I shall be out for dinner this evening, Lady Courtney. I'm sorry not to have let you know before, but I've just had the invitation."

"Very well, Mr. Cameron," said Lady Courtney, coldly resigned, and her son added irritably,

"You seem to have nothing but last-minute invitations. Who is it this time?"

"I'm going fishing with Henderson and Vincent. They're taking supper."

Henry looked up with quick suspicion.

"Just the three of you?"

There was a slight hesitation before Angus replied slowly, "Henderson said they were asking Miss Fielding and Miss Cheriton. I don't know if they'll come."

Lady Courtney sighed.

"I'm afraid that Clare is still very much a tomboy. It has always surprised me that Mrs. Fielding allows her to run about with the young masters as she does."

Henry laughed contemptuously.

"Clare is just as she was at fifteen. Nothing in her head except games and cars and fishing. I shouldn't have thought this sort of thing would amuse Miss Cheriton much, I must say."

"I don't know that she's coming," repeated Angus. Frances had not been sure either.

"Go fishing? Me?" she exclaimed when Nick invited them.

"Why not you?" demanded Clare. "Benenbeck's a heavenly place and you should have a go at fishing if you're going to give country life a fair trial."

"Not my line," replied Frances decidedly, but Nick said, "Come off it! You're too young to have a line. Anyway Clare wants to come. You needn't fish if you don't want to. Bring your tatting if you like."

"Do you go out in boats?" Frances demanded, and on hearing that Benenbeck was a river and you fished from the bank or in waders she agreed to join the party, announcing that she would take a book and all her warmest clothes.

"A fine sporting spirit," remarked Clare rudely. "How do we go, Nick?"

"Patsy's car. Cameron's coming too, by the way. And Delia's packing supper."

Clare sighed with pleasure.

"It's far too long since I went to Benenbeck in Patsy's car with one of Delia's picnics."

Nick grinned at her as he departed and Frances looked with interest at her cousin's pleased face.

Patsy's car was a very ancient Bentley. It was bright red in colour and greatly beloved by its owner and the boys of Ledenham School, though regarded less favourably by Patsy's occasional lady passengers, except Clare who liked cars of character.

It drew up with noisy flourish at School House early that evening and the three young men got out. Angus clean and tidy in neat fishing garments; Nick and Patsy frankly disreputable. Clare bustled out wearing her oldest slacks and windjammer and exclaimed happily,

"Gracious, Patsy! Haven't you had that sweater washed yet?"

"It's only the dirt that holds it together," explained Nick, and they all turned as Frances came out to join them. Her slacks and her suede jacket were scarlet, new and exquisite, and she carried a white blanket coat and a scarlet leather "bucket".

"Help, Frances!" cried Clare. "Where do you think you're going? You can't take a white coat in Patsy's car! Wait!" and she rushed into the house taking the white coat with her.

"Do you mean to say we're going in this?" asked Frances, regarding the cherished Bentley with dismay.

"You're going in it and you'll like it," said Patsy firmly.

Frances handed the scarlet bucket to Angus and tying a silk scarf over her hair, remarked resignedly that if this was her fate she must face it, but she felt too young to perish either from accident or exposure. Clare appeared again and held out an ancient burberry.

"Here—put this on," she commanded. "It's Richard's and fairly filthy, but at least it will keep the oil out."

"What oil?" asked Patsy indignantly, and Nick added, "And it won't be so startling for the fish."

Frances obediently belted herself into the coat, investing even that dilapidated garment with an air of elegance, and they arranged themselves in the car, the two girls in front to share the protection of the windscreen and Nick and

Angus with the rods, baskets, coats and rugs in the back.

Benenbeck was a fine trout-stream about ten miles from Ledenham whose owner, an old boy of the school, was hospitable in the matter of fishing permits for the staff, and from the first time that Clare and Richard, aged fifteen and thirteen respectively, had gone fishing there with Nick and Patsy such expeditions had ranked high amongst their greatest pleasures.

It was, as Clare had said, a long time since she last went to Benenbeck in Patsy's car and she had got out her tackle and made her preparations with almost more than her usual zest. But the sight of Frances in her exotic clothes, the goggling devotion in Angus' face and the amused admiration displayed by Nick and Patsy damped her spirits, and she sat in the car silently taking herself to task.

It was not that she grudged Frances the admiration of Nick and Patsy she was sure. She did not feel in the least sentimental about either of them and had seen unmoved their attentions bestowed upon various young ladies from time to time. But it looked as though this expedition, instead of following the usual gloriously fishy, messy and hilarious pattern was in danger of turning into a party for entertaining and admiring Frances. And this, thought Clare, gloomily, was liable to happen to every one of the things she had looked forward to this term. Not that Frances meant to be a wrecker, she just naturally was one, because her startling beauty absorbed everybody's thoughts and attention whenever she was in sight.

They bundled themselves and their tackle out of the car and Angus for a moment forgot even the lady of his heart when he stood beside Clare gazing with gloating fisherman's eyes at the river. Clare had brought a rod for Frances and as she put up her own and selected her cast, Frances stood with her hands in the pockets of Richard's old mac while all three young men persuaded her to "have a shot at it", assembled the rod and issued instructions.

"I'm going right down to the willows and I'll work up," said Clare at last. "Is that all right?"

"O.K." said Patsy. "Wherever you like." And she went off leaving Frances being helped by everybody to make trial casts.

"I hope I'm not just being plain jealous," she thought miserably, "but it is a bit much to have things like this spoilt," and she thought too of a small, unworthy private worry which had nagged at her intermittently ever since Frances' arrival.

They were in nice time for the evening rise and as Clare made her way downstream her unhappiness receded and was forgotten altogether as she grew absorbed in her fishing. After a time she became aware of Nick, who had waded across the shallows and was fishing quietly a little way out from the opposite bank, and as she came round a bend in the river she caught sight of Angus' red head moving further up. It was nearly two satisfying hours later that Nick, rod in hand, joined her, wearing his peaceful fishing grin.

"How've you done?"

"Not so bad," said Clare complacently and showed him five good trout. Nick peered at them and turned out his own catch.

66

"Beaten you in numbers, but not in weight. I've got seven but only two big 'uns. What about food?"

"About time," Clare agreed. "Where's everybody?"

"Angus isn't far up. I haven't seen Patsy and Frances for ages. He probably took her up to the clear stretch."

They collected Angus, who was looking happier and "more of a person", Clare thought, than she had ever seen him, and having congratulated him on his six good ones they made their way to the car.

"Is it the usual place and a fire, Nick?" asked Clare.

"Sure," said Nick, "and grilled trout thanks to the favourable fates. Not that Delia counted on that, of course."

Clare laughed and explained to Angus,

"Delia has the most ample ideas about picnics and no faith at all in our ability to catch fish."

Angus smiled politely but his look of peaceful happiness had faded and he kept glancing uneasily up the river. They carried rugs and baskets of food to a sheltered little hollow where blackened stones and ashes showed that many picnic fires had been made, and while Nick arranged his fire-place Clare began unpacking the food.

"Do you suppose they've fallen in?" she asked when the fire was well alight.

"Is it Patsy?" jeered Nick. Clare laughed.

"He might have thrown Frances in if she disturbed the fish."

"That might be," agreed Nick, "and then he'd have a remorse, poor chap, when he remembered to notice she wasn't there any more."

Angus continued to fidget and grew more gloomy.

"Should I go and see if they've missed the place?" he asked at last.

"They couldn't miss it," said Nick.

"And you'd probably disturb Patsy in his best run of luck," added Clare. "I wouldn't risk it myself, hungry as I am. We won't wait though, Nick." And together they proceeded with reverent care to the cooking of the trout, taking no further notice of Angus who lit his pipe and went to stare mournfully at the river.

Before the trout were ready Patsy and Frances made their appearance walking towards them down the river path. They appeared to be deep in conversation and when they were within hailing distance and Nick's bellow urged them to hurry, they waved cheerfully without increasing their pace. Frances' hair was blown into untidy curls and though Richard's old mac could hardly have looked more battered than it was when she put it on, her shoes and the scarlet trousers showed marks of water and mud.

"You almost look as if you might have been fishing," said Clare, looking with a return of friendliness at the dishevelled figure and the bright eyes and cheeks.

"I have been fishing," replied Frances, "and I've caught a small trout and a very small trout and an eel."

"And lost two casts and broken her line," added Patsy.

"I'm sorry you felt it necessary to say that," retorted Frances coldly. "I've walked for miles and I'm worn out and I should have thought a bit of encouragement would have been in order. Where is the powder room, Clare?"

"I'll show you," said Clare getting up. Frances collected the scarlet bucket from the car as they passed it and remarked,

"I feel a mess. I'll find a tree and then do some repairs."

When she had run a comb through her hair Clare said,

"Now stop. Make-up looks awful out here. So do smart clothes really. A bit of powder and you're right."

Frances looked up and paused.

"O.K." she said briefly and returned her equipment to the bucket.

The trout, fresh out of the river, cooked and eaten in the open air were delicious, and Delia's picnic was as good as her picnics always were. The party was sharp set and pleasantly tired, and they ate their meal in companionable ease with very little said. It was when large mugs of steaming coffee had been passed round and Nick was lighting the girls' cigarettes that he said to Frances,

"Well—are you a convert to country life?"

"Certainly not," she replied with decision.

"You've enjoyed this though, haven't you?" asked Clare.

"Oh yes—quite. But that doesn't prove anything. I dare say even Patsy tolerates a theatre from time to time. *Julius Caesar* at the Old Vic perhaps."

"Coliseum," Patsy corrected her mildly.

"H'm, h'm," began Angus. "There isn't any need for Miss Cheriton to be converted is there? I mean—there's probably a lot to be said for town life."

Clare, mindful of Lady Courtney's warnings said kindly,

"There's no use trying to keep up the formalities Angus. Everybody's forgotten who Miss Cheriton is and they've never heard of Miss Fielding."

Angus blushed and bowed courteously.

"Thank you," he said. "It's not very nice to feel yourself a stranger."

Frances glanced at him with a gleam of amusement.

"I'm obliged to you, Angus. I don't see either why I should be forced to be a country lifer."

"Every reason," said Nick firmly. "If you only know town life you're only half alive."

Patsy sat up and knocked his pipe out.

"Whether Frances likes country life or not," he said, "you can't expect her to admit she likes it."

"Why not?" asked Clare.

"Too proud."

Frances flushed a little.

"I've never known anything like the—the smugness of people who live in the country and happen to like it," she said angrily. "There's no virtue about it and certainly no cleverness." She got up and added, "Can't we go home? I seem to have been sitting on very hard ground for a very long time."

"Yes," said Clare. "Time to go."

The packing up and the drive home took place in a rather uncomfortable silence. When they drew up at School House Clare said,

"That was grand. Thank you, Nick and Patsy. And compliments to Delia."

"We'll do it again soon, or something like it," said Nick. "Sorry we badgered you, Frances. Forgive us, won't you, and come out again?"

Frances laughed. "I expect so," she said, "and—thanks, all."

The girls went in and Clare began tidying and putting away the fishing gear while Frances hung about and watched her. It seemed, Clare thought, a very small display of crossness on Frances' part to have left behind it such a heavy cloud of discomfort. She herself had found nothing to say which would dispel it and she worked away at her tidying, wondering whether to ignore the episode or to say something, not serious, about it. Frances settled it herself by saying as Clare finished,

"Sorry I was cross and flattened the party, Clare. A bad lapse of poise." She spoke lightly and laughed a little but her eyes were honestly distressed and Clare said quickly,

"Forget it! It was nothing at all."

"Well—it felt as though it was something."

"I think Nick and Patsy were shaken because they'd annoyed you. They were only fooling of course. Not getting at you."

"I suppose not," said Frances slowly.

"Surely you don't think they meant it, you chump?"

Frances hesitated.

"Well—in a way I think they did. Not that they meant to be snorky. But you all feel pretty contemptuous of anyone who isn't keen on games and sport. Except Henry."

"I don't think I feel contemptuous," said Clare looking at her cousin, "but the only things we have here to amuse you are the country things, so I suppose I'm—anxious that you'll join in and enjoy them. So are the others."

"Oh well!" said Frances with a laugh and an impatient shrug of her shoulders, "I'll join in. As a matter of fact I enjoyed the fishing and the picnic. It does get my goat,

71

though, that it all needs such a hell of a lot of instructions."

"Instructions?"

"My clothes are wrong and my face is wrong and I don't know how to act. You know you're always scared that I'll upset Ledenham or let the show down, Clare."

"Your clothes and make-up do look a bit like fancy dress in these parts," replied Clare, feeling that this accusation was uncalled for in view of her own restraint and her very few hints. "Usually when you go to a new place you want to be told a bit what to wear. I would, if I stayed with you in London."

"Oh," said Frances carelessly. "No doubt you'd get by with your classic suit and your nice flowered silk."

There was a moment of silence and then Clare said, "Hell!" very quietly but with great emphasis, just as her father came through from his study.

"Hullo," he said, "I thought I heard Patsy's Peril. Good picnic?"

"Very good," said Clare. "Some nice fish. We ate most of them but there's one for your breakfast. Frances and I have been having a near-quarrel."

Mr. Fielding smiled at them both.

"You've reached the stage when you can snarl at each other have you? It's comfortable when it's established, as Trollope remarks somewhere. Any tea, Clare?"

Frances burst out laughing.

"I never thought of that!" she cried. "Polite self-control is off, Clare. But I'm sorry about that last crack. It was just being bloody—oh—sorry Uncle Hugh."

"I've heard the word before," he said mildly, and Clare

72

grinning said, "Not once, but again and again. Tea in a minute, Beak."

Frances went off to bed and Clare put an extra cup on her father's tray and carried it through to his study.

"Are you very busy, Beak?"

"No. Are you going to have a cuppa with me? Good. Cigarette?" Clare sat down and her father, having lit her cigarette for her, began filling his pipe and said,

"The picnic was all right was it? How did Frances like it?" Clare laughed.

"She went out in the most gorgeous and exotic clothes, but she got quite nice and untidy. I think she liked it. Patsy took her off and presided over her efforts."

"Patsy did? I thought he was a solitary and silent fisherman."

"So he is usually; but Frances is very attractive."

"Yes. She's a pretty girl," said Mr. Fielding moderately.

"There are one or two things I want to talk to you about," Clare said and brought forward her first item which concerned the matron's department of the house. When her father had dealt with it she went on.

"The next thing is silly really. Henry has asked Frances to go out with him tomorrow. The idea is to show her a bit of the Lakes, so they're starting immediately after lunch and not getting home till late."

"He didn't ask you?"

"No," said Clare.

"Well, if Frances likes to go there's no reason why she shouldn't, is there?"

"No—not really. Certainly not enough to stop it. I just

73

thought I'd tell you."

"Duly noted," said her father.

There was a pause. Clare looked rather uneasily at the fire for a moment and then she said,

"Beak—there's a friend of mine who wants to come." Mr. Fielding turned his calm gaze at her and saw that she had flushed a little.

"That's nothing unusual is it? Your friends, also Richard's, Alison's and Mike's come like an ever-rolling stream."

"True," said Clare laughing. "But this is a bit unusual. This, Beak, is a follower, to put it bluntly."

"I've seen a few of them about too," said her father mildly. "Is this one likely to be more successful in his pursuit? Who is he?"

"Yes," said Clare, "I think he is, perhaps. His name is Nevill Crichton and I knew him in Edinburgh. He's been doing his National Service in the Far East so I haven't seen him for more than a year, but we've been writing and I heard today that he's coming home and—and he wants to come."

"Well, my darling, let him come by all means."

"Do you think—you don't think it should be put off till Mummy comes home?"

Mr. Fielding smiled.

"I think you'd be adequately chaperoned."

Clare laughed and hesitated a little.

"I sort of feel," she said diffidently, "that the atmosphere is a bit—well, abnormal. Mummy being away and everything."

Her father met her eyes.

"I don't think there's much in that," he said decidedly. "A young man who is properly in love doesn't need a carefully set stage. You'll be busier and less peaceful without Mummy, but he'll take things as he finds them. Tell me more about him."

Clare told him about Nevill; how promising he was as a surgeon and as much as she knew about his family, and then she got up.

"I'll tell him to come then. Thank you, Beak. I hope you'll like him."

"I'm sure I shall if you do. Does Mummy know?"

"Sort of," said Clare. Her father smiled and held out his hand.

"Come and give me a hug. Bless you, darling. I hope he's good enough."

Clare went up to her room and taking a photograph from one of the drawers of her writing-table and a letter from her pocket she sat down. The photograph showed a young officer in tropical uniform. He was tall and a little angular with dark hair and a thin intelligent face which wore a cheerful, rather lop-sided grin and Clare smiled in sympathy as she looked at it.

The letter said:

"My darling Clare,

I have been perfectly restrained for a very long time because I don't hold with chaps marrying before they can support a wife, and I have a horror of long, vague engagements or understandings. I think though that you have known well enough about my feelings for you and I hope it isn't wishful thinking on my part which makes me think you like me a bit. I'll be in England almost as soon as this reaches you. May I come to Ledenham?

Yours,

Nevill."

Before she went to bed Clare wrote a very brief note telling Nevill to come when he liked, but she thought about it for a long time before she wrote it. However sure a girl may feel that a young man is so genuinely and permanently in love with her that he will want to marry her she does not know it until he tells her so. Clare had been sure enough of Nevill's feelings and her own to be puzzled and a little hurt when he left Edinburgh without asking her to be engaged to him, and though his letters had come regularly and often, and had told her of all that he was doing, of his plans and ideas for his future as though it was her right to know and he counted on her interest, he said nothing of love. She had come to understand pretty well why he did not and today's letter did not much surprise her and made her very happy, but at the prospect of Nevill coming to Ledenham for the first time now, she was haunted, and angry with herself for being haunted by thoughts of Frances.

It was true, as she had told her father, that the atmosphere was abnormal. At least enough to be a threat simply as a potential interruption to the happiness of having Nevill at home. Every one of the young men who had come in contact with Frances had been to some extent changed by her, and the stability and friendships and fun of home had been disturbed so that poor Clare felt that they would never again be uncomplicated and young as they had been before Frances came. There was Nevill and so long as there was Nevill there would be no room for regrets about the past. But, this was the crux and Clare looked at it firmly, would Nevill be changed by Frances too? She got up and went to her writing-table. Her father was perfectly right. Nevill must come and see her as she was. If he loved her enough Frances would not change him, and if he was ever going to be susceptible to the attractions of other women it might as well be Frances and better now than later.

CHAPTER 6

"THERE'S a young man coming to stay," Clare said to Frances next morning.

"What a lot of young men we have about the place," replied Frances indifferently. "Who is this one? Another promising young schoolmaster?"

"No. This one's a doctor."

"Oh? That'll make a change. They tend to be a bit earnest and tell you about operations of course. When is he coming?"

"I'm not sure. He's on his way home from the Far East," said Clare. "He's a friend of mine, actually. Not a school visitor."

Frances, who had an eye for colour and design, had taken on the arrangement of flowers for the house, and as she enjoyed doing it and had plenty of time she produced such enterprising decorations that Clare felt that the familiar rooms looked quite self-conscious. This conversation took place while she was composing a bowl of mixed flowers for the dining-room table, and she was giving most of her attention to her colours till something in Clare's voice made her look up.

"Special?" she asked.

Clare hesitated and gave herself time for a moment's thought by carrying vases to the sink and filling them noisily with water. If she admitted that Nevill was "special" she knew that Frances would be friendly and interested and perfectly innocent of any desire to spoil things for her.

But it was not what Frances did, it was what she was that fascinated people, and she could not prevent it however much she might want to.

"Special?" repeated Clare, carrying the vases back to the table. "I don't know yet."

"Don't you?" said Frances and suddenly smiled her warm, radiant smile and said as Alison might have done, "Oh Clare, it would be lovely if he was! I'd love to be here when you get engaged."

"Would you?" said Clare surprised. "Why?"

"Well—it would be so exciting. Hardly anybody I know has got engaged—nobody I know well. And you see I haven't got anybody of my own to get excited about. An 'only' misses all that."

She looked very young, and Clare, who was a devoted member of a devoted family, was filled with compassion.

"Poor Frances," she said, "I must say I'd hate to be an only. Still I suppose it has its compensations hasn't it?"

"What?" demanded Frances.

"Oh—more clothes and more travel and—and a higher standard of living all round I suppose."

Frances turned back to the flowers and made no reply.

Directly after lunch she came down wearing her most sophisticated "country" clothes and a good deal of make-up and drove off with the equally elegant Henry in his shining car. She waved carelessly as she went out and said,

"Back sometime. Possibly late as we're having dinner out," and Clare watched her go with an uneasy conscience. She had refused the opening which Frances had offered in that moment of young expansiveness, partly because she was surprised by it and did not recognize at once that it was an appeal for family intimacy, and partly too because she was not ready for confidences about Nevill.

She felt restless and, as it was a fine day and a half-holiday, she went out to watch cricket and immediately met Angus who had also seen the departure of Henry's car and looked very gloomy indeed. He was pleased to see Clare and turning to walk on with her he cleared his throat and said with elaborate carelessness,

"I see your cousin is away out with Courtney."

"Yes," said Clare, "Henry is showing her a bit of the Lake District."

"That'll be a long run."

"Quite a long run, but it's a fast car."

They went on for a little without speaking and then Angus said suddenly,

"She—Frances—is the most beautiful girl I've ever seen."

"She's the most beautiful girl I've ever seen, too," said Clare.

"Yes," said Angus, "but—it's different. I'm—I'm desperately in love with her, you see."

"Oh blast!" exclaimed Clare, and then seeing Angus' startled face, "Sorry, Angus. What I mean is—I thought you might be, but as there's nothing I can do about it I wish you hadn't told me."

"I'm sorry," said Angus stiffly. "I didn't expect you to do anything about it and I didn't intend to bother you with it. It just came out. Good afternoon," and he walked rapidly away.

Clare with a flushed and contrite face looked after him

and then said "Hell!" and went to her favourite bench under a huge plane tree and sat down.

Cricket failed to grip and she was pleased when presently Nick sat down beside her.

"You look disgruntled," he observed. "What's biting you, chum?"

"I'm afraid to open my mouth. I've put my foot in it twice today—badly."

"Too bad," said Nick. "If you'll proceed with me to the copse I'll give you a cigarette and you can tell me all about it."

The copse was the recognized refuge where masters and their guests retired to smoke, and though the boys were naturally aware of the custom and indeed no effort was made to conceal it from them, it had become established that while cigarettes and pipes smoked anywhere else about the fields constituted a Bad Example, and a flaunting of forbidden fruit before their deprived eyes, the same smoked in the copse were reasonable grown-up indulgences.

Clare and Nick therefore adjourned and lighting cigarettes watched the cricket from a greater distance.

"Now, what about your feet?" said Nick cosily.

"Well—I've snubbed Angus and he's taken umbrage."

"Dear me! What had poor Angus done? Did he confide in you his grand passion?"

Clare laughed.

"The only way to deal with you Nick is to keep absolutely mum. I've never known such a leap-to-conclusioner."

"And usually right," agreed Nick complacently. "What was your other danger?"

"Never mind my other danger."

"Oh? Cagey are you? Very well. Returning to Angus' heart—you really did start something when you imported your beautiful cousin you know."

"You're telling me!" said Clare.

"I saw her driving off with Henry," went on Nick. "Henry looked like a cat making off with the cream and Frances waved, a sophisticated, patronizing wave."

"Everybody saw her driving off with Henry," said Clare. "That's what set Angus off."

"Well I suppose it's set me off to some extent. I witnessed their departure and then I saw you and I thought thank God there's Clare. We can have a good comfortable natter and forget sirens and satyrs."

"I suppose you want me to listen to your boyish confidences now," said Clare rudely.

Nick turned his back and moved to the far end of the bench.

"Take that back, will you?" he said with cold dignity.

Clare sighed. "Brick number three I suppose. O.K. Cancel." Nick returned and went on with the conversation.

"I'm not in love with Frances. I know my place, or rather my face too well, but—"

"What on earth do you mean?" cried Clare indignantly. "There's nothing the matter with your face. It's a perfectly good face. Sweet in fact."

Nick laughed aloud.

"Clare, I adore you! If there were more trees between us and all these ruddy boys I'd kiss you. But you see how it is. It's one of these round, moon-like unromantic faces and you look at it with the calm affection of a sister—or an aunt. You are unmoved. You wouldn't tell Henry his face was sweet."

"No indeed," said Clare shuddering. "It isn't. But it's not romantic either, Nick. It's sleek and smug and getting fattish. Anyway, if you want to fall in love with Frances you do it. I'll back you."

"A good offer but no, thanking you all the same. I'm not denying that when I saw her first I felt as though someone had hit me over the head with a stuffed eelskin, but it fizzled out pretty quickly. But—Clare—I rather suspect that Patsy's gone in."

"Patsy!" exclaimed Clare. "No! Not really. He's a what-d'you-call-it—hates women."

"Not him," said Nick decidedly. Clare looked at him with interest.

"Cave man stuff, you think?"

"No, no," grinned Nick. "Nothing violent or dramatic. Quiet inevitability if anything."

Clare burst out laughing.

"Well she'd be a lucky girl if she got Patsy or you, Nick. And I believe she'd settle down and be very happy and good as a wife."

"She would with the right chap," agreed Nick. "She's a nice kid. Only you don't always see it behind the facade."

Clare had a return of her remorse and said,

"Oh poor Frances! And I snubbed her too a bit this morning."

Nick looked at her amazed.

"What on earth is up with you? You're not a snubber as a

rule—far otherwise."

Clare, to her great annoyance, felt herself blushing and saw a sharpening of interest and enlightenment in Nick's eyes.

"Well, well!" he said.

"Blast you, Nick! You're jumping to conclusions again. Go away."

"It's all right you know," said Nick. "I don't split."

"I know you don't. I'll tell you. I don't know if this is it or not. I haven't seen him for more than a year, but he's coming back to England now and he's coming to stay with us."

"Darling Clare," said Nick gently. "I hope he's something like good enough, because you're special. Is he coming soon? Before Mrs. Beak comes back?"

Clare laughed.

"Beak said I'd be adequately chaperoned. Yes, he'll be here quite soon I think. But I wish that Mummy was here and it was a bit more—peaceful."

"Yes," said Nick. "You've a good deal on your plate one way and another. But it won't matter. Nothing does if it's the real thing. I thought," he went on, smiling at her, "that there was a sort of glow about you this term. Extraordinarily becoming, if I may say so."

Clare got up and smiled back at him affectionately.

"Thank you for kind and boosting words. I will now leave you. I dare say the School is announcing our engagement to itself by now."

"I dare say," agreed Nick. "Not for the first time, though possibly the last. All possible good luck, Clare. Let me know, won't you?"

"Of course. And thank you, Nick dear. I feel a good deal less harried."

At eight o'clock next morning as Clare went downstairs the telephone rang.

"May I speak to Miss Clare Fielding?" inquired a well-known voice and Clare's heart thumped.

"Hullo, Nevill," she said.

"Clare!" cried Nevill in London. "Look—when can I come? Can I come by train today?"

"Yes," said Clare and explained about trains and where she would meet him.

She went into the dining-room with bright eyes and smiled at her father.

"Nevill's coming today, Beak."

"Is he?" said her father smiling back at her. "How is he coming?"

"Train from London. I thought I'd meet him at Leyburn."

"Yes. Do that. Take Tishy and don't hurry home." Clare looked at him surprised, and he laughed.

"You needn't think I've forgotten all about it, Clare. One doesn't. You'll have a lot to talk about and there isn't much peace for you here."

"True," said Clare. "But there's Frances."

"Shake her off," said Mr. Fielding calmly. "She won't mind."

Frances had been brought to the door by Henry fairly late the night before and had gone up to bed immediately after telling her uncle politely that she had enjoyed herself very much and thought the Lakes were lovely. She came down to breakfast just as he left the table, still wearing the look of reserve which had closed her face at the end of the flower-room episode and Clare felt a mixture of compunction and a slight exasperation that anyone should need handling on the day that Nevill was coming.

"You enjoyed your day, did you?" she began cheerfully.

"Quite," replied Frances coolly. "I like good cars and four-star hotels, and Henry is sufficiently amusing."

Clare found no reply to this and presently Frances said,

"Are we doing anything today?"

"Nevill Crichton is coming—this afternoon."

"Oh—is he the doctor boy-friend? How is he coming?"

"He is the doctor and he's coming by train. I'm going to take Tishy and meet him at Leyburn."

"Ah," said Frances. "Tishy being definitely a two-seater vehicle. And yet he's not special."

Clare flushed and felt that she was being heckled.

"I didn't say he wasn't special," she said. "I said I didn't know. I'm still not sure, but he may be."

There was another pause and she tried again.

"I haven't seen him for over a year. He's been overseas. And so, you see, we need to talk to each other."

Frances glanced up with friendlier eyes and then closing down again she said:

"No doubt. Well—don't worry. I'll keep out of the way."

"For heaven's sake, Frances, don't take that line!" cried Clare, but there was nothing more that she could usefully say to such a stony face and she gave it up, thinking that it was one of these tiresome things that would or would not come right of its own accord.

Frances was not much in evidence during the morning and disappeared as soon as lunch was over, so Clare left herself plenty of time to meet Nevill's train and drove slowly to Leyburn, glad to be alone with the docile, friendly Tishy. When she drew near to the town with more than half an hour to spare she pulled up by the road-side and, lighting a cigarette, thought about Nevill. Attempts to remember what he looked like, to see him with her mind's eye, were never satisfactory, but she got a clearer picture of him when she recalled scenes and incidents. She smiled as she thought of the first time she had seen him. She had just been transferred to a surgical ward and had stood, her hands behind her, as a famous specialist went round, with Nevill as house-surgeon in attendance. Later, as a theatre nurse she had worked with him, and it was during that time that she began to know that they liked each other and they had met off-duty at somebody's party. It was not very long before his appointment as house-surgeon came to an end and he disappeared to his National Service in the Far East. but they knew each other very well by that time. She wondered about his plans. He was a very good surgeon. People who knew regarded him as outstanding and Clare thought that he must not be allowed to settle down in some ordinary dead-end job in order to make money to marry on.

She drove to the station and stood with her hands clenched in her pockets as the train pulled in. There he was, tall and thin and burned dark brown by the tropical sun and, seeing her, he ran along the platform and dropping his baggage seized both her hands.

"Gosh, Clare!" was all he said and she found no words at all. He took her arm and held it closely as they went out of the station and when she led him to the car he grinned and saying "Tishy!" patted the bonnet as if greeting a friend.

"I'm glad you brought Tishy and nobody else," he said as they got in. "How long is this journey and when must we arrive?"

They turned off the road into a little valley where Clare sometimes fished, and Nevill swept her into his arms.

"God—it has been a long time," he said. "I've been kicking myself half the time because I didn't ask you to be engaged to me before I went. You did understand though, didn't you?" he added anxiously.

"Not quite at first," said Clare. "It might have been just an—episode."

"But—my darling love—it couldn't have been."

"No, I didn't think so when the letters kept coming."

Clare had thought, not very clearly, that they would go on from the point at which they had left off when Nevill went abroad, and that in the course of a few days they might be engaged, or, if the nightmare happened and he like others was changed by the loveliness of Frances, it would all be over. But she knew as soon as she saw him that she had in fact engaged herself when she wrote telling him to come to Ledenham and that he was far too much in love, and too grown-up and decisive for any delay or hesitation. They were engaged, said Nevill firmly and would now go straight home to see her father. Also he had brought a ring for her from Burma. She could have another if she didn't like it, but it would do to go on with. The ring was a very beautiful square-cut zircon and Clare exclaimed with delight.

"Nevill—it's the loveliest stone I ever saw! What a colour—and so clear and delicate. How did you know about the size?" Nevill hugged her closely.

"I thought it was like you—delicate and clear and a lovely colour," he said and then he laughed. "There was a girl married to one of the permanent staff who was about your size and had thin hands rather like yours. She tried it on for me. In the presence of her husband," he added solemnly.

They drove up to School House, through crowds of boys and masters, in time for tea and Mr. Fielding came out to meet them.

"Sir," said Nevill as soon as they were in the drawing-room. "I know Clare has told you about me. Have we your permission to be engaged?"

Mr. Fielding smiled. He was pleased with what his expert eye had told him about the young man, and he liked the direct and forthright approach—a good balance to Clare's slight hesitancy.

"So far as I can see if it's what Clare wants, yes," he said. "If further inquiry brings to light anything wrong about you it's off. But I hardly expect it. Clare, you must write to Mummy tonight and so shall I. It won't be easy to prevent her from coming home at once."

"Oh I wish she was here," said Clare.

The three of them had tea together and it was not till they had finished that Clare exclaimed,

"Frances! I'd forgotten all about her. Where is she, Beak?"

"Frances?" said her father vaguely, "I've no idea. Gone out

somewhere I dare say."

Clare went to look for her cousin but she was not in the house or garden. Mrs. Higgins in the kitchen had not seen her, but since she had seen Nevill and had caught sight of Clare's ring, she was not disposed to be concerned about Miss Frances. Mrs. Higgins had been the mainstay of the School House kitchen for a long time and it was clearly her due to be told at once about the engagement by Clare herself, and to have Nevill presented to her with proper ceremony. It was not till she went upstairs to change that Clare thought about Frances again. She was not in her room, but she came up soon afterwards and Clare finished dressing and went to see her.

"Frances—where have you been? I've been quite bothered about you."

Frances was standing by her dressing-table looking pale and rather miserable.

"There was no need to get bothered," she said, "I told you I'd be out of the way."

"That's rather beastly of you I think," said Clare. "Not friendly."

"Sorry," said Frances. "One does one's best. I've been out with Angus actually, in his car."

"Angus? Till now? Wasn't he in school?"

"He wasn't. Whether he should have been I wouldn't know." Her glance fell on Clare's ring and she said "Hullo! Do I gather that the boy-friend is special?"

Clare was worried, but she laughed a little and holding out her hand to show Frances the ring said,

"Absolutely special."

"Nice work," said Frances. "It's a lovely stone. Clever of him to find something that suits you so well. I'll come down and have a look at him in a minute."

She entered the drawing-room just as the gong sounded and Clare, with interest but no uneasiness, watched Nevill get up to meet her. He shook hands, smiling at her.

"I've seen that smile before," thought Clare. "It's his doctor one—kind."

CHAPTER 7

WHEN Angus walked furiously away from Clare on the cricket field the day before Nevill arrived he was so overcharged with the emotions of love for Frances, hatred of Henry and resentment of Clare's snub that he felt physically ill. He might have hit Clare if she had been a man and felt better for it, and he might easily have gone and relieved his feelings by weeping on his bed. What he did was to get into his car and drive savagely about, seeing nothing but Frances smiling up at Henry Courtney and that did him no good at all. He drove back to Little Campion rather late for dinner, which was a glum and almost silent meal tête-a-tête with Lady Courtney. She glanced uneasily at him from time to time but her main feeling towards him was irritation with his gloomy silence and that was, moreover, mixed with apprehension about her son, who had gone off looking, she considered, like an infatuated calf, to drive about the county with the Cheriton girl.

Angus went up to his study after dinner knowing vaguely that a good deal of work was waiting for him there. There were three piles of corrections to be done and lessons to be prepared for next day and he sat down at his table. But pictures of Frances being driven away by Henry in his shining car, Henry with his silk scarf and intolerable moustache, came between him and his papers and he sat there for hours in tormented idleness. He heard the car come back and Henry slam the front door and climb the stairs, humming some luscious love-song and he jumped up and, pouring himself a stiff whisky, disposed of the corrections in a burst of furious activity.

Next morning Angus cut chapel in order to have a last minute look at the day's teaching, but he went into school knowing himself ill-prepared and in a very bad temper. For the first part of the morning it happened that he took junior sets and the work was sufficiently easy and the boys sufficiently docile and unobservant for his lack of preparation to pass unnoticed.

During break, while coffee was consumed in the common room, Henry was in splendid form. One of the masters who admired him observed that some people evidently had what it takes, driving off with the prettiest girl in England.

"England!" cried Henry, radiantly bonhomous. "In the world, m'boy, I should say," and knowing looks were exchanged. Nick Vincent flushed and looked unhappy, Patsy read the newspapers with an expressionless face and the little Chaplain looked rather anxiously at them and at the grim, white-faced Angus. The Cameron campaign had clearly struck a snag.

"Cameron, you look uncommon bilious," said Henry gaily as the bell sounded the end of break, but the Chaplain interrupted with a loud hail,

"Henry—a word with you," and under cover of the general movement he muttered, "Lay off that boy now, Henry. It isn't fair to tease him. You don't know what his troubles might be."

Henry laughed loudly.

"Oh I know what his troubles are all right. He needs to be bounced out of them, silly young pup."

Angus went in to face his top set. They were a clever lot of sixth-formers who would be trying for scholarships presently and they were keen on their work and accustomed to an atmosphere of discussion. To Angus, a really good mathematician, the work itself was simple enough, but he was an inexperienced teacher and he had not assembled it in his mind, or given any thought to the words in which he could best explain it. He therefore floundered, and in his embarrassment grew angry. He was exceedingly and most unfairly rude, and he swept out at the end of the period leaving behind him a sullen, resentful and contemptuous lot of boys.

His last set on that unhappy morning consisted of cheerful and moderately gifted persons who were being driven hard towards the General Certificate of Education, ordinary level. Their ordeal was drawing near but even so they did not co-operate with any great sincerity and they were always delighted with anything that caused a diversion— and there is no better potential diversion than a green, new master. Angus had kept them in hand so far, because everybody regards an international athlete with respect, and anybody hesitates to go far in annoying six foot four inches of rugger player. Also when he had prepared his lessons he drove them at a speed which left little time for dalliance. This morning, however, he was not only unprepared, he began the period by giving them corrected papers which belonged to another set. There was an instant uproar, ranging from the righteous, "Please, sir, I think there must be some mistake," to uninhibited laughter and comments on the work done and the marks gained by other people. The papers were distributed with lightning speed, and were passed and thrown from one boy to another in a pandemonium of noise and movement. In fact there was a full-blown riot and Angus was helpless and panic-stricken.

The door opened and the noise subsided as Hacket, the school porter, appeared at Angus' side, silently handing him a notice to read. This was a thing which happened frequently and surprised no one. Angus took the paper and saw printed in large capitals,

"ROAR AT THEM, SIR."

"Thanks, Hacket," said Angus.

"Thank you, sir," said Hacket and went away.

The noise immediately surged up again and Angus inflated his lungs.

"QUIET!" he roared.

There was an astonished silence and he, forgetting everything but the present crisis, seized his advantage.

Two persons were helped back to their places by a large and painful hand, four others were ordered to report to their housemaster, and for the remainder of the period a chastened set bent its noses meekly to the grindstone.

The encounter left Angus exhausted but in a healthier frame of mind and, when his troubles returned to sit heavily on him again, his first thought was that he had been very rude to Clare Fielding who was a particularly nice girl and could never have meant to hurt his feelings. He accordingly went round to the School House to see if he could find her to apologize and make friends again, but Clare had gone to meet Nevill and he was turning away disappointed when Frances appeared from the garden.

"Hullo, Angus," she said, looking pleased to see him.

"Hullo," said Angus. "I was looking for Clare."

"Clare's gone out. Would I do instead?"

She was very lovely and gay and Angus gazed at her with hungry eyes.

"No," he said, "I mean, yes, of course—that is—I wanted to apologize to her for being rude yesterday."

"Gracious, Angus!" exclaimed Frances. "Whatever were you rude to Clare about?"

"Well—I—I really can't tell you that."

"Mysteriouser and mysteriouser!" Frances laughed and looked up at him. "You can grovel to Clare another time. What are you doing now? Or what are you going to do when you've stopped talking to me?"

"Nothing," said Angus dizzily "Why? Do you mean—"

"I'm bored," said Frances plaintively. "I'm all alone. Couldn't we go somewhere?"

They went out in Angus' car. Angus was due in afternoon school at four forty-five, but he forgot about it. Frances was very friendly and unbelievably sweet and they talked a great deal and had tea in a pub and went rather further from Ledenham than they thought they did. On their way home Angus suddenly saw where he was.

"By gum!" he exclaimed stopping the car. "We're at Benenbeck."

"Benenbeck?"

"Yes—look! That's where we had the picnic and that's where you practised casting."

"So it is!" said Frances. "Let's have a look at it again."

He helped her to climb over the wall and she looked at

him with her blue eyes shining and suddenly she was in his arms and he was kissing her wildly.

"Angus darling!" gasped Frances. "Go easy for heaven's sake!" In her circle girls expected to be kissed and she herself had been kissed a good deal. Angus was attractive and she rather liked him and was not at all displeased that he should kiss her.

"Frances my darling," said Angus at last. "You can't think how I love you. I think I worship you. But I never thought you could care for anybody like me. When will you marry me? I've no money—could you wait for me?"

"Marry you?" exclaimed Frances, surprised and amused, and looked up at him. He was standing with his arms round her looking down, his face so transformed with love and delight and his eyes so filled with undefended tenderness that she dropped her own eyes with a feeling of shock. Nobody should see him like that except one girl, and she was not the girl.

"Oh, Angus!" she cried. Angus drew her closer, but she pushed him back. "You mustn't. You mustn't, Angus—I didn't mean it."

"You didn't mean it, my darling? What didn't you mean?"

"I didn't mean you to love me—really. I don't love you—I couldn't marry you."

"You kissed me," said Angus. "You let me kiss you and you kissed me back. Surely—that couldn't happen unless you loved me and were—were going to marry me?"

There was a pause before Frances said in a small voice,

"Yes—it could I'm afraid, Angus."

Angus' arms dropped from her.

"You don't love me, Frances?"

She shook her head,

"It was only fun—and because you're nice. You are nice, Angus, but I don't love you."

Angus had turned absolutely white. He looked at Frances with an expression she never forgot and turning round walked away up the river path.

He was shivering with shock and a blinding combination of grief and rage and shame, and when he had rounded a bend in the path and was out of Frances' sight he threw himself down on the grass with his face in his arms.

It seemed a long time before he stopped being wholly absorbed in feeling. When he began to think again he wondered where Frances was and got up. She was quite near, sitting quietly on the bank with her back to him watching the river, and when she heard him move she got up and he saw that she had been crying.

"Angus," she said hesitantly. "I'm so sorry about this that I can hardly bear it. You may not believe me, but it's true."

"I'm evidently very green," said Angus wearily. "I didn't know that a girl like you let any man kiss her like that unless she was going to marry him."

"Or else I'm green," Frances said rather bitterly. "Let's go home, Angus. I can't say any more than that I'm sorry."

They walked back to the car in silence and Angus drove fast and stopped at School House without a word.

"Don't get out," said Frances. "Good-bye Angus," and she ran quickly into the house.

Angus went automatically to Little Campion and as soon

98

as he went in Henry met him.

"Where the hell have you been, Cameron?" he demanded.

"What the hell has it got to do with you?" demanded Angus in his turn.

"Do you realize, you fool, that you cut the whole of afternoon school?"

"God!" said Angus putting a hand to his head. Courtney looked at him, puzzled and with an increasing hostility.

"What's the matter with you? Have you had a smash? Or are you tight?"

"No," said Angus, "I'm all right. I must see the Headmaster about cutting—it was quite unintentional."

"But what have you been doing?" persisted Henry. "You can't behave like a lunatic and give no explanation. After all in a way I'm responsible for you."

Angus turned and stood towering above him.

"You are in no way responsible for me, Courtney, and I'll ask you to mind your own business."

"It is my business and the business of everybody belonging to the School if you can't behave yourself. And a good deal my business because you were seen driving away with—Miss Cheriton hours ago and I've been pretty worried let me tell you. Now you come back in this state. What have you been up to, damn you?"

"You filthy little swab," said Angus quietly. "I've a good mind to knock your block off."

Henry moved hastily back towards a protective table, but at that moment the front door opened and the Chaplain came in. He was not wearing his customary look of geniality.

"Do you want the whole of Ledenham to know that two of its masters are quarrelling?" he asked coldly. "Cameron, go up to your study. I want to see you in a minute, but I'll have a word with Courtney first."

"You can clear out, Cameron," said Henry furiously. "I won't have you in the house another night."

"Go on, Cameron—up you go," said Mr. Perry, and Angus turned on his heel and went upstairs. The Chaplain drove Mr. Courtney back into his own study and closed the door. Henry was trembling.

"I don't know by what right you walk into my house and interfere in my affairs, Perry."

"Then I'll tell you," said the Chaplain crisply. "I've been anxious about Cameron for some days and when I saw him driving across the grounds a few minutes ago it was plain that he was in some bad trouble. He was a happy enough chap when he came, so we may take it, I think, that he's met his trouble here and—"

"He's an oaf," said Henry interrupting. "His trouble is that he's been setting his cap at Frances Cheriton and no doubt she's turned him down as flat as he deserves. I'm only afraid she's had some ghastly experience with him."

"Rubbish!" said Perry roundly. "If he's in love with Miss Cheriton he's as much right as anyone else to 'set his cap at her', as you call it. It's his own affair and if he's been snubbed, that's his affair too. But to talk about ghastly experiences in connection with that decent boy is rubbish."

Henry smiled unpleasantly.

"Decent boy!" he said contemptuously. "What do you

know about him?"

"I've seen a goodish bit in and out of common room, Courtney." Mr. Perry went on. "So have others and we don't forget Tomlinson. There's a nasty taste about."

Courtney turned on him savagely.

"There's a nasty taste about this damned interference of yours. What are you getting at?"

The Chaplain held up his hand.

"Stop. I'll have no personal wrangling with you. If you want to complain of my interference you can do it to the Headmaster."

There was silence for a moment and then Courtney said more quietly,

"You've misunderstood. Cameron has nothing to complain of. I've mocked him a bit, but he's so damned callow he needs a bit of training. This business is different. He cut afternoon school and when he came in looking half-dead—or drunk, I tell you I got a hell of a fright."

He turned away and taking out his handkerchief passed it over his forehead. Mr. Perry stood looking at him and then said,

"Well now. I heard you telling him to get out of the house. Do you mean that?"

"I never want to see the brute again," said Henry vehemently.

"You realize what it means if you turn Cameron out, do you?" asked Mr. Perry.

Henry shrugged his shoulders.

"Tittle-tattle of course."

"A little more serious than that I think. You've been a bit

too rough in your mockery you know, and some of it's been pretty public. It would be better if you could get Cameron to stay here till he can make a proper move to decent digs and give this a chance to die down. Better for you as well as for him than if I take him into my spare bedroom in an obvious emergency."

"I couldn't care less what happens to Cameron," said Henry. "I would recommend the Beak to get rid of him at once. He's practically unbalanced."

"Rubbish," said the Chaplain again, very sharply. "Pull yourself together. He's a perfectly good youngster as you very well know. I don't think you'd enjoy the Beak's searchlight on a recommendation for his dismissal. Come on now, Henry. Patch the thing up and let the boy have a chance to change his digs quietly and decently."

There was rather a long pause. The Chaplain was short and stout, untidy and almost ridiculous in appearance. Henry Courtney, nearly a head taller, nearly twenty years younger, elegant, and in his own way undeniably handsome, stood before him and found that he could not meet the steady eyes which looked at him through the thick, round spectacles. He turned away and threw himself impatiently into a chair.

"All right," he said curtly. "He can have his chance. But I hope to God he gets on with it. I can't stand much more of him."

"Good," said the Chaplain. "I'll go up to him now and take him out to dinner." And he climbed the stairs to deal with Angus. He had never before penetrated to the quarters allotted to the paying guests at Little Campion and the expression of distaste on his kind and tolerant face showed something of his feeling as he entered the comfortless dingy little study; but he smiled at Angus.

"Well, boy," he said, "this is a shemozzle."

Angus was standing gazing blindly through the window and he turned round slowly.

"I've made a fearful hash," he said miserably.

"You're not the first," said Mr. Perry calmly.

"Did you know I cut afternoon school?"

"Oh yes. That's been done before too. Also," with a slight grin, "others before you have had riots in form. I hear you got it under control quite quickly."

Angus looked up with a little gleam of amusement. "That was Hacket," he said, "I was flummoxed."

Mr. Perry smiled

"Hacket's an old hand. He knows all the dodges. Now I want you to come and have dinner with my sister and me and we'd better get along or it will be spoiled."

Angus hesitated.

"It's very good of you, sir. Thank you. But I don't think I can. I've got to pack up and find somewhere to sleep and I've got to see the Headmaster."

"Also you've got to eat," replied Mr. Perry. "You won't move from here tonight and—"

"But Courtney said—"

"Courtney has unsaid it. You'll stay till you can find another suitable place."

"I don't want to stay."

"I dare say not. You will stay, however, and give the School a chance at least to pretend it doesn't know there's been a row between you and Courtney."

Angus was silent but he looked obstinate and Mr. Perry, longing for his dinner, waited.

"I'll have to see the Headmaster," said Angus at last, "and I think it will be better if I leave the school at once."

"You can see the Headmaster when he's had his dinner and you've had yours and he'll deal with that."

Angus allowed himself to be lead away and they got into his car and drove through the town to the house which Mr. Perry shared with his sister.

Miss Perry was older and taller than her brother and almost the only resemblance between them was the odd angle at which they wore their spectacles. She was a notable, even an inspired cook and she kept house exceedingly well. The rest of her life, almost completely solitary, was occupied with her two Irish wolfhounds and a varying series of hobbies and handicrafts and she showed no interest whatever in the human race, though she was unfailingly kind when it came her way. A great many people in Ledenham liked to have tea with the Perrys, to be fortified with feathery soda bread and soothed by their hostess's impersonal and incurious kindness, and Angus was fortified by a very good dinner now, and soothed by gentle and not unamusing conversation about dogs and the scenery of Scotland from the viewpoint of a painter in water-colours, since sketching was Miss Perry's current hobby.

When Angus left to go to the Headmaster, Miss Perry remarked as her brother shut the front door, "Nice boy. Well brought up," and drifted away, while the Chaplain turned towards his study. Until she brought him a tray of tea at ten o'clock neither had any idea what the other would do and no desire to know, and Mr. Perry, who found human squabbles and problems tiring though interesting, reflected gratefully, as he often did, that there could be nobody more restful to live with than Letitia.

He went to the telephone and told Henry Courtney that Angus would return to Little Campion after seeing the Headmaster, and would stay there till he succeeded in finding a suitable alternative.

CHAPTER 8

AS Angus pulled up at School House he encountered Patsy Henderson.

"Hullo," said Patsy. "Coming to see Nick?"

"No," said Angus heaving himself out of his little car and not looking at his friend. "Got to see the Headmaster."

Beneficent as the Perrys and their dinner had been, his appearance was still far enough from normal to startle even the phlegmatic Patsy.

"No need to worry," he remarked. "The Beak's quite good at remembering his own youth. He'll tear one strip off you and forget it. Come and have a drink afterwards."

"Thanks," said Angus. "I'll have to get along afterwards."

And without saying anything more he went towards the Headmaster's study. Patsy looked after him curiously and went into Nick Vincent's room, his usually impassive face wearing a disturbed expression.

Reverberations of Angus' escapade and vague rumours of a row rolled round the school. Boys discussed the new bloke's incalculable temper and wondered what happened to masters who cut school, since presumably even the most junior could not be beaten. A good many husbands told their wives about it, in some cases adding darkly that they suspected a hell of a row between Cameron and Courtney, or that they had seen Cameron drive off with the Cheriton girl, and several wives remarked that the girl was clearly a man-eater and was sure to make trouble sooner or later.

The Chaplain who never showed any surprise whoever

called on him at whatever hour may have found it more difficult than usual to conceal some sign of it when Patsy Henderson arrived at ten o'clock, but he succeeded and Miss Perry, appearing with her brother's tea, produced an extra cup and saucer with no more fuss than if it had been ready in her pocket.

The two men sat down together and Patsy said,

"Wondered if you could tell me what's up with Cameron?"

"Speaking on behalf of the Cameron supporters?" There was a short pause.

"Not entirely."

"Ah," said the Chaplain. He finished filling his pipe and, as he lit it, he glanced through the smoke at his young friend with eyes which showed comprehension and a great deal of affection. Humphrey Perry had an apparently limitless store of affection of the rare kind which demands nothing in return and of which the recipients are often hardly aware; but Patsy, silent and reserved, he loved like a son, discerning in him a particular sweetness of character as well as a shrewd, penetrating intelligence.

"I don't know that I can give you many facts," he said. "You've probably heard already that Cameron cut afternoon school to go motoring with Frances Cheriton?"

Patsy nodded briefly and the Chaplain went on, "I can tell you, though one hopes, perhaps vainly, that it won't get about, that he's also had a most almighty row with Henry, who was for turning him out of Little Campion forthwith but has now agreed to keep him till he can move in decent order."

"That was you, I suppose," said Patsy.

"Yes, it was. I saw Angus driving across from School House looking like death so I charged in. I'm afraid he's taken a bad toss over that really exquisite child, poor chap. I don't blame him. I suppose one of the compensations of advancing years is that one is no longer subject to that particular kind of toss, but when one sees a girl like that it seems almost a pity. Such a waste."

"Some don't outgrow it," observed Patsy, glancing across with amused eyes.

"True. Most of us have other things to think about though."

There was another short silence while both men smoked their pipes and looked at the fire which was so welcome on this May evening, and then the Chaplain went on quietly,

"Cameron, poor boy, has gone off to the Beak with his mind at least half set on getting out of the place as fast as possible."

Patsy looked up quickly.

"The Beak won't let him, will he?"

"No, I don't think so. He'll handle him all right. I've never known anybody with a surer touch. But it'll be an uphill pull for Angus one way and another. He's got the boys' backs right up and Henry's a bad enemy, and then there's his broken heart too, of course."

"You think it is broken?"

"Yes—for the moment, and he's had a real shock of some kind. I think," he added in reply to Patsy's unspoken question, "that Angus is quite as green as he looks, even greener maybe, and that young Frances isn't far ahead of

108

him." He laughed suddenly. "She's more self-possessed and aims, of course, at a quite terrifying sophistication, but I had Sunday supper with them the other night and she was sweet. Chattering to the boys and backing up Clare and the Beak like a good 'un." Patsy smiled, but said nothing.

"I fancy," said the Chaplain, "that she was not averse to a little flirtation and Angus lost his simple wits and they had a head-on collision. Shattering at the time for both parties, but nobody's fault and no lasting harm done."

"I must get along," said Patsy knocking out his pipe and rising to his feet. "Thanks, Hum."

"You're welcome," replied Mr. Perry. "We'll have to get that boy on his feet again."

Patsy nodded.

"We'll do it. He's a good chap," and the Chaplain, left alone, thought kindly about the pains and problems of youth.

The dinner gong sounded at Little Campion a few minutes after Angus and the Chaplain left the house and Henry Courtney pulled himself together and went in to face his mother. The encounter between Angus and himself had taken place in the hall and had not been altogether silent, and Rogers wore the expression of a man endeavouring to conceal inquisitive glee. Lady Courtney glanced sharply at her son and said coldly:

"Where is Mr. Cameron?"

"He's gone to dinner with Perry," replied Henry without looking at her.

"Indeed? He might have mentioned it. Rogers, remove Mr. Cameron's place."

"Very good, m'lady. Will Mr. Cameron be here for breakfast?"

Henry looked up quickly.

"Naturally," he said angrily.

"Very good, sir," said Rogers injured, "I thought it best to make sure."

He left the room and Lady Courtney went into action.

"May I inquire the reason for this disturbance?" she asked majestically.

Henry moved irritably.

"What disturbance?"

His mother eyed him with icy severity.

"There is no need to be rude, Henry, and no use trying to pretend that nothing has happened. My home has been disturbed by a noisy and unseemly quarrel and I consider that I have every right to expect an explanation—and an apology."

Henry with the utmost reluctance embarked on explanations. They were not well received.

"Mr. Cameron is an uncouth young man," said Lady Courtney, "and I am not altogether surprised to hear of misbehaviour. I cannot, however, understand why his being absent from his duties should lead to a quarrel between him and you, Henry. It is the Headmaster's affair."

There was no reply. They finished their dinner almost in silence, but as Lady Courtney got up to leave the room she said,

"Henry, it looks to me as though you are in danger of making a fool of yourself."

He looked at her angrily.

"What on earth can you mean?"

She returned his look with equal anger and the likeness between them was very strong.

"That girl," she said, "you are both in love with her—that is the trouble. Don't imagine it can't be seen—quite clearly."

Frances was quiet and rather pale during dinner and almost immediately after the meal was over she said that she had a headache and would go to bed.

"Can I get you anything? Aspirin?" asked Clare

"No thanks. I've got aspirin if I need it."

Clare looked rather anxiously at her and Frances smiled and said:

"I'm quite all right. Don't fuss, Clare."

"Very well. I'll bring you some hot milk later on," said Clare and Frances made a face and went away.

"What did she do this afternoon—do you know?" asked the Headmaster. Clare, who was pouring out coffee, looked up surprised.

"Is that a polite query, Beak, or do you want to know?"

"I should like to know, if it doesn't inconvenience anybody," replied her father mildly. Clare hesitated.

"I'm not quite sure about the inconvenience," she said, "she was out with Angus Cameron part of the time. I don't know where or for how long."

"Long enough for Cameron to miss afternoon school anyhow."

"Yes. I was afraid he must have done that."

"I must go in a minute," said the Headmaster. "Forgive

111

me, Nevill, but Clare is doing a job for me while her mother is away."

"Shall I clear out?" asked Nevill.

"No, no. Clare—Perry rang up to tell me that he fished Cameron out of a row with Courtney this evening. Fortunately before blows were exchanged."

"Oh dear!" said Clare.

"He also says," continued her father, "that he hopes he's patched it up till Cameron can find other digs and move in decent order, but the chap's in very poor shape. Looks as if he's had a bad shock. Do you know anything about this?"

Clare said slowly,

"I'm afraid Angus is very much in love with Frances."

"And Henry also seems to be attracted," remarked the Headmaster. "Yes. A little surprising I think, though she's a pretty girl of course," and he went away.

"She's more than that," said Clare. "She's devastatingly lovely. Don't you think so, Nevill?"

Nevill grinned.

"Very, very pretty. I outgrew dumb blondes myself in my first year, but I've always understood that schoolmasters are slow to develop."

Clare laughed aloud.

"Poor Henry!" she exclaimed. "But she isn't dumb, you know."

The Headmaster was in his study when Angus knocked at the door.

"Come in, Cameron," he said. "I thought I'd be seeing you tonight."

"Sir," said Angus. "I have to tell you that I cut the whole

112

of afternoon school today."

"I know you did. Why?"

"I forgot about it," said Angus miserably.

"Sit down," said the Headmaster. "You're looking downright ill, man. What is all this?"

"I can't very well tell you, sir. I'm very sorry. I really think it will be best if I go at once."

There was silence. Angus stared at the carpet and the Headmaster stared at Angus and then he said:

"Do you consider that cutting two periods is a serious enough matter to warrant your leaving the school short of a mathematics master? At this stage of the certificate term?"

"No, I don't, sir. Not that."

"Neither do I. So long as you're fit for your work, Cameron, you're bound to do what you've undertaken to do—teach here for this term. Any private trouble is your own affair and a man should at least do his best to keep it to himself."

Angus was silent and the Headmaster went on,

"You probably hardly realize how serious it would be for the School if we lost you now. And for yourself. You started well. I think you have it in you to make a very good schoolmaster. It would be a great mistake to throw it away."

"I hadn't thought about it properly," said poor Angus. "I only felt that I had made such a hash of everything that you'd be better without me. Courtney said—" he stopped.

"Have a cigarette or light your pipe if you prefer it," said Mr. Fielding. "I usually have some tea about this time and I'm going to see if it's ready."

113

He went out of the room for a few minutes and presently Clare entered with the tea-tray.

"Hullo, Angus," she said.

Angus got to his feet.

"Clare—I tried to find you today. I wanted to apologize for being such a—a boor yesterday."

"Well I've been wanting to apologize to you," said Clare, "I was a boor-ess. We'll take it as said shall we?"

She smiled at him very kindly and gave his arm a little quick pat as she left the room.

The Headmaster did not miss much that went on in the School and he knew most of what had happened to Angus in the short time he had been at Ledenham. Knowing that he had been out with Frances that afternoon, and having seen the subdued silence of the girl during dinner and the shocked, unhappy face of the boy, he had a pretty shrewd idea of the kind of scene which had taken place between them. When their conversation was resumed over cups of tea nothing was said about Frances at all and very little about Courtney. The Headmaster said that he thought Courtney's household rather a difficult one for a young man to fit into, and that as they had got across each other it was certainly best for Angus to look for rooms elsewhere. He did not appear to think it a very serious matter and pro-ceeded almost at once to talk about schoolmastering in general. He was an expert and he talked well, and Angus grew interested and presently was talking himself, asking questions and finding his mind clearing on problems of teaching and discipline and the handling of boys. He began to understand something about education and what school masters might do for their boys besides getting them through the G.C.E., and the fascination of the job dawned upon him. Mr. Fielding saw the shock and misery leave his face and the colour begin to come back, and at last smiled and said,

"Now you must get along and make peace with Courtney. Stay on there till you find a suitable place to live. It doesn't matter if you dislike each other, but it matters if you show it. You'll find that Courtney realizes that."

Angus got up and flushed with embarrassment.

"I'd no idea it was so late, sir! I'm sorry to have taken so much time."

"That's all right. We've had a useful talk. You're on your way, Cameron—nothing to worry about. Put your back into it and you'll make a good schoolmaster."

Angus drove slowly back to Little Campion thinking about this last remark. Did he want to be a good schoolmaster in a good school? To spend his life among boys, working with men like the Beak and the Chaplain, Nick and Patsy? He would never be rich, but he would never have to think of "making money" and he thought that there could hardly be a better way of life for him than this.

As he put his car away and turned towards the house the thought of Frances returned to him with a pang, but it was a less bitter pang and his face was more peaceful than that which Courtney showed when he opened the door of his study.

"Courtney," said Angus, "I'm very sorry about all this. I apologize for losing my temper."

Henry bowed coldly.

"There are things which can't be forgotten," he said, "but I have agreed to allow you to stay on here for the present. If I turned you out you could hardly remain in the School of course." Angus looked at him without speaking and he flushed a little, but went on.

"I think myself it would be better for the School if you did leave now, but that's not my decision."

"No," agreed Angus. "It has nothing to do with you. I'll do my best to leave your house as soon as I decently can and meanwhile I'll try to keep out of your way."

"You owe my mother an abject apology," said Henry, "and I hope you will contrive to avoid upsetting her again."

To Angus, fresh from his adult talk with the Headmaster, it was suddenly clear that Henry, the exquisite, the confident, the impeccable Mr. Courtney was more rattled than he was himself; and, moreover, that he was trying to save his face and to unload his guilt in a manner which could only be described as childish. He said nothing more, except to murmur as he turned away a stately assurance that he would make his apologies to Lady Courtney in the morning, but he felt as he mounted the stairs that he had grown up a bit and was comforted. Courtney on the other hand had seen his involuntary flash of amusement and, understanding, turned back to his study far from comforted and angrier than ever.

Only one more of the reverberations of that day need be told.

It was about nine o'clock when Clare took the tray of tea into her father's study and had her word with Angus. Like everyone else she was a good deal shaken by his appearance and she did not think that a quarrel with Henry Courtney, even if it were followed by severe words from the Headmaster, would account for it. There must have been a crisis of some sort with Frances she thought, and felt more than a little angry with that young lady till she remembered that she as well as Angus had looked disturbed and miserable.

She heated some milk and took it upstairs. There was no reply to her knock on Frances' door, but she had quick ears and heard a sound as of somebody lying down quietly.

"Foxing," thought Clare irritatedly and went into the room and turned the light on. Frances sat up in bed and glared. Her pretty face was pale and she had obviously been crying.

"If I'd wanted you to come in I'd have said so," she said angrily.

"I've brought you some milk," said. Clare, "and I wanted to come in." She put the cup of milk on the bedside table and sat down on the edge of the bed.

"Frances," she said slowly, feeling that this was something that needed more experienced handling than she could give it. "Angus Cameron is downstairs with the Beak and—"

Frances sat up again.

"What's he saying?" she asked quickly.

"I don't know what he's saying. He'd got to see Daddy about cutting afternoon school. Also he's had a blazing row with Henry."

"Nothing about me?" asked Frances.

"Not so far as I know. Anyway he wouldn't, would he?"

"I don't know. Probably not. He's very much a gent," said

Frances in a peculiar tone of mingled contempt and respect.

"All the same," said Clare more firmly, "he's in a bit of a mess. He's very miserable and he's made quite a hash of things one way and another, and his chance of staying on here permanently will depend on whether he can get right quickly. If there's anything you can clear up for him I think you ought to do it."

There was a silence. Clare could not help thinking impatiently of Nevill alone in the drawing-room and resenting the necessity of spending time and thought on the affairs of other people when her own were so absorbing.

At last Frances said, "There isn't much for me to clear up. Angus is simply not grown-up enough, and too Presbyterian to have an ordinary friendship with a girl. We'll be keeping out of each other's way, I fancy, from now on." She spoke in a hard voice and Clare got up.

"That's it, is it? I see. Poor Angus! Well—I hope your head will be better. Good night."

She went downstairs again and Nevill said,

"You look a bit grim. Is it the unhappy young man?"

"Frances," said Clare. "She's been flirting with him and I suppose he thought she meant it. Blast her."

"Well don't worry," said Nevill calmly. "It comes to all of us sooner or later. How old is this bloke?"

"Oh—twenty-three or four I suppose."

"In that case I think Frances might be excused for expecting him to know his way about. Especially as she probably moves in knowledgeable circles herself."

Clare flushed a little and turned away.

"That sounds beastly," she said crossly. "I hate know-ledgeable circles."

Nevill turned her firmly back to face him and put his arms round her.

"My darling girl! Be your age and your nice self," he said. "It can't be all that easy to be Frances you know. She's not at all a bad kid, but she's the kind that almost every man she meets makes a pass at. Repeat—almost."

"She needn't encourage the passes," said Clare.

"Ah—but it's not so much that. She's naturally so seductive that she'd have to be very discouraging to put people off. Anyhow she may enjoy a bit of dalliance from time to time, and who shall blame her?"

"You sound very—experienced."

"So I am," said Nevill promptly, "I'm a normal man, twenty-seven years old—brighter than most, if I may say so, and I should take a poor view of myself if I wasn't experienced. I've been about and got my experience and now you've cropped up, quite different from anything that's happened before."

There was a pause, and then Clare went on,

"All the same, Nevill, I don't see why men and girls shouldn't enjoy themselves together without emotional complications."

"Well," said Nevill, "it does happen of course, but it's much rarer than you think. You're the type that can do it, and you've been brought up in an environment that is conducive to it. But it's not altogether natural—it's a cultivated plant, and I don't think you should blame Frances much, if at all. Incidentally," he went on, "she

119

looks to me as if she'd got a considerable shaking up herself, as she would if she was just being cheerfully flirtatious and Cameron turned out to be shatteringly earnest." Clare had a vision of Angus' solemn face and his nervous clearings of the throat and laughed a little and then she remembered Frances' appeal to be allowed "in on it" if Nevill were "special".

"Poor Frances," she exclaimed. "I believe I've been a beast to her. I must try to get it right."

"Cheer up," said Nevill. "People have got to get things straightened out for themselves in the end."

Mr. Fielding came in very soon, remarking that his evening seemed to be over before it had begun.

"Have you soothed Angus?" asked Clare.

"Soothed and stiffened I trust. He'll be all right," said her father and they left the affairs of Angus, Frances and the School for what remained of the evening. Clare, however, before she went to sleep turned her honest mind to Frances, and Nevill's remarks about her, and to her own reaction to Nevill's "experience". She remembered certain experiences of her own which she had hitherto regarded with shame, because they had been a falling short of her belief that kissing should never happen unless one were engaged. Not only had she fallen below her standards in the matter, she had actually enjoyed it and she grimaced at herself now and decided that she had been very near to a most objectionable, self-righteous prudishness. She had been unusually lucky in having her platonic friendships with Nick and the others, and she went to sleep resolving that she would get on terms with Frances tomorrow.

CHAPTER 9

THE ordeal of making his apologies to Lady Courtney turned out to be less severe than Angus had expected.

He had gone up to his study the night before determined to take hold of his job and to begin at once to make up the ground he knew he had lost; and when at last he went to bed he thought that the apology to Lady Courtney would, so to speak, wind up the Little Campion business. After it had been made, however it was received, all he would have to do would be to exist there, almost completely detached from both the Courtneys till the time came when he could leave the house.

He went down early and had finished a hurried breakfast when Lady Courtney entered the dining-room. Angus got quickly to his feet.

"Lady Courtney," he said, "I owe you an apology. I do apologize most sincerely and I hope you will accept it." He was looking at her with steady eyes and he saw that she was old and in some way deflated. It was a moment before she spoke and it seemed to cost her some effort.

"I accept your apology, Mr. Cameron," she said. "Such a scene could not fail to shock me, but I believe that the fault was not entirely yours. Perhaps not even the greater part of it lay with you."

"Oh poor thing," thought the kind-hearted Angus, "she's quarrelled with Henry." The Courtneys were nothing to him, he was worse than nothing to them and it would be a sad thing if the mother and son were unhappy in each

121

other on his account. He did what he could.

"I'm very sorry, Lady Courtney. I don't think it was really anybody's fault exactly. I'm afraid Courtney has found me irritating and it just—sort of blew up. Anyhow I'll move as soon as I can."

Lady Courtney made one of her stately inclinations of the head. The interview was over and Angus went forth, free to make what he could of Ledenham.

As Angus stood up to face Lady Courtney, Clare tapped at the door of Frances' room and went in.

"Beak reports that Angus is soothed and stiffened," she said cheerfully. Frances who was doing her hair looked round and her face cleared.

"Oh thank goodness!" she exclaimed. "He's—all right, is he?" Clare burst out laughing and in response to Frances' look of surprise said,

"It sounds so absurd—as though he was a timid and shrinking maid."

"Well," said Frances drily, "he was a bit like it I must say. All the same, I felt a—well a mixture of a worm and a tart I suppose."

"Let's forget him now, anyway," said Clare. "I'm engaged to be married and Nevill's here. Come on, Frances, I want to make the most of it."

Frances thought she had never seen anyone look so happy or so alive and though she had always admired her cousin's spare, unpretentious good looks they seemed to have been transfigured into real beauty. Her own face softened and cleared into friendliness and affection and she smiled warmly at Clare.

"You're besotted," she said, "but it suits you. Evidently there's something in this engagement business. I must try it sometime."

There followed a week which for Clare was a time of unclouded happiness. Nevill was there. Her father provided a secure background of understanding affection and there were satisfactory messages of pleasure and excitement from her mother, Alison and Richard, of welcome from Nevill's family and of outraged protest from Michael to whom any hint of romance was anathema at this stage of his life.

The news of her engagement flew round the School as quickly as news always did. The Fieldings were popular and the school community small enough and sufficiently intimate to feel a particular, personal interest in their family affairs, and for Frances, though she did not fully realize it, Clare's news could hardly have been more timely. Ledenham had not seen much of her as yet, and though no fault could be found with her manners and she had shown nothing but friendliness to those whom she had met, she was too pretty, too startlingly expensive and exotic to be easily digested. The rumours and speculation about her connection with whatever had happened to Cameron circulated in an atmosphere which already contained seeds of suspicion and resentment, and it was fortunate for her and, in the long run for Angus too that Clare provided such a happy diversion. The people who came to congratulate her and see for themselves what sort of young man her Nevill was, saw Frances in a new light, very much a part of the School House family and supporting her cousin with unaffected pleasure. She played a very useful and sensible

123

part during that week and a new relationship grew up between the two girls which they never afterwards lost. Neither of them had ever thought of the tie of cousinship meaning anything, but their intimacy and mutual confidence was based on their common heritage and blood and though Frances' golden beauty had come from her father's family, Mr. Fielding, watching the two, began to see resemblances between them, likenesses of bone and movement and, more gradually, of mind, as though they had been dormant in Frances till contact with her cousin brought them to life.

To Frances the relationship with Clare and being in the centre of the family at such a time were altogether new experiences and she was too absorbed to dwell on the memory of her scene with Angus, though she did think of it with concern for him and some rather puzzled doubts about her own part in his troubles. To Clare the new friendship was like that between herself and Alison, except that Frances was more her equal in age and maturity and contributed a gay and resourceful help from a store of knowledge and experience far beyond, or at any rate utterly different from Clare's own. It was Frances whose tact and skill averted the danger of Nevill's visit being swamped by socialities, Frances who so organized things that Clare was free to spend her time and thoughts with Nevill, and Frances who persuaded her that the School and School House could get along without her for a few days while she went to Edinburgh to visit his parents.

"Heavens! Clothes!" Clare cried in despair when the visit was settled. "I have none! I meant to get things before I came home and then Mummy was ill so I didn't. What am I to do?"

"What sort of people are the Crichtons?" asked Frances in business-like tones.

"I don't know. He's a judge and they live just outside Edinburgh."

"Well," said Frances. "You're only going for a few days. We'll manage. What have you got?"

Clare's wardrobe was undoubtedly at a low ebb. Frances went through it with swift and ruthless efficiency and Clare, whose interest in clothes was careless and intermittent, watched her meekly and, recognizing genuine skill when she saw it, thankfully left her cousin to it. They had picnics and parties, fishing and golf, and there were times when Clare and Nevill disappeared blissfully together in Tishy and Frances meanwhile sent a few orders to London shops and worked steadily and skilfully, altering and adapting. She said very little about it and Clare gasped when she saw her transformed garments displayed ready for packing.

"Heavens, Frances!" she cried. "How on earth have you done it?" Frances looked complacently at her handiwork.

"It isn't so much. Only for a few days."

"But so lavish. There's everything," cried Clare. "I don't know how I'm to thank you." And she hugged her cousin warmly. "This is the nicest thing anybody could have done for me."

Frances was pleased.

"It was fun. Let's see how they look."

"It's a good job," said Clare, trying on and surveying the

125

effects, "that I didn't do the shopping I meant to do. You've made these things far more distingy than anything I'd have bought. I now know what it must feel like to be dressed by Hartnell."

Frances burst out laughing.

"Poop!" she cried. "You don't know what you're talking about."

"Well I'm not an authority," agreed Clare, "but I can recognize distinction when I see it. You have the flair. Why don't you become a top-line designer?"

"I might, I suppose, do it quite well. The trouble is that though it's fun dressing you I'd hate to have to do it for most people. Think of Lady Courtney as a customer."

"Well—you must take my trousseau in hand. I'm getting bitten by clothes."

"Good," said Frances, "dawning of clothes-consciousness and not before time. My life has not been altogether spent in vain."

A fortnight after Nevill's arrival in Ledenham Clare returned from her visit to his family and Frances who had, as the highest mark of gratitude and esteem, been given the freedom of Tishy, met her at the station. As Frances, in slacks, her hair blown about by the wind and Clare, elegant in her transformed town clothes, crammed her luggage with some difficulty into the little car, the same thought suddenly struck them both and simultaneously they broke into laughter.

"I must say you look your part all right," said Clare wiping her eyes. "Did my elegance terrify you?"

"Sure," said Frances grinning, "and I hope you feel thoroughly over-dressed and vulgar. Do you want to drive?"

"No—carry on."

"Well—how was it?" asked Frances.

It had been very good and Clare had much to tell.

"Nevill's coming back when this job is fixed up," she concluded, "and we think we can be married in October. Now you. How've you got on and how's everything? It seems ages since I went away."

"It isn't," said Frances. "Everything's ticking over nicely. You haven't been missed at all."

"Well I'm glad of that. Have you been bored?" Frances grinned.

"No. I've made steady progress with my education." Clare looked at her inquiringly and she went on. "I was a gracious hostess on Sunday. Preacher at lunch and four boys and Patsy and what's-his-name the history man for supper."

"Good for you. I didn't know Beak meant to have anyone in for supper."

"He didn't, till I pointed out that there was no need to fall behind schedule just because you were away."

Clare laughed.

"Go on. What else?"

"Oh—I went to chapel. Lady C. gave me the dirtiest look I ever saw and Henry—well Henry was definitely peculiar." She stopped and Clare, who always watched the road whoever was driving, transferred her gaze to the driver. Frances was driving very easily and well. The pushed-up sleeves of her jersey showed her slim arms and hands browner than when Clare saw them last and her whole body looked relaxed and contented. Her expression was amused and slightly puzzled and when Clare asked,

"How was Henry peculiar?" she glanced round and grinned.

"He was flustered. Off his balance—and he blushed."

"No!" said Clare. "He couldn't."

"He should be past it," agreed Frances, "but I assure you he did. He was wondering whether he dared leave mother and walk home with me, I think, and then while he was dithering I went off and Angus fell in and walked along with me."

"Angus!" cried Clare.

"Yes indeed—Angus. He blushed too, but it's more natural for him and he was really very nice and sensible, Clare."

"I'm glad to hear it. What did you talk about?"

"Well—he said, rightly, that we were bound to meet and he thought it best to get it over. We couldn't have the whole School watching us avoid each other. And he said he was sorry about that ghastly day. He didn't want to talk about it, but he knew he'd been an ass. So I said 'thanks—O.K.' and we were home. A brief encounter."

"Good for Angus though," said Clare.

"Yes. I thought so. Patsy says—" Frances stopped again and Clare glancing round wondered if she imagined a heightening of her colour.

"What does Patsy say?"

"Oh—he said he thought Angus had begun to see what

matters and what doesn't. In other words he's grown up a lot."

"Patsy said that?"

"Well—something like that."

"Quite a speech for Patsy," remarked Clare thoughtfully. "I do want to solve the Henry mystery though," said Frances, "I don't get it."

It was not till late that night that Clare and her father found themselves alone.

"Everything has been peaceful, I gather," she said. "And it sounds as though Frances has been good."

"She's been very good," said Mr. Fielding. "I've really got quite fond of her. She didn't try to do too much."

Clare smiled, knowing his loathing of officious helpfulness. He was looking thoughtful and presently went on.

"I wouldn't say that everything's peaceful."

"Oh? What's up?"

"Hard to say. A sort of unease. Henry seems to be exceedingly bad-tempered and quarrelsome."

"How do you know?" asked Clare curiously. She always found it puzzling how her father knew all he did about the School and the common room. He did no spying, he had no use for snoopers or tale-bearers or even for gossip, but he was never anything but fully informed.

"Oh—I really can't tell you," he said vaguely. "One sees things and hears odd snippets and they add up."

"What about Angus?" asked Clare. "He's done a very sensible thing about Frances," and she told the story of the walk home from Chapel.

"Yes—that was sensible," agreed Mr. Fielding. "He is

having a pretty tough time I think. It's difficult to get right with boys if you've got wrong and he did get himself thoroughly disliked, poor chap. But he'll get through I think. I suspect, though, that Courtney isn't helping. He seems to have got his knife into Cameron to quite an extraordinary degree."

"I'm afraid that's Frances," said Clare. Her father took out his pipe and looked at her sharply.

"That must be nonsense," he said. "A man of Henry's age and experience isn't knocked off his balance by a pretty girl as easily as that."

"I think you underestimate Frances' attraction."

"Well if she's flirting with them all tell her to stop it," said the Headmaster, "but I don't think she is. It can't be that."

Clare felt vaguely uneasy as she went upstairs to bed and resolved that the most useful thing she could do was to keep Frances fully occupied and carefully and continuously "grouped". But she found that it was more difficult than she expected to control her cast.

The day after her return was the day of the Upton Match. It was always the first school match of the term and since Upton was their nearest comparable neighbour the two schools were intimate rivals and the matches were always well attended and sociable.

"Tidy clothes," Clare told Frances. "Nothing like Speech Day of course. About 'Inspection' level."

"What on earth's that?" asked Frances. "Don't tell me—d'you mean a garden party frock?"

"Well—I usually wear the best of my ordinary cottons,"

said Clare, "and a hat if it's very sunny—and if I happen to have one."

It was a day of blazing sunshine and Frances appeared in a frock which was the "simple cotton" interpreted with genius regardless of expense. It could hardly have been simpler, but the fit, the cunning extra fullness of the skirt and above all the colour, lifted it astronomically above everything to which Ledenham was accustomed. Frances wore high-heeled white sandals, so delicate as to be hardly visible, and she carried a large white hat. Clare gazed at her and nearly groaned aloud.

"What's the matter?" demanded Frances. "Don't you like it?"

"Like it? It's heaven! Nobody will look at the match of course."

"Oh hell," said Frances crossly. "Why should they?"

This was one of the occasions on which Clare's hostessly duties kept her very busy. There was a large party, including the Headmaster of Upton and his wife, for lunch at the School House, and Frances was an able and comfortable lieutenant, but on the cricket field, while Clare was still tied to the V.I.P. party, she drifted away and was thereafter to be seen either surrounded by young men or walking about with one or other of them. It seemed to Clare that she herself spent the day having the same conversation with hundreds of people. An inquiry about her mother and then her beautiful cousin and then her engagement in that order. It was a change, but hardly a relief when she was seized after tea by the mother of a boy in School House. Mrs. Leigh had had three sons in the

School and considered herself a privileged parent, and she lived near enough to Ledenham to visit it often and to know everybody in it.

"Clare, my dear," she said authoritatively, "come and talk to me. I've been missing your mother and I'm behind-hand with all the gossip."

Clare hoped that her instant mustering of caution did not show as she allowed herself to be led away to a more remote chair. It was really pretty simple of Mrs. Leigh, she thought, to imagine that she'd believe the suggestion that Mummy told her the School gossip.

"Now," said Mrs. Leigh. "You've been working away like a Trojan all day. I don't know how you do it. Relax and have a cigarette and be comfortable."

Clare accepted the cigarette and leant back rather wearily. It would now begin again, she thought—Frances. But it didn't. Mrs. Leigh lit her cigarette, inhaled deeply and said,

"Now tell me about this sinister new maths master."

"Sinister new maths master?" repeated Clare idiotically, turning astonished eyes to her companion.

"Yes—this Mr. Cameron," went on Mrs. Leigh briskly.

"John says he really is a horror. He'd had a frightful drinking bout and was missing for a whole day and went about looking like death. Don't pretend you don't know about it, Clare. Of course I get it all from John—he tells me everything, we're such pals—but I just want to know how bad it is. Boys exaggerate so."

Clare managed a laugh, all her wariness well forward.

"John must be a prize exaggerator," she said. "It's absolute nonsense, Mrs. Leigh. Mr. Cameron is a perfectly nice young man."

Mrs. Leigh shook her head.

"Oh no, my dear. There was a lot that John simply couldn't have made up you know. There's certainly something very far wrong. And the boys are terrified of him—they never know when he'll fly into a rage and be violent."

Clare said, "Well if you've been hearing things like that you ought to be talking to my father, not me."

"Talk to the Beak?" cried Mrs. Leigh with a shriek of laughter. "I wouldn't dare! I'm terrified of the Beak."

And well you might be, thought the Beak's daughter grimly, if you went to him with that tale. But Mrs. Leigh had not finished.

"Seriously though, Clare, I have been worried—and I am worried. You know I've had to bring up those three boys alone since my husband's death and it's a terribly heavy responsibility."

"I know," said Clare. "It must be a very heavy load."

"Yes. Well—hearing all this from John I really didn't know what I ought to do, so this morning when I got here I waylaid that divine Henry Courtney. He's always so human and understanding and I said, 'Now do just keep this under your hat' and told him the tale."

"Well I hope he laughed at it. I'm sure it's all it deserves," said Clare, wishing it had been anyone else.

Mrs. Leigh shook her head.

"Oh no. He couldn't."

"What did he say?"

"I don't think I can tell you that, my dear," said Mrs.

Leigh with a sort of smug importance. "Henry Courtney and I know each other very well and he spoke confidentially. It's a matter, you see, of avoiding scandal. As he said, if the Beak heard of it officially he'd have to take notice of it officially and then it would all come out. I think that the man will just quietly disappear from Ledenham you know. Henry hinted as much, and said I mustn't worry. Of course he had to turn Cameron out of his house!"

Clare sat in dismayed silence. Nothing that she said would change Mrs. Leigh's opinions, even if she said right out that Henry was a liar which was impossible as well as useless. She would tell the Beak of course, but must she first warn this ghastly woman? She thought about it with some panic and decided that "when in doubt, say nothing" was the best policy, but she could not leave without saying something for Angus.

"Mrs. Leigh—I think there is a bad muddle about this," she said. "I don't know Mr. Cameron very well, but I like him and I know my father thinks he is good. He's inexperienced of course. I believe that—that he's had some private trouble since he's been here, bad news I think, and I expect it was then that some of the boys started rumours about him. They do start silly rumours sometimes you know."

She had done her best, but Mrs. Leigh only smiled knowingly and shook her head.

"I know all about boys' rumours. Heavens I ought to with three of them! I'm afraid this is more serious. But" suddenly gay, "let's not talk of horrid things any more. Tell me about this young man of yours. Are you very happy? Of course you are!"

Clare escaped from the fusillade of arch congratulations as soon as she could and looked about for Frances, but the charming blue figure was some distance away with Henry Courtney in attendance, and she turned, feeling rather sick and unhappy, to do her duty by Mrs. Carr of Upton.

The match was nearly over and Clare felt that she had been staring at those white figures running about on the sunny green field for a life-time and talking politely till her throat was dry and her head filled with hot sand when Frances came, and leaning over the back of her chair murmured with a note of laughter in her voice,

"Clare—people aren't staying for dinner are they?"

"No—why?"

"I'm going out. Dining over at Riverdale with Henry."

Clare said urgently, though still quietly,

"Oh, Frances—don't! I can't explain now, but—"

Frances laughed outright.

"It's all right. I know all about it and it is funny. Don't be so solemn, you ass. 'Bye," and she was off, walking lightly across the grass towards the house.

Clare made a movement to get up and follow her, but the match ended and everybody was getting up and coming to say good-bye. By the time she was free to go to the house herself she knew that it was too late. Henry had disappeared as soon as Frances did and they would have gone at once. She felt quite badly upset and when Patsy, who had been umpiring, ran after her and said,

"Clare, come and drink. Where's Frances?" she shook her head and was infuriated to find tears coming into her eyes.

135

They were almost at the door of the Zoo and she was neatly steered through it and up to Patsy's study. He shut the door and taking her by the arms put her gently into his best chair.

"What you need," he said comfortably, "is a nip of whisky and a cigarette."

CHAPTER 10

CLARE wiped her eyes, took a comforting pull at her cigarette and sipped whisky. She disliked it a good deal but it drove the tears back and steadied her lip.

"Sorry," she said. "That was very silly."

Patsy was standing against the mantelpiece filling his pipe and without looking at her he said,

"Trying day I should think. Saw you in the thick of all the old trout. Nevill all right?"

Clare laughed a little.

"Oh yes! Nevill's all right. Aren't you having a party?"

"Thought of it, but I hadn't asked anybody else. Doesn't matter. Nick'll probably look in." He lit his pipe and looked at her inquiringly. "What's up?"

"I don't know if I ought to tell you," said Clare doubtfully.

"Well you don't have to. Where's Frances? Or don't you want to tell me that?"

She hesitated and then said,

"She's gone to dine at Riverdale with Henry."

"You don't mind do you?" asked Patsy.

"In a way I do," she replied with a troubled face.

Patsy drank some beer and sitting down turned his very direct gaze on her and said,

"Henry is pretty bloody-minded at present. Have you been getting wind of that? I saw you being hauled off by the Leigh menace."

"Well, yes," said Clare. "She's been getting tales from her

revolting brat and—and—"

"Took them to the sympathetic Mr. Courtney," concluded Patsy grinning.

"I shall have to tell Beak about it. There seems to be some —beastliness going on. I'll go, now, Patsy and you can still have your party. Thank you very much."

"Don't hurry—the party's off. Have another cigarette."

Clare said she wouldn't and got up, but Patsy had more to say.

"You know Perry and Nick and a few other people have been keeping a sort of eye on Angus don't you?" Clare nodded. "Well, clear it with the Beak and then, if you can, you might let one of us know what you've got."

"All right," said Clare, "I'll do that. But I've nothing definite you know. Just dirt really." Patsy nodded and as he opened the door he said, "You needn't worry about Frances you know. She's all right. Just likes to be a bit devilish now and again."

"Oh I know that. But there are better people than Henry to be devilish with."

"Not so devilish devilish though," said Patsy grinning. "But he isn't dangerous, Clare."

Clare went into the house by the route which took her past the study, but the "engaged" sign was on so she passed on and did not see her father till dinner, for which he was unusually late.

Mr. Fielding had gone straight to his study after the match and was signing his letters when Miss Wills entered wearing the severe expression which meant that something required discretion.

138

"Lady Courtney is on the telephone, sir," she said. "She wants to see you if you can spare a few minutes."

"Now?" asked the Headmaster surprised.

"If possible."

"Oh. All right. Tell her I'll go round in a minute."

"She would rather come here, she said, sir."

If the Headmaster's thought had been uttered it would have been something like "Lor'!" but he merely said in an expressionless voice.

"Very well. I'll have the letters ready when you bring her in."

He could not imagine why Lady Courtney should want to see him immediately in his study and he wasted no time in speculation, but when he rose ten minutes later to receive her, his polite greeting concealed considerable curiosity and a sharpened observation.

Like Angus on another occasion he thought she looked old, and her movements as she arranged herself in the chair he placed for her were clumsy and almost fumbling. He had never liked her, but he felt sorry for her now and his voice was kind.

"Is there something I can do for you, Lady Courtney?"

"I think so," she said heavily. "If you will."

"If I can—certainly," he replied and waited.

There was a pause and then she leant forward and said,

"Mr. Fielding—you should send your niece away from Ledenham."

Whatever he had expected it was nothing like this, and for a moment he was completely taken aback and then anger began to rise in him. Lady Courtney was going on,

"It is an extraordinary thing to say, I know, and a very difficult thing to say. But I think it right that somebody should tell you that she is doing infinite harm here."

Mr. Fielding was accustomed to controlling his feelings and he did so now.

"Lady Courtney," he said, "I think that if you had given more consideration to whatever is troubling you, you would not have come to me. That is not a thing that should be said."

She lifted her hand in its white glove as though she moved something out of her way.

"I can assure you I have considered it very carefully and I can see no other way. I would have avoided it if I could."

"In that case," said the Headmaster, "I must hear what you have to say."

It was very difficult for her but he gave her no help and she fumbled for a moment with her bag and her handkerchief.

"Miss Cheriton is a very pretty girl," she began at last, "I don't know how much she intends it but she—she simply bewitches people." Her voice rose a little and she spoke hurriedly. "I think she does it deliberately, that she is wicked. She has the most terrible effect."

The Headmaster looked at her with dismay and then said firmly,

"Lady Courtney this is really the most arrant nonsense. Frances is a very young girl, but she is a lady and quite incapable of such conduct as you suggest."

"You are deceived," said Lady Courtney, "I know I am right."

140

Mr. Fielding had a fleeting memory of Clare telling him that he underestimated Frances' powers of attraction, but Lady Courtney was going on,

"I must say it, I suppose. Mr. Fielding—that extraordinary behaviour, a breakdown really, of Mr. Cameron's was entirely due to Miss Cheriton. Both Mr. Vincent and Mr. Henderson are infatuated, and Henry is—is desperately unhappy and unsettled. He—he is quite unlike himself. His work and his judgement—he—there is no other word for it —he is bewitched."

Some laughter had now to be controlled as well as anger, but the Headmaster did not altogether conceal his amusement. "I really can't," he said, "regard my young niece as a serious danger to the common room. If she flirts she does it no more than a pretty girl is entitled to flirt, and if my assistant masters lose their heads about her or anyone else they must find them again. Certainly they'll have no protection or sympathy from me against a little girl of twenty. You should say to Henry what the young say to each other, Lady Courtney, 'Be your age'."

Lady Courtney began making the collecting movements of one about to depart.

"It was a great effort to come to you," she said coldly, "and I am sorry you refuse to believe what I say, and receive me with flippancy."

"I don't refuse to believe you. I do think you have been troubled and are therefore seeing things out of proportion."

"That may be so. It may also be that you fail to see things which are serious because of your affection for your niece. I believe the situation to be so grave that since you will not

141

listen to me I shall go to Lord Leyburn."

They were both standing now.

"My dear Lady Courtney," said Mr. Fielding. "I do beg you to consider what your son's feelings would be if you went to the Chairman of the Governors with this. Henry may be behaving foolishly, if so it will pass, and he would have every right to be very angry indeed if his mother told the story of his folly. It would be almost unforgivable."

The old lady was standing very still, looking, he thought, really frightened.

"He is out with her now," she said.

"Well—what of it?"

She shook her head slowly, and said again,

"He is so unlike himself. I have never seen him so unlike himself. I am—alarmed."

Mr. Fielding paused, and then said,

"I can't possibly speak to Henry about this—unless of course it came to a question of marriage between them. But I'll have a word with him when I see a chance. Don't worry, Lady Courtney. This will pass. But for Henry's sake you must not speak of it, and I must remind you too that it is very wrong and, I may add, dangerous to make such allegations against a young girl."

Clare was waiting for him in the drawing-room when he went through.

"Sorry I'm so late," he said. "You can ring now. Is there soup? Good—we'll have some sherry with it."

"Frances is out," remarked Clare.

"Is she? Oh, yes—she's dining with Courtney of course."

Clare wondered how he knew but she did not ask. He

probably saw them as they drove off. Her father put a glass of sherry beside her and went to his own place.

"This is very nice," said Clare. "I hope it's all right. Patsy gave me a whisky a little while ago. Do they mix?"

"I didn't know Patsy served whisky. Why did you drink it? You don't like it do you?"

"It was a bracer-up."

They went on with their soup in abstracted silence.

"Why did you need bracing?" asked Mr. Fielding suddenly.

"Oh," said Clare, "I'll tell you all about that later."

Her father smiled at her. "More anxiety?" She nodded. "Oh well—let it wait."

They had their coffee just outside the french window which led from the drawing-room to the garden. The only sounds were the singing of the river and occasionally distant, cheerful voices from the boys' part of the house, and Clare, with great distaste since the subject seemed particularly sordid in this peaceful setting, told her story.

Her father listened in silence and when she finished he said quietly,

"I'm sorry you heard it, my dear. That sort of rumour-mongering is very nasty. All I can say is that it very seldom does much harm—in the long run."

She looked surprised and he went on,

"Quite soon people get on to the fact that the Mrs. Leighs of this world aren't reliable you know."

"Yes—that," agreed Clare. "I wasn't worrying about her —but it's Henry. What is the matter with Henry, Beak?"

"Well," said the Headmaster drily, "according to his

mother, who ought to know, he's bewitched."

Clare looked completely astonished for a moment and then laughed aloud.

"Really, Beak! This simply gets more and more crazy."

"Yes it does," he agreed.

"Were you and Lady C. having a heart-to-hearter before dinner?"

"I'm afraid so."

"Well—come clean. What is all this?"

When she had heard most of what Lady Courtney had had to say she was silent for a moment, and then said rather anxiously:

"You know, Beak, Frances really doesn't lead them on— or not much. Nevill says," she hesitated and her father looking amused said,

"What does Nevill say?"

"Well—he says she's the kind of girl who is so seductive that it's really hard work discouraging people."

"He's immune, I take it?" said her father.

"Oh, he says he outgrew dumb blondes long ago, but schoolmasters are slow to develop."

Mr. Fielding was seldom heard to laugh aloud, except for a genial noise which his family called his social laugh and which expressed no genuine amusement, but he did so now. He had barely recovered when Frances' light step was heard and she came through the window.

"There you are," she said. "I thought the house was empty. Are you still drinking coffee at this hour?"

"The coffee's finished," said Clare, "but we're daringly drinking liqueurs. Would you like one?"

"Lovely," said Frances. "I'll get a glass."

The Headmaster looked very much at ease in his chair, and his pipe was drawing peacefully when Frances brought her glass and sat down.

"Uncle Hugh," she remarked, "I've never seen you lounging before."

"You don't know what goes on in his study," said Clare darkly.

"I resent that," said Mr. Fielding drowsily. "I'm a hard-working man. I don't see why I should be hen-pecked when, for once in a way, I sit down."

"No indeed," said Frances, and patted his arm kindly, looking as she did so very unlike a predatory female, or a sorceress.

"Had a nice time?" he inquired, without opening his eyes.

"Quite nice," said Frances. "Well—rather boring actually. Clare, Henry's asked me to go to a ball at Leyburn, but I said I'd find out if you were going. Are you?"

"Oh," said Clare, "I'd forgotten all about it. Yes, of course you must go. But you don't want to go with Henry, Frances—he's a loathsome dancer."

Mr. Fielding opened his eyes.

"What's wrong with Henry's dancing? He's usually an efficient chap."

Clare gave a shrug of distaste.

"He plasters himself on to you and glides meaningly about." Frances gave a hoot of laughter and said,

"Well if we want to go to this dance without Henry we'll have to get cracking. Nevill will be here. Who else? Patsy?"

Clare had thought that Frances' acquaintance with Patsy

appeared to have ripened during her absence in Edinburgh and a small impulse of mischief led her to say, "Nick's the man for a dance. Nick's dancing is an absolute poem and he's terribly good at a party. We'll get him." She thought Frances' face fell a little and, relenting, went on, "If Patsy likes to come too of course, we can dig out another girl—or they can."

"That sounds fine," said Frances. "So long as Henry doesn't tag on."

"Frances," said her uncle opening his eyes again. "Are you playing fast and loose with Henry?"

Frances turned a startled face to him.

"Fast and loose!" she exclaimed.

"He means flirting, or playing him up," explained Clare.

"I don't mind at all," went on Mr. Fielding mildly. "He's old enough to look after himself. I just wondered."

"Oh," said Frances, still rather puzzled and a little uneasy. "Well—no, I'm not. Or not much anyway. Why, Uncle Hugh? Do you—do you think I've been behaving badly?"

The Headmaster heaved himself out of his chair and smiled at her.

"No, child, I don't. He's not a very reliable chap though in some ways." He said good night and departed.

"Golly," gasped Frances. "What a rocket!"

"A rocket?" said Clare. "Surely not. It wasn't meant to be."

"Well it felt like one to me. I'm all shook up. Not a scolding rocket—a warning one." She lit a cigarette and after a moment went on. "It's the habit of authority I suppose. Daddy—I don't suppose you really remember him

146

much—he's always pouring out streams of scoldings and warnings and it doesn't mean a thing. And one mild little word from Uncle Hugh shatters me. What would it be like if he was angry? Wrath of God I should think."

Clare smiled.

"Something like it perhaps if he was really angry. He meant the warnings though, Fran. Henry is a bit—nasty you know."

"Yes," said Frances thoughtfully. "I think he is rather. And I wasn't going to ignore the warning. But it may be a bit tricky shaking him off. He never does or says anything to justify sweeping out, but there's a sort of persistence, all meaning-like. Very rum."

They were silent and Clare was wondering whether to bring out the gossip about Angus when Frances added with an air of finality.

"He's up to something. I don't know what. I must just try letting him down gradually without fussing."

"That'll be the best thing," agreed Clare, "if you can manage it. He's being very bloody about Angus."

"How?" asked Frances. "I know he hates him, but what can he do?"

"All sorts of things," Clare said grimly. "Mocking him in common room, laughing at him with boys, steadily throwing dirt. Lots of little things—but they mount up."

She went on to tell Frances about her talk with Mrs. Leigh and with Patsy, but Lady Courtney's interview with the Headmaster was something which she felt she could not tell. It had been too personal an attack on Frances, and, besides that, the fact that the cold, confident lady was

147

sufficiently agitated to do anything so unexpected was in itself alarming.

Frances said slowly: "It's rather beastly isn't it? And not very easy. If I'm not clever about it—dropping Henry I mean—it may make things worse. I think I'll have to stall a bit."

Clare agreed.

"You don't want any sort of crisis."

"No," said Frances. "Slow freezing tactics I think."

CHAPTER 11

NOTHING had been heard of Angus since the day when he made his apologies to Lady Courtney and left her to begin his new leaf, but there had been no further drama and his life had become a hard and rather a painful grind. It happened that he never did hear the talk and rumours concerning his alleged habits with regard to drink and even drugs, though they were very wide-spread and much canvassed for a time.

"Of course it's drugs," said one knowing 15-year-old to a friend who was usually credulous. "You can see it by his eyes. He'll have another brain-storm soon, you'll see."

"I've never been near enough to see his eyes," replied the friend simply. "But," he added, a puzzled scowl gathering beneath the overhang of rough, mouse-coloured hair, "what I can't understand is how a chap who drinks or drugs can play rugby like this chap can."

He was not alone in his dilemma. The majority of the School never believed in the drink or drugs theory and came nearer to the truth in regarding Frances as the cause of the storm, but they were almost unanimous in their dislike of poor Angus, and wholly unanimous in their mistrust of him as a master liable to blow up without cause and to be unjust in his wrath. Angus was unhappily aware of their hostility and as he was a friendly young man and, moreover, beginning to be aware of his boys as individuals, mostly likeable, the fact that he was on bad terms with them and had to control his sets by sheer authority and punishment hurt him a good deal, though his control was successful. The problem of his living accommodation was solved, curiously enough, by Miss Perry, who in the course of a conversation about it murmured "Mrs. Crump" and left the room.

"Of course," said her brother. "Why didn't I think of it?"

Mrs. Crump was the object of much sympathy in Ledenham at that time as her husband, a postman, had recently been killed in a particularly stupid road accident, and in due course, Angus transferred himself to her rather airless little house, too far from the school for convenience, and to her substantial, but very plain cooking. But he spent three very strange weeks in Little Campion before he did so.

They were weeks which he afterwards remembered as almost completely silent. Courtney never addressed him at all. Lady Courtney, largely for the benefit of Rogers, tried to maintain some conversation at meals, but it was uphill work and never very successful. Angus was sorry for her. She had never been friendly to him and was chilly and repressive to the last, but he thought that Henry was behaving abominably and being thoroughly unkind to her, and though there was nothing he could do about it he hoped that they might recover when he left them.

The people who were "in the know" and inclined to be well-disposed to Angus were very kind to him. He had a good many invitations to meals which gave him relief, though it seemed that much as Courtney resented his presence he resented his absence on these occasions even more, and getting to know his colleagues and their families as he did was the pleasantest thing that happened to him.

The Cameron supporters did all that they could, though as Mr. Perry said, things mostly had to be left to time and to Angus himself.

"He's a good chap and eventually that'll get through. But it'll take time and you can't hurry it."

Meanwhile Angus, grinding along and sorely tried, discovered growing up within him an overwhelming ambition. He had by no means forgotten Frances. The thought of her was often and painfully with him, but whether he was still in love with her or not he hardly knew. The ambition, however, as it grew pushed her farther and farther away and left him with no other desire than to get through this bad patch and establish himself in Ledenham. This was his job and his place; these were the friends he wanted to live with; and his whole self was concentrated on the task of overcoming his present difficulties and securing his foot-hold.

Patsy, as part of the campaign, put him on to taking nets practice. Angus was not a particularly good cricketer, but he had an athlete's natural skill with any kind of ball and that, combined with his size and his competent grace of movement, made him impressive. He was also, as he was beginning to realize, a born teacher, and applying this ability to cricket-coaching did him a certain amount of good in the School. His first real break, however, came through Nick Vincent who discovered that he could climb.

"You've never mentioned this before," said Nick rather indignantly. "What have you done?"

They were spread about Patsy's study with mugs of beer

151

and Angus was very tired and suffering from one of his more discouraging days.

"Oh—not very much," he said indifferently, but ruthless questioning elicited the information that he had in fact had a good deal of experience and had accomplished some formidable climbs.

"It was just some chaps at the University," he said deprecatingly. "We used to go regularly for a bit—Cuillins mostly."

"Was that Lawrence McPhail's lot?" asked Patsy curiously.

"Yes," said Angus, mildly surprised.

"And McPhail's been to the Himalayas," said Nick, "and I remember hearing him speak of one Cameron as a chap he'd like for an expedition. That would be you, I suppose?"

Angus blushed.

"He had an idea of it," he said apologetically, "but it never came to anything."

"Well, I must say, Angus, you are a chump," Nick said severely, and brushing Angus' protests aside he went on,

"From now on you can dam' well help with the Climbing Club."

Within twenty miles of Ledenham were hills which presented a range of nicely graded climbs. There was nothing big and nothing to tax the expert, but it was an ideal training ground and here Angus found himself nearly every Sunday for the rest of the term. Immediately after chapel he rushed to change, and his little car, full of food, climbing gear and boys hurried in company with Nick's similarly loaded jeep to what was very much his element.

While he was there he forgot everything except the hills and his delight in climbing. Even the ambition was temporarily submerged to such a depth that he failed to see how much his skill and leadership were doing for him.

"He's absolutely top-class," Nick told Clare. "I've never climbed with anybody better and he handles the chaps a treat. You should come and do the Needle with him, Clare. You've never done it and you'll never have a better chance."

"I'll come," said Clare, and in due course she did, but not till some weeks had elapsed.

There now began what Clare later described to her mother as the "haunted period", when it seemed that the house was never free of Henry Courtney and dealing with him became a major pre-occupation for herself and Frances.

It began with the Leyburn Ball. Urged by Frances, Clare had, as she said, "laid it on with Nick" by the house telephone before she went to bed on the night when the party was first mentioned; and she was very glad she had done so when Henry dropped in after morning School the following day.

"Clare, my dear!" he said, his usual patronizing greeting. "How well love suits you! Charming! And the young man—he flourishes I hope?"

Clare, making appropriate noises, led him to the drawing-room and gave him a cigarette.

"I just dropped in," said Henry, "to talk to Frances and to you about an idea I had for the Leyburn Ball. Is she in? Did she speak of it?"

There was something odd about Henry and Clare found it embarrassing. He looked excited and restless, and he seemed all of a sudden to have become a surprisingly intimate and affectionate friend of her own.

"Frances told me you had asked her to the ball," she said, "but I'm afraid I've arranged our party for it."

"Frances didn't say so," said Henry quickly.

"No. She didn't know about it till after she came home," replied Clare truthfully.

Henry eyed her suspiciously.

"Who is going in your party?"

"Really, Henry!" Clare exclaimed. "What a strange thing to ask!"

"Not so very strange surely, unless there is some reason why you don't want to tell me."

She looked at him very directly.

"No reason at all. When I've been at home I've always gone to the Leyburn Ball with Nick Vincent's party. We're going again to what will probably be my last one and Nevill, my fiancé, and Frances are coming with us— naturally."

"Well, Clare darling—don't be so up-stage and grand," said Henry with a placatory smile. "I couldn't be more in favour of a gathering of old friends, but I had rather set my heart on dancing with you and Frances, and I just wondered if another old friend might not join in."

Clare swore inwardly but kept her head.

"It's really Nick's party," she said. "Ask him if you like. I should think it might be difficult to find an extra girl. But of course you could bring your own partner," she added

154

with some malice.

"I could do that of course," he agreed. "But my idea was rather a special dinner for four—you and your young man, Frances and myself, before the ball. Couldn't that still be done? We could join the others afterwards, but it would just be my private little celebration of your engagement, my dear."

"It's very kind of you, but—no, Henry. I'm sorry, but we can't possibly do that. Nick's party is dining together. He always does it and I couldn't upset the arrangement. I wouldn't want to anyway," she added, looking at him with clear eyes. "Of course you are an old friend too, but you've always been more grown-up than the people who are in this party. If you'd ask us to dine another time we'd be delighted."

There was a pause before Henry said with artificial lightness,

"Well—there's nothing for it I see but to connive with Frances. She may be able to persuade you—she has her own ideas about a dancing partner I know."

Clare was baffled by his persistence and by the jaunty tones which strove to suggest a special relationship between Frances and himself while his eyes were so uneasy.

"Frances can't throw the party over when she's accepted," she said bluntly. "Henry—I'm sorry, but there are people coming to lunch. I must turn you out I'm afraid."

He got up at once, but as he opened the door he fired a parting shot.

"You know, Clare my dear, I know perfectly well how

155

Vincent's parties are arranged. You do it. Why are you determined to keep me out?"

This was so near the truth that Clare decided to lose her temper.

"Henry," she cried, "I am engaged for the Leyburn Ball. Frances is engaged for the Leyburn Ball. Ask us to something else if you like, but now—please, go away."

When she reported this visit Frances rumpled up her hair and swore.

"Blast Henry—what am I to do with him? Clare, for goodness' sake don't look so cross."

"I'm not cross," said Clare indignantly, "at least, I am a bit. You let us in for this muddle—you'll have to get out."

"But I don't know how I got in," cried Frances.

"Well—you flirted with him I suppose, and there you are."

"I didn't really," Frances assured her earnestly. "I've flirted ever so much more than I ever did with him and no ill-feeling." Clare could not help laughing but Frances still looked solemn as she went on, "At first he was amusing and it was fun to dress up and go to lavish pubs. And then I thought I might just pay him out a bit for being so bloody to Angus, and last night I went mostly because he'd been so peculiar and I wanted to find out why."

"And did you?"

"No—not really. I think he wants to marry me, but I'm not sure."

"Do many of them ask you to marry them?" asked Clare curiously.

Frances shrugged her shoulders.

"Quite a lot. Nobody very nice. You are lucky having Nevill, Clare. You look so comfortable with him."

"Cheer up," said Clare. "No need to give up hope for a year or two yet."

Whoever falls in love, or whatever crises occur in the private lives of its members, a school goes steadily on its way. Boys are taught and fed, play their games, and are entertained, and on this first day of the "haunted" period a small company of actors visited Ledenham. Three of them stayed at School House, three more were spread amongst other houses, and it was the imminence of their arrival which had enabled Clare to get rid of the unwilling Henry. The company worked hard all afternoon preparing their stage and rehearsing on it, and when the School House trio returned and were being comforted with tea, Henry arrived again. Clare felt testily that her hostessly poise was being stretched to danger point, and firmly introducing Henry to the actors she placed him beside the leading lady, gave him tea and turning to resume her conversation with the leading man said,

"Where were we?"

The eyes of the leading man were dancing with amusement, and as he neatly picked up the thread of talk they met those of the leading lady. She was not very young, nor particularly beautiful but she had charm and experience and before the fascinated eyes of the youthful hostesses she dealt with Henry very much as a spider deals with a fly. She enticed him with provocative flattery, detached him from the rest of the company with a low voice and expressive eyes, and when she had completed the

157

wrapping up of her parcel she rose with a wide, mischievous smile and dismissed him.

"My dear man!" she cried. "You have kept me talking for hours! I must rest. Go away at once, Mr. Courtney, or you will ruin the play."

And Henry went. One attempt he did make to speak to Frances, but he had no chance. He was swept out of the house on the tide of the leading lady's determined skill. When he had gone she paused on her way towards the stairs and looking at the leading man frankly giggled. He nodded at her.

"Very nice," he said grinning.

"But you must put the poor man out of his agony," she said, shaking her head at Frances. "He's in a very bad way you know," and she went on upstairs to her delayed rest.

"That was wonderful," remarked Frances earnestly.

"Yes," said Clare drily. "Pity we can't keep her longer. She's better than a watch-dog."

Everybody went to the play and during the interval everybody streamed out of the hall and stood about in the warm scented evening air, smoking and exchanging easy, familiar talk. Nick, with Patsy and Angus following more slowly, hurried to speak to Clare.

"Look, Clare," he said quickly. "Both the Brownlow girls will be at home for the dance. All right if we ask Angus?"

The Brownlow girls were old and tried friends and Clare was delighted.

"Oh yes! What a very good party! But, Nick," she went on in a hurried mutter, "Henry's trying to muscle in." Patsy had now joined them and when Nick said, "Oh lor'! Well

158

he can dam' well muscle out again," he added, looking at her rather intently,

"If you have any trouble refer him to us."

"Don't hesitate," put in Nick and Clare laughed.

"I won't," she said and turned away in time to hear Angus say to Frances, "I didn't know you had done any climbing."

"Frances," cried Nick indignantly. "Have you been holding out on me too?"

Frances lit up with laughter. She took Nick's arm and said with exaggerated mock affection,

"Darling Nick! Of course I wouldn't hold out on you."

"Away with your blandishments, woman! Can you climb?"

"Not what you'd call climbing," said Frances. "I had a bash at it one holiday in Switzerland and that's all."

"Did you like it?" asked Patsy.

"Not while I was doing it. Too frightened. You get a very pure and glorified feeling when you're safely down though."

"Another candidate for the Needle, Angus," said Nick. "Clare's booked and Frances can be next in the queue."

Frances looked at Angus with dancing eyes.

"You wouldn't drop me, would you?"

"No," said Angus primly. "My climbing-conscience is too strong." They were exchanging smiles of amused understanding when Henry came up and Clare saw him flush with a look of savage anger and slowly whiten. He smiled with an effort at gaiety which hardly succeeded and said,

"Hullo everybody. Quite a good show. What are you all

159

talking about in your huddle?"

"Climbing," said Nick quickly. "You're not a climber I believe, Henry, but you see before you a clutch or gaggle of mountaineers who are going to scale the heights under Cameron's leadership."

There was a tiny pause before Henry said,

"Well, I hope he gets you all up and down safely. I wouldn't care to risk it myself. Frances—I've been trying to get hold of you all day. Come and talk to me."

Frances hesitated and he was holding out a hand as if to take hers, when Patsy remarked,

"Bell, chaps, mustn't be late," and Nick began a general movement of bustle which carried Frances with it.

"Another time, Henry," she said over her shoulder, "I don't want to miss this."

Henry turned without a word and walked rapidly away from the hall while the others filed silently into it. It is difficult after all to improve on Lady Courtney's description of her son's state of mind He was bewitched; and Frances was perhaps not entirely free from blame, though Lady Courtney had, not unnaturally, made a mountain of guilt out of a very small molehill of mischief. Henry Courtney had been a spoilt child, a conceited boy and a too-comfortable young man, not quite so clever as he thought he was. His unusual position in Ledenham was entirely satisfactory to him. His wealth, his mother's title and his long connection with the place gave him a social standing which he enjoyed, largely because it was different from that of his colleagues; and he saw himself, with no unfulfilled ambitions, as the controlling influence in the affairs of the School.

He had decided, carelessly, to get rid of Angus Cameron as he had got rid of his predecessor. Angus was, he considered, a stolid, stupid sort of lump who might nevertheless stick obstinately to unsuitable ideas of his own and he was not a desirable colleague. And he had decided, carelessly, that an affair with the Headmaster's quite startlingly beautiful little niece would be a pleasant pastime for the summer term. Particularly since her deliciously sophisticated appearance and manner suggested that she "knew all the answers" and was ready to be amused by the only man-of-the-world in this remote country place. Both of these careless little plans had gone wrong. Angus proved to be a much tougher proposition than the unhappy Tomlinson; Frances proved to be less forthcoming than she at first appeared. To poor Henry's amazement and dismay he fell violently, even madly, in love with her and since he was, still essentially a spoilt child, those two, somehow entangled with each other, became an obsession and, in fact, he was bewitched.

Frances was the object of all his thoughts and desires. Angus, objectionable enough in his own right, he saw with clouded eyes as a threat and a rival, and Clare assumed a new significance as an enemy who, for some unknown reason, was determined to get in his way. At the play he had been humiliated in public between them, and he left them with something not far short of murder in his heart.

161

CHAPTER 12

AFTER the play a party gathered in School House to drink coffee, eat sandwiches and talk about it, and it was late when Clare finally shut her bedroom door and was free of people at last. She sat down, lit a cigarette and allowed "the Henry business" to burst its banks and flood her mind. Henry had been a menace all day and the scene outside the hall was a genuine scene. It had been very brief and very little had been said, but his looks and manner had made it almost frightening and Nick and Patsy and, she thought, Angus, were all aware of it.

She felt that the situation was too difficult for her and she longed for Nevill who always understood things and even more for her mother, whose capacity for staving off crises never failed. There was nothing definite enough to take to her father, nothing really that demanded action from anybody, and she decided that the policy of keeping Frances "grouped" was the only one. Combined with Frances' own "freezing tactics" it might cool Henry off and detach him without a fuss.

When Henry called at School House next morning he was told that Miss Clare and Miss Frances were shopping in Leyburn. When he called in the afternoon he found a party of girls playing tennis, and when he rang up in the evening the young ladies had gone out with the Headmaster to dinner.

Clare's efforts were bound to fail in the end. They held Henry for three days but in that time, far from cooling off

162

as she had hoped, his fever and his anger rose steeply.

On the fourth morning by cutting chapel and arriving unexpectedly early he caught Clare herself unawares. There was nothing left of the affectionate friend as he began,

"Clare, you have prevented Frances from seeing me for nearly a week. I intend to see her and I intend to know the reason for your behaviour."

Clare mustered her courage and her wrath and faced him bravely.

"Henry—you are extremely rude. You have no right whatever to speak to me of 'behaviour' in this way."

"I have every right when you are deliberately keeping Frances from me."

"I do nothing to prevent Frances from seeing you when-ever she wants to. We have been very much occupied in the last few days." This last remark, she thought, sounded weak, but she hoped it might at least suggest that they had not been avoiding him purposely. To admit that they had would make the thing altogether too important. Henry did hesitate as if he had a moment of doubt, then he said,

"Well, Clare—I suppose I must accept that. Can I see her now? No—I'm due in school. When can I see her?"

"Come in before lunch if you like," said Clare coldly, and when he came she made no attempt to turn it into an ordinary social call, but let Frances go to him alone as though to an interview. They spent half an hour together and then Frances, puzzled and uneasy, went to find Clare.

"Clare," she said. "This really isn't funny." Clare looked at her inquiringly and she added, "Oh—he doesn't say anything."

"Well," said Clare irritably, "he must have said something. You didn't sit in silence did you?"

"No—but he just spoke as if we'd been kept apart lately by an unkind fate and went right back to that bloody ball. When would I dine with him and plan how we could escape from your party, and a lot of meaning laughter as if we were a pair of happy intriguers. Honestly, Clare, I'm baffled. I don't know what he wants."

"If he wants to marry you I wish he'd say so and get it over," said Clare. Frances stared before her with wrinkled brows.

"I think he doesn't want to risk it till he's sure of me," she said at last. "He may not want it at all. He may just want to have me in tow. But I can't understand it, or why he's got this Angus complex mixed up with me."

"I don't either—quite," Clare said. "I suppose it's because he thinks Angus is a rival. What about dining with him?"

"Well—of course I don't want to. I stalled a bit, but it was the same as when I said 'no' about the ball. He laughed and took it that I was being, what d'you call it—capricious—or else loyal to you. In the end I said I'd go this evening. I'll be as boring as possible and hope he'll get tired of it."

They looked at each other and Clare said:

"I don't like it."

"No," agreed Frances. "Neither do I. But I just feel that the only thing is to keep it absolutely flat."

When Henry called for her that evening she was ready for him and they drove away at once. Frances knew that one of her attractions for him was her smart, sophisticated appearance and that he had immensely enjoyed being seen with her in the various "lavish pubs" where he had taken her to dine. Following her policy of killing the affair through dullness therefore, she had taken some trouble over her toilet that evening. It was hardly possible for her with her beauty and her wardrobe to look dowdy, and in any case neither pride nor wit would allow her to be too much unlike her usual self, but she did contrive to look a good deal less smart and very much less exotic than usual, and she saw that Henry was instantly aware of it. His reaction was immediate and unexpected.

"Frances, darling," he said as they drove away. "Let's not go to Riverdale tonight. I think this is the evening for a quiet pub I know where we can talk."

"Oh," said Frances, rather taken aback. "But—I like Riverdale. I'd rather go there."

Henry laughed tenderly.

"So she shall then, bless her. Lots of times. But I'm going to take you to rig choice tonight."

Henry's choice was a quiet hotel which catered with solid comfort for fishermen, and it gave them a very good dinner in a dark and rather gloomy dining-room where they were almost alone. After half an hour in which Frances was dull and Henry perhaps found it rather uphill work to maintain his usual level of gallantly flirtatious pleasantries, he leant forward and said:

"My lady is pensive. Why, I wonder?"

"Not particularly," said Frances. "No reason why I should be."

"Ah—but you are, you know," said Henry. "You are not

offended with your humble servant are you?"

"No—of course not."

"Then—could it be, dare I think, that you have been missing me as I've been missing you? We have been so apart lately."

"Oh no, Henry," said Frances briskly. "It's only a day or two since I had dinner at Riverdale with you."

"More than that I think. And I have felt that something has come between us. Something, or someone, threatening to spoil things for us."

"You're imagining things," said Frances firmly. "There is nothing to spoil. You have taken me out sometimes and you're doing it now. This trout is very good."

"Frances, you are not being open with me. There is something. Our friendship, our feeling for each other is a lovely thing, don't let us allow anyone to spoil it. Clare has a hand in this. Why is she determined to keep me out of her party for the ball? Why is she so—hostile?"

"Clare isn't hostile. This is nonsense, Henry. The party was arranged—why should it be disarranged?"

Frances was having no success. However she stalled, however bluntly she spoke the truth, however flatly she failed to reply, Henry remained firmly in position one. There was something unspecified but special between them. Clare was plotting against them, and in some way the root of the matter lay in the party for the ball. Frances felt that Henry was, throughout, striving to make her say something particular; to get from her an admission by word or action or look, but she could not discover what he wanted her to admit. She got up as soon as they had drunk

166

their coffee and he made no attempt to prolong their sitting, but to her dismay when they were in the car he turned it away from Ledenham.

"Oh, Henry," she said. "I think we should get back. It's late enough."

"Nonsense! It isn't a bit late, my dear. We'll have to part soon enough." Presently he reverted to the ball, and asked her directly who was going in Clare's party.

"It's Nick's party," said Frances wearily. "He arranged it," and she told him the names of the people Nick had asked.

"Cameron!" exclaimed Henry. "I thought so! Even Cameron rather than myself. I tell you, Frances, there is a very strange conspiracy against us. Cameron has lived in my house. I know him better than anyone and I know him to be unfit to be here at all, far less associating with you."

"Really," began Frances, but he went on,

"You know that. You had a terrible experience with him. I know it all, and of other things, and yet he is allowed to stay here."

"Henry," said Frances coldly. "Please take me home at once. You are talking nonsense and I don't like it. There is nothing wrong with Angus Cameron and I had no terrible experience with him."

"I'm sorry. I shouldn't have mentioned it. Of course, I know of it, but naturally you don't want to talk about it. Forgive me, Frances, don't be stiff with me."

He turned to compliments and told her how enchanting she was—"the kind of girl who can drive men mad, my lovely Frances".

167

Frances felt trapped and somewhat alarmed, but he at least drove on, and eventually they turned towards Ledenham. When they stopped he said:

"Till next time—very soon, Frances."

"Thank you, Henry," she answered. "But—it seems to me that it will be better if I don't come out with you again."

"Ah—you're feeling defeated, my dear. The opposition is having its effect. Clare is too much with you."

"Clare has nothing to do with it. I simply don't want to."

"You're very loyal—but I know your feeling. Be strong, my lovely Frances, this will come right for us."

Frances did indeed feel defeated as she went indoors. "I've just about had it," she said to Clare. "I think he really must be bats. I won't go out with him again. I wish I need never see the creature again. If he gets angry and tries to take it out on Angus—well, Angus is bigger than me."

On the following day Mr. and Mrs. Clayton gave a large and comprehensive cocktail party which was attended by almost all the masters and their ladies, including the Fieldings and Frances. It was obvious to most of the party that Mr. Courtney was monopolizing Miss Cheriton, and to some of them that Miss Cheriton was not altogether happy to be so conspicuously monopolized. Several people attempted to rescue her but Henry was tenacious. He either returned promptly to her side or refused to leave her, and when Frances herself walked away he went with her.

That evening Mr. Fielding unexpectedly took a hand. They were having their coffee in the garden after dinner when he took off his spectacles and, looking at her kindly, said, "Is Henry Courtney bothering you, Frances?"

Frances started with surprise and flushed a little.

"Well—he is a bit, Uncle Hugh," she said.

"Does he want you to marry him?"

"He hasn't said so. I don't know what he wants."

"But he won't leave you alone? You should have let me know about this, Clare."

"There wasn't really anything definite enough to let you know," said Clare. "He's just being a pest, and I didn't think you could do anything about it."

"I could always ask him his intentions," said her father drily.

"But I don't want to marry him," protested Frances hurriedly.

Mr. Fielding laughed.

"If you did I certainly wouldn't ask him his intentions. Few things can be more off-putting. Don't go out with him again, Frances, and avoid seeing him alone if you can."

"Are you going to—say anything to him?" asked Frances.

"I'll see how it goes. He's hung about a good deal and I won't have your name coupled with his any more."

He had risen to go and was lighting his pipe when Henry himself came through the drawing-room.

"Ah," he cried gaily. "I thought I'd find you here. What a thing it is to have a garden in weather like this."

"You were looking for me, Courtney?" asked the Headmaster pleasantly.

"On this occasion, sir—no. I came to fetch Frances, as this seemed to be the evening for a little expedition we had promised ourselves. She must see the local 'Falls' while she is here."

"She must indeed," agreed Mr. Fielding smoothly, "but not tonight. She is tired and I forbid it. By the way, Courtney, I've been meaning to get hold of you. As you're free you might come along with me now."

He led the way into the house, talking as he went so that Henry had no choice but to follow him or make a scene, and the girls were left looking at each other with wild surmise.

When the two men reached the study and sat down the Headmaster opened fire without delay.

"There is something I must say, Courtney, which is not quite pleasant, but I'll make it as little unpleasant as I can. I don't want you to see so much of my niece. She is very young, and while I am responsible for her I am anxious that she should not see more of any one man than she does of the others who come about us."

In the short silence which followed this statement Mr. Fielding became aware as Clare had done that Lady Courtney had not spoken of the bewitchment of her son without reason. He was white with anger and making visible efforts to control his voice as he said,

"I am not aware, sir, that I have seen more of your niece than others have. I have, in fact, been strangely prevented from seeing her, though I have reason to believe she wished to see me."

"I fancy," replied the Headmaster calmly, "that she has been out alone with you on a number of occasions, and has begun to find it embarrassing as it makes her appear to be on specially intimate terms with you. In any case the point is that I don't approve of—"

Henry had risen to his feet.

"This is quite extraordinarily offensive," he said loudly. "Who has suggested to you, or to Frances, that there has been anything improper in my attempts to give her pleasure? Somebody has been making mischief."

"Nobody has suggested it. I am not suggesting it for a moment."

"But you most certainly are suggesting it. I must tell you that my occasional drives and dinners with Frances have been all pleasure to her as well as to me. She has always been delighted to accept my invitations, till a week or so ago when Clare, for some reason which is beyond my comprehension, decided to prevent her from seeing me."

The Headmaster had also risen to his feet and was the taller man of the two. He said coldly,

"There is no need to go on with this conversation I think. I say again that I have not the slightest reason to suspect anything improper in your behaviour, but you have been causing Frances embarrassment and I therefore ask you to refrain from seeing her alone."

"Embarrassment!" exclaimed Henry. "Did she say so?"

"She did."

"I don't believe it."

"In that case I must say that I order you to leave her alone, and if necessary I shall take steps to ensure that you do." There was a pause and he went on, "Come, Courtney. Let's have no storms in tea-cups. Think kindly of the need to protect a young girl's reputation and leave it at that."

"No," said Henry slowly, "I don't think we can leave it at that." He sat down again and took out his cigarette case, and the Headmaster, watching him intently, noticed the unsteadiness of his hand when he lit his cigarette and the changed manner towards himself. However Henry might over-estimate his own importance he had never before failed to pay an almost exaggerated deference to his Headmaster, and his little, hostile intrigues, of which Mr. Fielding was perfectly aware, were carried on behind a façade of respectful affability. The noisy rudeness of the last few minutes had passed, and with his cigarette alight, Henry appeared to have recovered some of his self-control, but when he began to speak again there was no deference in his tone.

"It has been in my mind to have a talk with you for some time," he said, "and the subject has some connection with your accusations against me which makes it necessary to deal with it now."

"Very well," said the Headmaster. "But keep it short please. I have an appointment." He had not sat down again, and instead of returning to his arm-chair he now moved over and sat at his desk, switching on a lamp which cast a bright and searching light on Henry, and established the atmosphere of an official interview.

"It is my duty as one of the senior members of common room," said Henry deliberately, "to protest against your appointment of Cameron and to demand his instant dismissal."

This seemed remote from the subject of Courtney's attentions to Frances, and the Headmaster had to conceal a flash of amusement, but there was no pause before his reply.

"The appointment and dismissal of staff is my affair," he said. "No member of common room has any say in the matter. Any complaint by one master against another which is serious enough to warrant my attention must be placed before me in writing. If that is all, Courtney, I will wish you good evening."

This had something of the effect of a douche of cold water, but Courtney, though a little breathless and with a tendency to gasp, was not finished yet, and with a moderately successful laugh he said,

"I really must advise you to consider a little before taking this extremely dictatorial line. My standing in Ledenham is longer than yours, you know, and I may perhaps be allowed to remind you that I have a certain amount of influence one way and another."

"Several of you have been in the School longer than I have, but the question of standing and influence doesn't arise. The Headmaster has the authority."

"I have access to the Governors and I shall use it."

Mr. Fielding's hand moved on his desk and he paused for a moment, and then he said,

"Any one of you has access to the Governors and you are free to make use of it at any time. But you must understand that if an assistant master complains of misconduct in his Headmaster, he puts the Governing Body in the position of having to choose between them. Either the Headmaster goes—or he does."

As he finished speaking the door opened and Nick Vincent appeared.

"I'm sorry, sir, if I'm too soon. I thought—"

"All right, Vincent, Courtney and I have finished. I take it that both these points are settled then, Courtney. Good night."

"I'm sorry, sir," said Nick again when Courtney had left the room, "that I barged in like that. I thought you rang for me."

"I did," replied the Headmaster easily. "We'd nearly finished and I didn't want to wait. Now, about Benson."

They went straight on with their business, but Nick confided to Patsy later that Henry had clearly been on the mat.

"He looked mighty queer," he said. "The Old Man must have torn a hell of a strip off him. I wondered if he'd been told to lay off Frances."

"Your imagination'll land you in trouble one day, Nick," said Patsy.

Nick chuckled.

"Clare calls it leaping to conclusions."

"Same thing. Equally dangerous."

"Waffle! Anyway I wish somebody would haul Henry away from Frances. He doesn't look nice and that was an exhibition at the Claytons' tonight."

"For all you know she likes him," said Patsy. "And if you have visions of you or me or some other chap barging in, you can lay off it."

"She didn't look pleased tonight. I don't think she likes him very much and he is definitely very queer you know," insisted Nick. Patsy had removed his pipe from his mouth and was regarding it with mild interest.

"Everybody has to work things out for themselves," he

174

said. "You know that yourself, Nick, with boys. Same thing here. Frances has got to make up her own mind what sort of girl she is and who she wants for her friends. Nobody has any right to butt in."

"Well I don't think you're altogether right. She's young, and Henry can turn very nasty as you jolly well know, Patsy."

"The Beak doesn't miss much and Clare's as sound as they come. They're the people who can take a hand if necessary. We keep out."

"Clare," said the Headmaster when she appeared with his tea. "I want a word with you when Frances has gone up."

"She's gone now. Wait till I fetch another cup."

When she returned with the cup her father said,

"What is Frances' feeling about Henry? Do you know what sort of terms they're on?"

Clare was pouring out tea and as she handed her father his cup she said,

"As far as Frances is concerned the thing amounts to a very mild flirtation—now over—and going out with him half a dozen times. What Henry's feelings are is anybody's guess. He's very stewed up, but it all seems rather indefinite —and queer. Did you ask him his intentions?"

"I warned him off," said Mr. Fielding, "and he was certainly very strange." He told Clare about the interview and finished. "She is not to see him alone again—that's an order. Pass it on to her."

CHAPTER 13

THE Headmaster had not been altogether surprised by Henry's attack on Angus, though the connection between it and the subject they had been discussing was remote enough to amuse him a little. He had known, as he had told Clare when she returned from Edinburgh, that Courtney was not leaving the matter of Cameron's appointment alone, and that a good deal of the boys' hostility to Angus and their distrust of him was being "fed", as it were, by him.

He knew Courtney very well, his habit of intrigue and disloyalty to himself, and the fact that he was often a trouble-maker both inside the common room and between boys and masters. It is very easy among a lot of men working closely together to exacerbate irritation and split them into "sets", and it is equally easy to belittle a master to boys. A little amusement, some sympathetic suggestion that his authority is unfair or ridiculously hard, a hint that it is a recognized manly sport to rag an unpopular man, and the trouble is made. All this the Headmaster knew, and he used this knowledge along with a great deal more when he had to deal with the complaints and punishments, dis-agreements and arguments which formed a considerable part of his routine work. Courtney, of course, had his good points. He was a really able teacher, his affection for and rather peculiar loyalty to the School itself were unquestionable, and he played quite a valuable part in it, particularly perhaps in backing with all his money and his social gifts his belief in Ledenham's status and quality.

Angus, the Headmaster had assessed when he appointed him as a promising youngster. Academically and as an athlete he was good, there was no doubt about his character, but he was vaguely quaint and his actual capacity as a schoolmaster had to be proved. Mr. Fielding blamed him for no more than a youthful failure in "grip" when the storm broke over Frances and Little Campion. He had rather liked the way Angus responded when he talked to him, and he noted that he was accepted by the other young men, notably Patsy and Nick, and that the Chaplain liked him. It was, however, proving slow and uphill business for him to get out of this bad patch of unpopularity and, though reports of his work were good and he was holding his sets all right, the Headmaster thought that it might be better for Angus himself to make a fresh start in another school with the term's experience behind him.

The Upton Match seemed to open a new phase of the affair. The rumours had been so wild and obviously silly that there had been no need to notice them, but the new phase opened with questions and even complaints from parents. These had to be answered—it was not very difficult—and then there had been a slightly uneasy question from one of the School Governors who "didn't want to make too much of it, but had just heard something"; and then there had been the call from Lady Courtney. It all added up, thought Mr. Fielding, to something strange and unsavoury; Henry's intrigues had never before been savage. Courtney's attentions to Frances, which he had never liked, had amounted to persecution that evening at the Claytons' party and he had been both angry and surprised that a man, supposedly a gentleman, should allow himself to make a girl so conspicuous and so uneasy. Altogether he had accumulated considerable impetus for the rocket he had fired at Courtney, and he had enjoyed the firing which as a rule he did not, but he thought about it a good deal afterwards and wondered whether he could have found a better method of handling the interview. He had, it was true, silenced Henry nicely at the time, but he was convinced that it would not be the end of the trouble.

Clare, Frances, Nick and possibly Patsy as well as the Headmaster thought about Henry that night, and Henry himself, it must be presumed, had some thinking to do too, though nobody ever knew what his thoughts or feelings were when he left the Headmaster's study. He was in School next day as usual, and in the course of the day he made several attempts to get in touch with Frances. Clare had gone into her cousin's room after hearing of her father's scene with Henry and told Frances about it.

"Well," said Frances, "that's that isn't it? After that and the shame-making business at the Claytons', Henry's out."

"Yes," agreed Clare, "I only hope he'll stay out."

Frances said, "Oh surely! He couldn't do anything else, could he, after being ticked off by Uncle Hugh?"

But next morning before lunch Henry called at School House again. Clare was on her way downstairs when he knocked briefly on the front door and walked in, and Frances heard his voice as she left her room and waited out of sight.

"Clare," he said. "I must see Frances. There is some frightful misunderstanding."

"I'm sorry, Henry," said Clare, "but my father's orders are that you're not to see her."

"No, no! That isn't right. He doesn't want her to go out with me—this is different. He would realize—you must realize—that I must see her. I can't be cut off from her."

"No—the orders were quite clear. In any case I must tell you plainly that Frances won't see you."

"My good girl," cried Henry, "you don't know what you're talking about. Why are you doing this dragon act, Clare? Tell Frances I'm here and let her decide for herself."

"Frances has decided that she won't see you."

"I don't believe you, you know," said Henry. "And I am determined to see her."

He went away, but a few minutes later the telephone rang and he asked the man who answered it for Miss Cheriton without giving his name.

"But it's Mr. Courtney I think, Miss," said Higgins helpfully.

"I'll go," said Clare, but Frances said:

"No—I will. I must try to stop this."

"Frances," cried Henry in his study at Little Campion. "Look, darling, what is going on? Your uncle forbids me to take you out and Clare won't let me see you. What is it all about? We must meet and sort it out."

"No, Henry," said Frances. "I don't want to see you. That's quite final, so please don't come or ring up again."

"But, dear girl, you're not going to submit to this? I'm not, I assure you. Nobody has any right to stop our seeing each

179

other. You mustn't let your loyalty to the Fieldings—"

"It isn't that," said Frances. "It's me. It's no good, Henry. Thank you for taking me out and I'm sorry about this—unpleasantness, but it's finished. Good-bye," and she rang off.

"Well," remarked Clare. "You couldn't have been more definite than that."

"No—but could you hear him?"

"A bit—rather quacky."

"Well, you see, he still won't come to it. It's loopy."

The girls had an engagement to play tennis that afternoon and they went out early and stayed late. On their return Higgins, the houseman, told them with a face unconvincingly blank that Mr. Courtney had called for Miss Frances, and Clare went straight to her father's study.

"What am I to do?" she asked.

"You are not to see or speak to him again. Send Higgins to me."

When Henry called just before dinner, Higgins informed him stonily that the young ladies were "not at home", but the Headmaster would see him if he wished.

"No thank you," said Henry. "I won't trouble him—now."

Few men can ever have been so consistently snubbed as Henry had been that day. The common room considered that he had made an ass of himself and something not unlike a laughing stock of Frances at the Claytons' party, and nobody, even among his usual followers, was pleased to see him. The Chaplain when he addressed him was curt, but he held the view that a man should never be allowed to continue on the wrong road without at least some effort

180

being made to stop him, and he made a point of walking a little way with Courtney.

"Henry," he said. "This kind of thing isn't like you. You're behaving badly, man."

"What kind of thing?"

"You know well enough. You were a nuisance to Frances Cheriton at the Claytons. A man should never make a girl noticeable like that."

"You know nothing whatever about it," said Henry and walked away.

After dinner he made one more call and received one more snub. He went to see a Governor whom he knew well, an old boy of the School and a man who usually liked to be amused by the latest gossip and "Henry's little bits of dirt" as he called them. This time he may have heard gossip from other sources, because he greeted Henry without cordiality.

"I wanted to have a word with you, Bill," said Henry sitting down gracefully and speaking with a pleasant air of an anxious man seeking advice. "I really am most terribly bothered. This brute Cameron. The Beak seems to have no idea—"

"Courtney," said the Governor very firmly indeed, "the Beak knows his job, we'll leave him to do it if you don't mind. Would you care for a drink before you go? No? Good night then."

Henry drove home to Little Campion. As he went into the house his mother came out of the drawing-room and said, "Henry—there is something going on. I am very worried. Come and talk to me."

"I can't come now," said Henry coldly. Then he smiled and said with an effort at affectionate lightness, "Busy man you know! I'll see you in the morning. I have some news for you, but I can't tell you now."

Lady Courtney went slowly up to her bed where she spent a restless and unhappy night. Henry went to his study and wrote two letters which were placed on the breakfast table at School House next morning. They were inscribed "By Hand" and addressed to the Headmaster and Miss Cheriton.

Frances, having no other letters that morning, opened hers, first remarking cheerfully, "Unknown hand. Invitation I suppose."

Clare and Mr. Fielding heard her give a gasp and an exclamation, and as they looked at her she pushed her chair back and said, "Oh no! This is—too much."

She had turned quite pale and Clare got up and went quickly round to her. "Whatever's up, Fran?" she said, and Frances said, "Look at this. What am I to do?"

She was standing up and the Headmaster said,

"Sit down, child—let us see what's the matter," and held out his hand for the letter which Clare, who had read it, handed to him silently. She patted Frances' shoulder,

"Cheer up, Fran. It's all right. This really is the end of the muddle. Drink up some coffee, chum."

Henry had written,

"My darling Frances,

I have had a most tremendous wigging from your uncle who thinks we have been seeing too much of

182

each other, and as you know he has forbidden me to take you out again and, according to Clare, won't allow you to see me at all—an order which you seem to feel you must accept.

"I must say he did not give me much opportunity to explain matters, but in any case I felt I could not say much since you had clearly kept our secret. I quite understand, of course, your feeling that your parents should be the first to hear of our engagement, but the time has come, my darling, when it can be a secret no longer. You owe it to both of us to see that I am cleared of the suspicion of trifling with you which both Mr. Fielding and Clare apparently hold, and it must be made plain that nobody has any right or reason to prevent us from seeing each other.

"I am writing to tell Mr. Fielding of our engagement and I shall tell my Mother in the morning. Meanwhile, dearest Frances, you must be true to your feeling and to me. I shall see you in the course of the day.

Till then, my love,
H."

Mr. Fielding made no comment when he had read this letter, but put it down and, opening the one addressed to himself, read that also and passed it to Frances and Clare who read it together.

"Dear Mr. Fielding," it ran,

"Our talk last night misfired very badly. I was very much taken aback by your accusations and, I must confess, exceedingly angry. It was not till later that I realized the completeness of the misunderstanding. I had taken it for granted that both you and Clare knew my position with Frances and the understanding between us.

I tried several times today to have a proper talk with Frances, so that together we might clear the matter up, but she was upset and Clare was not helpful. I have therefore written to her as I am writing to you, to tell you that in justice to me the engagement must now be made known.

Yours sincerely,

H. M. Courtney."

"What does the M stand for?" asked Frances stupidly.

"Mervyn I believe," replied her uncle, almost equally mazed.

"What will you do, Beak?" asked Clare.

"I shall have to see Courtney. If he won't, or can't, see reason it will be a matter for a solicitor. But I hope it won't come to that. It may be, I suppose, a genuine misunder-standing—a very stupid one."

"It couldn't be," said Frances. "He's never mentioned marriage or an engagement. He couldn't misunderstand."

"Well, but if he doesn't—why has he written this?" asked Clare. "What good can he think it could do?"

"He may have some wild notion of sweeping Frances into it," said her father. "It is not at all sensible."

He looked at the large pile of letters which lay, still unopened, before him and said,

"I must go. I have to be in Chapel. But I'll come straight back and meet you both in the drawing-room. Be ready for me, Clare."

184

When he had left the room Frances said,

"I'll have to go away, Clare. I can't see anything else I can do. But oh—I don't want to," and she put her head down and wept. "It's such a beastly spoiling of this lovely place and—and all the lovely times."

"I don't see why you should go because Henry is an ass," said Clare bluntly. "Beak will deal with it and nobody need know. Come on Frances—Higgy wants to clear the breakfast. Go and tidy your face up and leave the thing till Beak comes."

CHAPTER 14

THE Headmaster, emerging from School House in cap and gown and walking briskly across to chapel, looked exactly as he always did and he probably felt it. Courtney's letter had come as a shock to him since it was so utterly different from anything that could have been foreseen, and he knew that it signified a state of mind which might well cause a good deal of trouble, possibly very serious trouble if Courtney failed to regain his balance. Both habit and training, however, enabled him to keep even serious worries in the background till the time came to deal with them, and he walked towards the vestry with his mind on a small piece of business which he had to clear with the Chaplain. He had dismissed Frances and Henry so completely for the moment that he was utterly taken aback when Mr. Perry overtook him and instead of speaking of the subject they had to discuss said gravely,

"This news of Courtney and your niece was unexpected, Headmaster."

Mr. Fielding turned to him and stopped dead.

"What on earth do you mean?" he said.

They looked at each other in dismay and the Chaplain said, "I'm afraid there is something very far wrong, sir. Courtney has just told me along with several others that he is engaged to Frances."

"Good God!" exclaimed the Headmaster. "What on earth does the man think he's doing?" They walked on slowly and he went on, "Perry, this really is a very unpleasant

186

thing. There is no engagement. There has never been any question of it."

"Well, sir. I think half the School has heard of it already, and Courtney seems to be telling the other half now." The Headmaster following his slight gesture saw that Henry was indeed talking gaily and with all the happy consciousness of a newly engaged man in the centre of a group of masters and boys.

"Well," he said. "All I can do now is bolt for cover. Can you ensure that Courtney comes to my study immediately after Chapel?" and he disappeared quickly into the vestry and thence, without a word more, to the isolation of his stall.

Of all the people who were in Chapel that morning none had failed to hear the news of Mr. Courtney's engagement and a good many of them were thinking of little else. To the masses a master's engagement was a moderately interesting and vaguely comic piece of news, and this one was not much more, though Frances' unusual beauty and "glamour" gave it some extra value; but a number of the more intelligent senior boys had been puzzled and somewhat embarrassed by Mr. Courtney's look of excitement and his determination to spread his news immediately. They looked at the Beak sitting in his stall and wondered if they only imagined that his appearance was sterner and more remote than usual. The masters at the back of the Chapel were quite sure that there was something unreal about this affair. It is not normal for a man to announce his engagement by getting up early and waylaying masters and boys on their way to morning

Chapel, and it is more common than not for him to feel some reluctance to make what is, after all, a private and intimate matter, generally known.

Patsy, Nick and Angus, after anxious glances at the impassive figure of the Headmaster, left the Chapel together at the end of the service and had walked more than half-way to the common room in silence before Angus said emphatically,

"I just don't believe it."

"It could hardly have been more publicly announced," said Nick. "Wishful thinking?"

"No, I've no wishes. The thing is wrong and I don't believe it."

"What do you think?" Nick asked Patsy.

"There's a stink about it," answered Patsy slowly, "but I don't know what it is."

"That was a strange scene outside the hall the other night," said Nick, "and" he added, looking meaningly at Patsy, "there was the business in the study as I told you."

Patsy looked straight in front of him and said flatly, "Keep quiet. All we can do."

The twelve minutes or so which the service lasted was Mr. Fielding's only opportunity to consider the position. During the psalm he thought about Frances. He recalled her arrival, so pretty, so much too well-dressed and made up, and with so often a look of discontent mingled with her air of sophistication, and he thought of her gaiety and friendliness over Clare's engagement and her companionable cheerfulness and readiness in the days when she had been his "housekeeper" while Clare was in

Edinburgh. During the lesson he thought of Henry Courtney as he always had been and as he had appeared in the last few days. On his knees he decided that if Frances was to blame at all over this imbroglio her guilt was so slight as to be of no account, and he would not have the girl she was becoming, so genuinely sweet and so potentially valuable, damaged by any spoilt, middle-aged egoist. When he picked up his cap and left the Chapel he thought he knew what to do and went straight back to the house to deal with it.

In his study he rang for Miss Wills and pressed a more remote bell which would bring Hacket the porter.

"Type a notice immediately please, Miss Wills. Two copies."

Miss Wills' pencil was already poised and it is greatly to her credit that it did not falter as she took his dictation, but for some time to come her expression remained at a new level of cold severity. Nothing had ever demanded such discretion as this unbelievable notice.

"A note for Mr. Clayton," said the Headmaster. "Type them at once. Hacket is on his way."

Within a quarter of an hour after morning chapel ended Hacket had pinned notices on the boards in common room and the prefects' room, and had delivered a note to the senior assistant master. The notices read:

"The Headmaster wishes it to be known immediately that the report of Mr. Courtney's engagement to Miss Cheriton is untrue."

The note to Mr. Clayton told him briefly to arrange substitutes for Mr. Courtney's lessons as he would not be in

School again that day.

"I expect Mr. Courtney shortly," said the Headmaster as he signed the type-written sheets, "keep him here till I come. And ring Lord Leyburn and ask him when I can see him. Any time today, here or at Leyburn."

Then he went through to the drawing-room where the girls were waiting for him.

"Now," he said as he shut the door, "I have some strange and unpleasant news for you, and we must be very quiet and sensible about it."

"I think I've heard it," said Clare. "Mr. Higgins had it when I went to the kitchen."

"Have you told Frances?"

"No, I waited for you. Who can have started this rumour, Beak?"

"Courtney himself has been triumphantly broadcasting the news of his engagement to Frances," said Mr. Fielding grimly. Frances started to her feet.

"Oh no!" she cried and Clare said, "But—he must be mad! Mustn't he, Daddy?"

"No. He isn't mad. This looks mad I agree, but Courtney is fundamentally a foolish man. His life has been so easy and he is so egotistical that I imagine he believes that Frances is half in love with him anyway, and that these shock tactics will sweep her into an engagement."

"And if not," added Clare, "the resulting mess will provide him with a ready-made revenge on us all."

"That's it I fancy."

Frances was still standing up, white and trembling and she turned to her uncle and said,

"Uncle Hugh, I must go away. Today—now. It's the—the only thing. I must be out of the way and—and not have to see people."

Mr. Fielding put his arm round her and drew her close to him.

"My dear child," he said, "believe me you will be better here with Clare and with me than you could be anywhere else. Trust us to take care of you and clear this thing up."

She burst into tears and he put her gently down on the sofa and Clare, with an unhappy, angry face sat beside her and patted her comfortingly.

"I haven't much time," said Mr. Fielding, "and I need your help, Frances." She began to dry her eyes and he went on, "I want you to cast your mind back and try to think if there was ever anything said—or done—between you and Courtney which might lead a silly man to imagine an engagement or an understanding."

Frances was still sobbing but she concentrated herself on an effort of memory.

"No," she said at last, "I've been going over it all—ever since I read that letter. He—he never said anything about—love—or marriage."

There was a slight pause, and then Mr. Fielding remarked in a detached voice.

"I am never sure how much young people indulge in love-making, kissing and so on, nowadays."

Frances blushed hotly, but she looked up at him and her tearful eyes were steady and very blue.

"People—some people—indulge in a good deal of it, Uncle Hugh. I have myself. But only with people I liked.

191

Never with Henry." She gave a little shiver and went on distastefully. "He tried once to kiss me, but I wouldn't let him and he—he was very—gallant, and kept on saying it must be just as I liked."

"Good," said her uncle more cheerfully. "Now we're all clear. The next thing is—what are you going to do with yourselves today?"

Clare gave a sudden laugh.

"We were going to take Miss Perry for a sketching expedition with Tishy and a picnic."

Mr. Fielding smiled. "Excellent," he said. "Nothing could be better. Get off as soon as you can."

He left them and Clare said,

"Cheer up, Frances darling. Scram upstairs and do your face and let's get out. This is ideal really. It's so ordinary to drive off with Letitia and her easel, and she never notices anything."

But Clare had one more instalment of the crisis to face before she escaped, when she was told that Lady Courtney was waiting in the drawing-room to see Miss Frances. She took no time to think but went straight in and greeted the old lady who was clearly upset and at a loss.

"I came—I thought I must come and see your cousin," she said as though she were striving to speak with her usual authority.

"I'm afraid Frances can't see you, Lady Courtney," said Clare. "She is a good deal upset. But in any case it will be better for you not to meet."

"Upset?" cried Lady Courtney. "Not see me? I don't understand you, Clare."

"I must try to explain then. Lady Courtney—Henry has written to Frances and to my father assuming an engagement, and he has announced it publicly, but there is no engagement."

There was a silence and after a moment Clare went on, "I can't at all understand why Henry has done this. There has never been any question of Frances marrying him."

Lady Courtney said with cold anger, "I knew he was in love with this girl of course, and it is plain what has happened. She has led him on and he, poor boy, has not seen that she was merely playing with him. I told your father that he ought to get rid of her. He refused to see, as others have seen, what sort of girl she is. Well—he will know now."

Clare got up and went towards the door.

"My father and I are satisfied that Frances is in no way to blame for this," she said. "I don't think there is any more for us to say, Lady Courtney."

The Headmaster was back in his study no more than twenty minutes after he had left it, and Henry Courtney was shown in by Miss Wills almost immediately. He still wore his expression of excited elation, but there was, too, a suggestion of slightly uneasy bravado and Mr. Fielding, regarding him with stern eyes, decided to let him have it without delay. He was seated at his desk but he did not invite his visitor to sit down.

"First," he said, "I am relieving you of your duties for the rest of this term. Arrangements are already being made. Secondly, you have been guilty of gross folly and misconduct which I shall report to the Chairman of the

Governors in the course of today."

Courtney began to speak but he silenced him and went on relentlessly, "Thirdly, your return to your post here after this term will only be considered if a full and public apology has been made to Miss Cheriton for your unspeakable impertinence. And finally, if she has any more trouble in this matter I shall put it immediately into the hands of my solicitors."

He waited, looking coldly at the wreckage before him. What Henry Courtney had had in mind when he announced that he was engaged to Frances will never be clearly known. It is probable that Mr. Fielding and Clare had come as near to understanding it as he did himself, and that he imagined the announcement would either bring Frances to his arms or prove, in Clare's words, a ready-made revenge if she rejected him. Whatever his thoughts had been and whatever he had prepared of bargaining, arguments or threats, the Headmaster's direct and comprehensive attack was something beyond his capacity. His smooth, urbane good looks had seemed a little tarnished during the last week and his usually confident bearing had become over-confident. Now his uneasy excitement left him suddenly, and he stood in the Headmaster's study bereft of his "personality" the essential, pitiful man. Mr. Fielding got up and went round to him. "Sit down," he said quietly and almost pushed him to a chair. He gave him a few minutes and then went on, "Courtney, you have made more of a fool of yourself than any man I've ever known. I don't want to make it worse for you than I need. My first object is to protect my niece.

194

When I am sure that she is safe I will help you if I can. But whether you can come back to Ledenham or not I don't know."

Courtney spoke for the first time. "What am I to do?"

"Give me a full apology which I will dictate to you and leave Ledenham today. Go abroad for a bit, and get in touch with me after the end of term."

"The Governors?"

"They will have to know about this. But they'll leave me to deal with it if I want them to."

"Very well," said Henry.

The apology was dictated and written and he left the house with hardly another word. It may be said now that he did leave Ledenham that evening, driving himself in his shining car which was well loaded with luggage, golf clubs and tennis rackets. A few days later Lady Courtney also left with ample luggage, travelling by train to join her sister at Torquay, and Little Campion remained empty, its furniture shrouded in dust sheets, for the rest of the summer.

The Headmaster lunched with Lord Leyburn and the matter as it concerned the Governors was quietly settled.

Later in the day he held two meetings, one with his assistant masters and one with his prefects, in both of which he read Courtney's apology and, declaring that the matter was now closed, left them without comment. When it was nearly time for dinner he went through to his drawing-room and found Clare alone. They had not met since the morning, and she looked up eagerly and said "Well?"

"As well as could be expected. Alcohol, Clare. Bring the

195

sherry. Where's Frances?" he added as Clare returned with the decanter and two glasses.

"She's gone to bed. She's really quite ill—she's got a bit of a temperature. I think it's mostly shock though."

"I dare say," said Mr. Fielding. He sat down with his sherry and a cigarette, and discovered that he was exceedingly tired. Clare said,

"You look pretty done up yourself, Beak. But can you just tell me where we've got to?"

Her father did not open his eyes, but he smiled.

"I'll tell you the tale in a minute. It's been quite a day, but the thing's finished. It only remains now to pick up the pieces."

CHAPTER 15

A DAY which began with Henry Courtney's announcement of his engagement, closely followed by the Headmaster's denial of it, and which ended with his apology and his disappearance could not fail to be a sensation of the first magnitude, and it would have been very unnatural indeed if it had not been talked about and discussed by everybody to the exclusion of every other subject. Inevitably people took sides in the matter; those who were inclined to support Henry regarding Frances as a man-eater, while her supporters declared emphatically that she was a thoroughly nice girl and they had always known Courtney to be a cad liable to turn dangerously nasty. After a few days, since no fresh fuel was supplied, the flames gradually died, and nothing was left except a slow smoulder of talk and feeling. The common room and its wives settled down to remembering that Henry Courtney was not a very reliable or lovable person and that his superiority had often tried them considerably, and Frances, though she was too pretty and smart to be altogether comfortable, had not been uppish or anything but friendly. Also she was obviously on very good terms with the Fieldings who were entirely reliable and sound.

It is probable that most of the common room came pretty near to understanding what had taken place and without taking much time to reach their conclusions.

Frances stayed in bed for three days nursing a genuine cold and a profound unwillingness to face the world outside her bedroom.

"She isn't really ill," Clare told her father, "but it was such a horrid shock I think she needs to rest a bit."

"So long as she doesn't take too long about it," he replied. "The sooner she gets back to normal life the better—and the easier for her."

"You don't think," said Clare hesitantly, "that it would be better for her to go away for a bit? She could go to Grannie for a week or so and come back."

"Clare," said Mr. Fielding decidedly, "if Frances goes now she will never come back, and I think that would be a disaster. I say with all humility that these weeks with us have transformed her."

"Yes," said Clare, "she is different."

"Well then—let her face this unpleasantness, complete her stay and consolidate the new Frances."

Clare laughed a little, but her father was usually right and she turned to the task of getting Frances back into circulation.

On the fourth day Frances got up and the two girls went out for a drive in Tishy. When they returned and were on their way upstairs to get tidy for dinner Clare was told that Patsy had called and was in the drawing-room.

"Oh good," she said. "That means they've got a plan on. Come on, Frances."

"No," said Frances. "You go. I'm not coming."

Clare had started downstairs but she stopped and looking back saw that Frances had blushed painfully and was almost tearful.

"My darling ass," she said, "you mustn't be like this! Come

198

on down and see Patsy. He's the most peaceful thing in the world next to Miss Perry."

"No," whispered Frances. "Not like this when he's waiting there by himself. Please, Clare! I—I can't explain it."

She ran into her room and Clare went down and found Patsy at the window staring out at the garden.

"Hullo," she said.

"Hullo," said Patsy. "How are things going? Frances better?"

"Yes, she's better. We've been out in Tishy. Come and sit down, Patsy. It's time for some sherry. Light your pipe. I am glad to see you—the last few days have been pretty bleak."

"Yes, they would be," said Patsy. "Clare, it's no good—pretending nothing's happened." She shook her head. "I don't want to talk about it and I'm sure you don't, but the thing is—can we do anything?"

"Yes, I think you can," Clare said at once. "It's really not easy for Frances to—to face people. She's been quite badly shaken up. I believe some sort of do with you and Nick would be the nicest way to begin."

"Well—let's line it up. A climb?"

"No," said Clare. "She's not fit for it. Let's go back to the beginning, Patsy, and have the Benenbeck picnic again."

"Right," said Patsy. "Tomorrow night."

The following evening the Bentley drew up at School House as it had done weeks before, full of Patsy, Nick and Angus with all their gear and Delia's picnic. This time Frances was already wearing Richard's old raincoat, her slacks were of neutral hue and there were no scarlet hand

199

bags in sight. She had tied a scarf over her hair and pulled it forward as though she would have liked to hide her face which was a little pale, and so uncertain that all three of the young men, and Clare with them, longed to get their hands on Henry Courtney.

They allowed no time for awkwardness, however. The girls were in and the car started within two minutes, and the worst was over. No time was lost either in getting to work at their fishing, and on this occasion Clare felt no resentment that the party's attention was concentrated on entertaining Frances.

Frances had a spell of fishing with Nick when she had finished her practice casts and they all separated for the serious business of the expedition, and she found herself later with Angus.

"You and I have both had an odd sort of time in Ledenham, Angus," she remarked. "How is it going for you now? What do you think of it?"

Angus did not hurry his reply, and when he spoke his voice was serious.

"I think I'm getting on all right. I don't know. It feels better, but I don't know yet if I'll be able to stay permanently."

"Do you want to?"

"Yes," said Angus without hesitation, "I do want to. I'm absolutely set on it."

There was a thoughtful silence, and then Frances said,

"The place sort of gets you, doesn't it? I don't know why. But I do think it's a very good life they have here."

"You think so too, do you? I know it's exactly what *I*

want but—I'd have thought you'd find it a bit dull."

"No," said Frances. "I expected to, and I did at first. But now I've got dug in and I hate the thought of going away."

"Well," said Angus heavily, "it looks as though we'll probably both go at the end of term."

Frances looked more like herself, with something of her customary brightness about her when they sat down for their picnic, and when the coffee went round she raised her mug in salutation and announced,

"I'm better. Cheers, dears."

"Attagirl," said Nick, and the others looked at her with friendly satisfaction.

The Benenbeck picnic was the first step but it was an easy one. To be swept rapidly away from the School House door in Patsy's Bentley with Clare beside her and to fish in peaceful surroundings with three particularly comfortable and friendly young men was very little of an ordeal, as Frances realized when she faced others more severe.

She had had what she called a winding up talk with her uncle when he told her of Henry Courtney's departure.

"So that's all over," he said, looking at her kindly, "and you have only to forget about it. I'm sorry it happened, Frances. We should have looked after you better among us."

"No," said Frances, "it wasn't that."

She was at the lowest ebb of both her desolation and her cold and she had gone on to say to her uncle, as she had said to Clare, that she felt she ought to go away.

"Do you really want to leave us?" asked Mr. Fielding, and she sobbed that she did not want to go but she thought it

201

would be better for everybody if she did. "I've made such a mess of it," she said as Angus had done. "I don't know how to—to face everybody and go on."

"You mustn't run away," her uncle had told her. "If you were to blame at all for this it was very little and everybody knows it. You've had a bad knock, my dear, but if you take it simply as an unpleasant part of the process of growing up it'll do no harm, and to do that you must go on as usual and ride it out."

With these words in her mind Frances went to Benenbeck and as she faced that and greater ordeals she thought about herself and how it was that things had gone so far wrong.

"It wasn't that I behaved badly," she said to Clare, "at least not very. But the fact is that Henry has had a really frightful disaster because of me. I can't forget that, or that I made Angus have a disaster too."

Clare for the second time quoted Nevill, who thought that Angus, and Henry very much more, should have been grownup enough to avoid such disasters. "And I can see," she added, "that it must be quite a job for anyone as pretty as you are to cope."

"Oh," said Frances, "it isn't prettiness."

Other people were pretty and managed better. Clare herself was pretty enough and attractive enough to have had all the young-man attention and fun that she wanted and now she was thoroughly in love and happy with Nevill. And Clare's young men were so nice. People like Patsy and Nick who were such good value and who were just as fond of her and pleased to be with her now that she was engaged. Frances did not find it easy to analyse the difference between Clare and herself, Clare's friends and her own. But she grappled with the problem honestly and in the end she came to the conclusion that one got the kind of friends one wanted and deserved, and if a girl was attractive enough to interest young men at all they too would, on the whole, be what she wanted them to be.

Knowing the sort of friends she wanted and beginning to know the sort of person she wanted to be, Frances mustered her courage and began by facing the world of Ledenham again. Going to Chapel was the worst ordeal as going to church always is in such circumstances. One is seen not only by proven friends but by those who are half-friends or not friends at all, and they have plenty of time to stare, to note every tremor, every uncertainty and add them to the store of material for gossip.

But it was not so bad after all. Paler than usual and with her self-confidence so rudely shaken she had, nevertheless, a new dignity, genuine and courageous, of which she was quite unconscious. She felt no hostile or inquisitive eyes on her and when, with Clare, she joined the church parade after the service, friends were immediately around her, drawing her back to normal.

Wherever she went in the days that followed, at the cricket teas which were a feature of that stage in the summer term, or at the inevitable cocktail parties, she was aware of Patsy. He never, of course, spoke of Henry Courtney, indeed he spoke very little and nothing that he did say had any significance, but his large, peaceful and friendly presence gave Frances more sense of support and security than even Clare's loyal affection or her uncle's approval.

It was now the middle of June and the tempo of the term quickened with the approach of Speech Day and the C.C.F. Inspection. Frances as a visitor was unaware of the piles of uniforms which were sent to the cleaners, of the bundles of surplices for the laundry and the hundred and one practical preparations for the climax of the school year, but she was aware of the mounting excitement, especially as Clare wrinkled her brows and moaned nervously over the ordeals of official entertaining which lay before her.

"It's not nothing," she said, "for anybody of my age to be hostessing Cabinet Ministers and Generals and things."

Frances considered. "I don't see that it's very different from all the other hostessing you've been doing, and you do it very well."

"Perhaps not. Beak says V.I.P.'s are easy on the whole, because they're usually so ready to talk. But I must say it's a strain. Thank goodness for Higgy anyway."

"What have you actually got on?" asked Frances.

Clare referred to a bundle of lists in her hand. "C.C.F. Inspection lunch. The General and his A.D.C. and the officers commanding the three sections of the corps. Five—that makes us eight."

"It's Greek to me," said Frances, "but don't try to explain. Go on."

"Tea after the Inspection—but that's done by the caterer in a marquee. Still, I've got all the politeries. Speech Day. Lunch—the Cab. Min. Lord and Lady Leyburn, Bishop and Bishopess—altogether twelve persons. Tea, caterers. About a thousand—or twelve hundred."

"What!" exclaimed Frances.

"Oh yes. Easily a thousand. Think of 500 boys each with two parents. Fortunately they don't all come."

"Golly," said Frances. "I should hope not! What do we wear for this jamboree?"

"You wear one of your simpler little numbers," said Clare firmly. "The rest of us put on all we've got."

They were giggling cheerfully when Miss Wills tapped at the door and came in with more papers in her hand.

"The Headmaster thought you'd better have the seating plan for your party in the hall, Clare," she said. "And here is the marquee plan. And what about the flowers?"

Clare held out her hand for the plans.

"What about the flowers? Sit down, Miss Wills. I've forgotten what happens about flowers."

"Well," said Miss Wills importantly, "Smith has enough in the greenhouses and kitchen gardens for the hall. Your mother usually sees to the arrangement," she paused inquiringly and Frances said,

"Could I perhaps do that?"

"It's rather specialized," said Miss Wills, who did not quite approve of Miss Cheriton. "You see, there is the play to be considered."

This was more Greek to Frances but Clare said,

"Oh I don't think there is much in that. It's only that they put on a play to amuse the parents in the evening of Speech Day, Frances, so the flowers mustn't get mixed up with the footlights and things. Yes, I'm sure you could do it. What about Chapel, Miss Wills? Does Mummy do it for Speech

Day?"

"Usually. Mrs. Clayton has done it and I expect she would be willing to help. The flowers for tea are the caterer's affair of course."

"Yes—well we'll see to the Chapel all right. Anything else I ought to be seeing to?"

"I don't think so. Did the Headmaster remind you that the parents of the Head Boy and the Head of House dine here before the play?"

"No—I'd forgotten that one. And the boys I suppose."

"Then that's all I think, Clare. I hope it all goes off all right. Oh—the Headmaster said about precedence. He wrote it out and it's with the plans."

She went away and Frances said,

"What on earth was the last bit? Precedence?"

"Oh," said Clare, "who sits on my right and who sits on my left you know. Funny that it should be an honour isn't it?"

Nick, who had a hand in most things, presently arrived to ask Frances if she would help with costumes for the play, and Frances found it not only a hilarious game contriving evening dresses with such material as the acting box and the wardrobes of various school ladies could provide, but the final stage in overcoming the "Henry episode".

"They look marvellous," she said one evening at dinner. "When I think of all the trouble we take about slinky underwear, and they come along in running shorts and we pin the frocks on top and some of them look quite chic. The hands and feet need a bit of tactful drapery."

"We seem to have acquired a useful new member on the

206

strength," remarked Mr. Fielding.

"Turns her hand to anything," agreed Clare cheerfully.

Frances laughed.

"I'd no idea boys were so lovable. You push them about and stick pins into them and they take it all with amiable grins and they don't titter. It's fun."

Mr. Fielding glanced at Clare and smiled, and when she took his tea in that evening said,

"I'm glad Frances stayed the course. She's consolidating very nicely."

"Very nicely," Clare agreed. "She's been frightfully good with those dresses and she's been making them walk properly and put their hands in their laps—and she's so nice with them."

"Why does she look different?" asked the Headmaster curiously.

"I'm not quite sure," said Clare. "She's abandoned the outsize ear-rings and things and she's not wearing quite so much make-up. But it isn't that altogether."

Mr. Fielding scowled thoughtfully. He disliked leaving questions unanswered.

"I think," he said, "that it is her bearing. She doesn't look now as though she's displaying herself and her clothes."

Clare scowled very much the same scowl.

"Perhaps it's that. It could be. And she doesn't look so confident either, poor Frances."

"She's getting rather more to be confident about if she only knew it," said her father.

As Frances made friends with the boys she helped to dress and wept with laughter over their "ladylike" deportment, she grew more and more interested and absorbed in helping Ledenham School to prepare for Speech Day and it was a shock when she was unexpectedly reminded of what now seemed a different existence.

It was the day of the C.C.F. Inspection and she and Clare were ready for the luncheon party which was the preliminary to the business of the day. The meal was ready, the table with its flowers and shining silver and glass waited with its chairs drawn out, while in the drawing-room, gay with flowers and its french window wide open so that all the garden seemed to be part of it, were drinks and cigarettes and an air of cheerful welcome. Clare may have been a little nervous, but she looked a very competent hostess as she glanced round and moved a chair or a table here and there, and when the Headmaster came in he smiled at both the girls with pleasure and a little amusement.

"I must say," he remarked, "I have a creditable pair of hostesses. Quite a treat for the General."

There was a sound of footsteps in the hall and a clatter of swords being taken off and placed on tables, and the three school officers entered the room, the third of them, to Frances' astonishment, being Patsy in Naval uniform who greeted them with slightly austere formality.

"This is a surprise," remarked Frances. "I didn't know you went in for fancy dress."

Patsy grinned.

"Duty," he replied. "Great shortage of Naval blokes in these parts."

A car was heard drawing up; the General was with them,

genial and easily urbane, and following him came part of Frances' past, a tall young man, beautiful, and as exquisitely uniformed and poised as A.D.C.'s usually are.

"Good God!" he exclaimed, the poise momentarily shaken by surprise, though he remembered to speak quietly. "Frances! What on earth are you doing here?"

"Oh! Hullo, Reggie," said Frances without enthusiasm. "I live here—for the present."

"Couldn't think what had happened to you," went on Reggie, in confidential undertones. "Your flat was silent and nobody seemed to have heard of you for ages. Have you married the Headmaster or something?"

Frances laughed aloud.

"Hardly. He's my uncle. The parents are in America."

"Oh—that explains it. But why here, my love? Fairly deadly isn't it? Hardly you, as they say?"

It seemed to Frances that Reggie's tactful murmur was extraordinarily penetrating, and that her uncle and Clare, as well as Patsy, who was standing near her, must all hear it clearly. She was hating it and her colour rose when her tormentor, as his habit was, went straight on without waiting for a reply, "Unless of course, darling, you find that schoolmasters amuse you. But could they?"

At this moment Frances was saved by the Headmaster who announced that their time was limited and swept them into the dining-room. She sat beside Patsy, her old friend Reggie at a comfortable distance, and Patsy for once opened the conversation,

"Old pal?"

"Yes," said Frances shortly. "Well—not a pal. Casual

acquaintance more. I used to dance with him sometimes."

"Beats me," said Patsy chattily, "where they find these chaps. You never see them in ordinary life, but every time a big service bug comes along he's got one of them frisking round. They do it very well, I suppose."

Frances laughed a little.

"You don't see them because you don't go to the right places. They're common enough in my sort of life."

The Inspection that afternoon was for Frances a significant occasion. It began when she and Clare in their pretty summer frocks walked across the great expanse of green grass and she saw the General step up on to the dais to take the salute, a solitary figure, remote and magnificent. Her uncle, equally alone and dignified in cap and gown, stood alongside and behind the General, gracefully rigid, even her old acquaintance, Reggie, looked as though he meant something. The band struck up, the march-past began and Frances watching had a sudden, surprising feeling of emotion, the feeling of all women who see men they know and love in service uniform, of separation and of something in which they can have no part. A lump came into her throat as she watched Patsy take his Naval section smartly by, as Nick came presently in Air Force blue, and, as men and boys she had come to know marched past her, unfamiliar, competent and remote, she blinked away a tear.

"Not bad," remarked Clare in a critical tone, devoid of any emotion whatever. "But I can never understand why boys look such odd shapes in Corps clothes."

CHAPTER 16

ON the day which came between the Inspection and Speech Day Nevill arrived, and for the next twenty-four hours he and Frances supported each other in the role of spectators. Either of them, thought Frances, would have been pretty completely at a loose end without the other since they alone had nothing to do but look on, and they were alone too, it seemed, in their ignorance of what Nevill called the form.

The day was completely devoted to the occasion. Everybody got up in best suits and wore buttonholes and soon after breakfast parents and visitors likewise clad in festive raiment began to arrive and wandered rather vaguely about with their sons, waylaying masters and breaking off conversations to watch the ceremonial call-over and to crowd into Chapel for the morning service.

The Headmaster, as calm as usual but somewhat abstracted, made a brief and silent appearance at breakfast, elegant in morning coat and starched linen, while Clare, though she showed no nervous qualms, was entirely absorbed by her responsibilities and looked through both her fiancé and her cousin with barely a sign of recognition.

"Well," observed Nevill, "now we know where we are. Unwanted. Temporarily, let us hope. Frances, let's have a look at this circus. D'you know what happens and when?"

"No," said Frances. "Not much, except that we're not to go to Chapel because there isn't room. There's a programme somewhere."

They had never before been alone for any length of time and Frances, wondering what Nevill was really like, found him companionable in a way that was new to her. She had always thought him attractive with his lean height and the lop-sided smile which made his very intelligent face charming, and the glow in his eyes when he looked at Clare had given her for the first time some understanding of the love which a man who is worth-while feels for the girl he is going to marry. He had, however, been nothing to her except Clare's young man until, as they went out into the sunshine together to look at Ledenham School's Speech Day their own relationship began. It was an easy relationship with no emotion or possibility of emotion in it beyond liking and friendliness, and Frances, who had known neither brother nor grown-up cousin, enjoyed it greatly and was well entertained. Nevill was in a state of more or less subdued hilarity as he surveyed the crowds of well-dressed parents stooping a little or looking proudly upwards as they conversed with their unnaturally tidy offspring, and he enlivened the proceedings for himself and Frances by joining in the game, as he said. They wandered about with the rest of the visitors discussing the School, its Headmaster, its staff and its customs and earnestly debating the future of their son, and presently their wanderings brought them to the cricket-field where the School was engaged in the annual Speech Day match against the Ledshire Gentlemen.

Nevill peered short-sightedly at the School XI which was fielding and said in a tone of rather worn husbandly affection,

"Look, dear, I can't quite see—is that Frederick bowling?"

"He has grown so tall," said Frances fondly, "but it must be him—he. He's the best bowler."

"And the best butter—batter," agreed Nevill, "but," shaking his head gloomily, "his reports are so invariably stinking. There's his form master. We'll have a word with him. Spends too much time on sport, that young man. All very well, I'm fond of sport myself but moderation is what I always say," and he fixed a stern eye on Patsy who, with Nick and one or two other members of common room, was playing for the "Gents". Patsy, towering and graceful in flannels, his pads on and his bat in his hand, received them without visible surprise and smiled at Frances' anxious-mother face as he said to Nevill,

"Getting your hand in? You'll be a prize specimen if you keep your form. And which of these disasters are you responsible for?"

"William," began Nevill pompously.

"Frederick," corrected Frances. "The handsome one. We're afraid you don't quite understand Frederick."

"Boy's got brains. Why can't you make him use 'em?" barked the father. "What we're paying for, isn't it?"

"They're all handsome," said Patsy sadly, "and they're all clever, only we don't seem to see it. I'd apprentice Frederick to a pirate if I were you. Your first wife is doing very well."

"Hidden depths," agreed Nevill. "I didn't know about all this social talent."

"Pity it's being wasted on a doctor. Any chap looking for a headmastership would be a safe snip with Clare as a

213

booster."

"If your ambitions run on those lines, Patsy, you should have been quicker off your mark," said Nevill firmly and Patsy's grin appeared.

"Me? No fear. Wait till you hear the Beak in action and then picture me in the part."

Nevill looked at him curiously.

"You're settled, are you? No ambition?"

"No," said Patsy. "Give me a good deep rut. Hullo— Nick's out. See you later," and he tucked his bat under his arm and walked away towards the wicket with his long, unhurried stride, pulling on his gloves as he went.

Frances and Nevill sat down and lit cigarettes, while Patsy centred his bat and straightening with it upright against his shoulder, glanced round the field and then pulled his cap on firmly and faced the bowling.

"Looks like action," said Nevill, sounding pleased, and as the first ball whacked towards the boundary. "It is action, by gum!"

Frances had been told by her cousin Michael before she met Patsy that he was a Test cricketer and she had heard a good deal about his prowess since, but she had never seen him play before and she found it startling. Patsy was hitting the bowling all over the field with ease and precision and the variety and sheer beauty of it so absorbed her that she did not see Clare and Nick who approached from opposite directions till Nevill said,

"Hullo, darling. Got a breather? There's a show on here."

"Yes," said Clare sitting down beside him. "I saw Patsy going in so I cut. Can I have a cigarette, please, Nevill?

Golly!" as a mighty drive sent the ball to the boundary. "He is going it. What's he up to, Nick?"

"He's learning them," replied Nick with satisfaction. "Wilson's bowling isn't quite so hot as he thinks it is and the fielding's been a bit slack, so he's just pointing it out, as you might say."

Nevill said,

"I'd forgotten how good he is. He's one of the very best to watch—beautiful really. Is he finished with Test cricket?"

"Might play in the 5th," said Nick, "if he can get in a bit of practice. Trouble is, cricket takes too much time for a chap with a job."

The whole Speech Day company had desisted from its wandering and stood watching, while the field raced hither and thither and the bowlers grew hot and near to despair and Frances, feeling ignorant as she listened to the knowledgeable comments around her, stared across at the authoritative, spectacular figure which was so familiar and yet unfamiliar.

The field changed over and she saw Patsy walk up to meet the other batsman and say something at which they both grinned.

Nick laughed.

"Point made, I fancy. He'll let them ease up a bit now," and when Patsy faced the bowling again the tempo was slower and the fireworks were over.

"Help!" cried Clare. "Lunch! They'll be coming in a minute. Come on, Frances. Oh dear! This really is it!"

"Stick it," said Nick encouragingly. "You're doing fine. Frances, you're coming to help with dressing and make-up, aren't you? Come and have grub early with us."

"Does it matter if I cut dinner?" Frances asked Clare. "All right then, Nick, thank you."

Clare's dreaded ordeal was over, so to speak, before it began. She had been more or less burdened by thoughts of the Speech Day luncheon party since her mother left her in charge and for the forty-eight hours before it she had suffered quite acutely from stage-fright, but her tremors left her before the party finished drinking sherry. Lord and Lady Leyburn and the Bishop and his wife were not, after all, formidable in spite of their importance, but kind old friends whom she had known nearly all her life who called her their dear Clare and wanted to look at Nevill; while the Cabinet Minister, who was the speaker and the principal guest, proved to be a genial individual who liked pretty girls and immediately launched a jocular flirtation with Frances which kept him happily engaged.

Clare shepherded her flock of Very Important Persons smoothly into their places in the Hall for the prize-giving and sat back in her chair with a small sigh of relief that the heaviest of her responsibilities was over. She wished that she could have listened to the speeches beside Nevill and Frances instead of being rather warmly wedged between two of the stouter V.I.P.s but it would soon be over, and she glanced along the row and smiled at them.

"Now," said Nevill, "for the Beak's Big Moment. He looks uncommon cool, doesn't he?"

Frances' prize-giving experience had been confined to those which she had perforce attended at her own school and, with the memory of her distinguished headmistress rising to read her report from a neatly typed sheaf of papers trembling slightly in her hand, she thought that her uncle did indeed look uncommon cool. She saw with something like anxiety, that he held only a scrap of paper which looked very much like an old envelope and she glanced along at Clare. Clare, however, far from displaying uneasiness was regarding her parent with calm affection and some amusement. When the slight stir of expectation in the Hall had settled, the Headmaster began to speak.

Whatever Frances had expected she had never imagined that a Headmaster in his Prize Day speech would make his hearers laugh till it hurt, but Mr. Fielding, in the course of welcoming the visitors, giving news of the year which was nearly over and of plans for the future not only did that, he also left them full of confidence in himself and enthusiasm for the School and all its ways. It was an accomplished, witty speech, a perfectly polished performance and Frances felt some sympathy with her friend the Cabinet Minister when he said that if he had known of the Headmaster's powers as an orator he would have hesitated to accept an invitation to speak after him.

"And well he might," remarked Nevill afterwards as they made their way towards tea. "They make too many speeches, these political blokes. After the Beak's his was just a resounding stream of waffle."

"I didn't think it was as bad as that," protested Frances, "but people here do things so well. Uncle Hugh and Patsy's cricket and Clare's hostessing."

Nevill looked across the crowded marquee at his girl, slim and young in her lovely frock and hat, smiling charmingly at the Cabinet Minister. She looked round for him and beckoned and he went over to join her.

"Husband deserted you?" said Patsy's voice beside Frances. She said, resigned,

"Gone back to his first. What are you doing here? I thought you were supposed to be playing cricket."

"Chaps must eat—and drink."

"How's it going?"

"Much as usual. Probably just beat them. They need it."

Frances was very happy. She looked up at him severely. "You were showing off dreadfully this morning. Lamming about like that!"

It was never easy to make Patsy rise. He had his own methods of dealing with challenges or mockery and it was with a "dead pan" face and a perfectly flat voice that he replied,

"A man has to do his duty, Frances."

"Nonsense!" said Frances. "You were just—"

"Miss Cheriton," said a rich, important voice behind her. "The time has come, my heart is breaking, but I must catch my train."

She turned to the Cabinet Minister to wind up their flirtation and to respond enchantingly to his mock tragic farewells, and when he had released her hand and gone away she turned again to Patsy who looked at her quizzically and raised an eyebrow.

"You were saying?" he said politely. "Something to do with showing off, wasn't it?"

Frances laughed outright.

"A girl has to do her duty, Patsy. O.K. One up."

There are one or two days in the lives of most people which remain in the memory as having had a particular quality of happiness, days which are remembered not only because of events, but even after the events themselves have been largely forgotten leave an impression of light and colour. Since Frances was happy in Ledenham, fond of her relations and the friends she had made, Speech Day could not fail to be interesting and entertaining, and with Nevill's companionship and the flattery of the Cabinet Minister to amuse her, events had been favourable. But the peculiar radiance which flooded the day was the beginning of falling in love. It was too soon for any doubts or pain, too soon for her even to understand what was happening; she was simply happy, and so lovely and feminine and young that eyes softened as they looked at her and smiled in sympathy.

She went after tea with Nevill and the others to watch the end of the match and Angus, whom she had hardly seen all day, came up and with neat management unusual for him, drew her aside.

"Frances," he began and then as if he suddenly saw her, "I say you do look marvellous! You always do of course, but is this a special frock or something?"

"Sure," said Frances cheerfully, "Speech Day Super."

"Oh that's it, is it?" he said, glad to have the matter explained. "I say, Frances, I wanted to tell you—I've been staffed."

"Staffed?"

He beamed at her with happiness as radiant if less beautiful than her own.

"Staffed! I've got the job permanently. Got the letter this morning."

"Oh, Angus!" cried Frances, "I am glad. How pleased you must be and how lucky you are! Now you'll never have to go away."

"I know. I'm terribly lucky. I wish you were staying too, though."

"So do I. Why don't they have girls on the staff?"

Angus suddenly laughed.

"That would hardly do," he said. "There are wives though, Frances."

She looked up and meeting his teasing eyes she remembered that dreadful scene at Benenbeck and smiled thankfully at him.

"You watch your step. I might take you up on that," she said warningly, but Angus was unabashed. When the match was over and the School just sufficiently beaten for its good, Clare, Frances and Nevill went back to the School House rather wearily.

"Nearly done," said Clare, "quite a quick dinner for these parents and I'm through."

"Are you absolutely whacked?" asked Frances. "It has been a day."

"Fairly whacked. I don't know why, quite. The Higs really do all the work. But, Frances, I don't believe I'll come to the Zoo after the play."

"No," said Nevill. "You'll come straight home and spend half an hour holding my hand while you drink a glass of hot milk and then you'll go to bed." Clare sighed.

"Lovely. Let's skip the next bit and begin now."

"Well you can at least have an interlude," said Frances. "Lurk in the old nursery and nobody'll find you. I'll see Higgy and have a look at the dinner table and so on."

"Oh, Frances—you are an angel—would you? But don't make yourself late for the Zoo supper."

"I won't," said Frances.

She talked to Mrs. Higgins and made a conscientious inspection of the preparations for dinner and encountering her uncle, who looked nearly as tired as Clare, she took a bottle of beer to him in his study and arranged that he would be undisturbed for half an hour. Then she rushed upstairs to bath and change and was nearly at the Zoo when she met Patsy in his dinner jacket.

"Am I late?" she said. "I've been organizing my relations."

"No, you're not late," said Patsy. "I thought you might be too shy to barge in among the bachelors by yourself so I came to fetch you."

There was nobody in Patsy's study when they arrived and Frances sat down thankfully and curled her feet comfortably up beside her.

"Extraordinary thing," observed Patsy bringing her drink to her, "how girls fold themselves up. Clare always does it too. Are you comfortable?"

"Very. You should try it—though there's rather a long way for you to fold perhaps." She took a cigarette from him and when he had lit it she went on. "What a long time it seems since I first saw this room. Do you remember? With Clare and Nick after a flick."

"I remember," said Patsy. "Sorry the time's seemed long. I thought you were quite enjoying Ledenham."

"I am. I love it. It isn't that the time's seemed long, it's only that rather a lot has happened in it."

Patsy was in a very usual position for him, leaning against the mantelpiece, his eyes on his hands as he filled his pipe, and he completed the operation and put the pipe in his mouth before he said,

"Been quite a lot of ups and downs this term. We aren't usually so eventful, but it all seems to be working out right. Clare's happy, Angus is in and you've enjoyed yourself."

"What about Henry?" asked Frances.

"Oh, Henry," said Patsy. "No need to worry about Henry. He'll turn up next term and go on as before."

The door opened and Nick, dressed for stage-management in old grey flannels and gym shoes, ushered in the two young wives who were in charge of costumes and make-up for the play and their husbands with them.

Frances felt that there was something a little depressing about Patsy's summing up of the events of the term, a settlement of Ledenham's affairs which established Angus and restored Henry and assumed her own disappearance, but the feeling was swept away before she was fully conscious of it by the cheerful party, and the evening which continued to go well for her.

Delia had provided one of her ample, slightly haphazard meals which was eaten in an atmosphere of friendly scramble while everybody discussed Speech Day. It was considered to have gone off well. The Beak, they said, smiling at Frances to assure her that no strain would be placed on her loyalty, had been in his usual cracking form and Clare had coped magnificently. But the Cabinet

Minister would not have been much delighted to hear himself placed without regret in the used speakers' bin, dismissed as another of those who talk far too much without saying anything, and make honest men wonder how they have got so high in the world.

"Gas," said Nick conclusively, "in sufficient quantity will lift almost anybody."

Frances pinned and stitched dresses over football shorts on bony frames, adjusted wigs and applied make-up to amiable faces with petal-like skins, whose brilliant eyes and luxuriant lashes needed little assistance from art, and then she went round to the front of the house to sit beside Patsy and see the results of her labours. The cautious deportment of her ladies and their tendency to huskiness made her giggle and there were unrehearsed appearances of disproportionate feet and elbows, but they were, she thought, surprisingly convincing compared to any girl attempting any male part.

"It shows a very sporting spirit," she said to Patsy later, "to let themselves be dolled up and made to mince about and behave like foolish females."

"Oh," said Patsy, "they don't mind making fools of themselves. Do it often enough anyway."

He spoke in a tone of tolerant resignation and Frances said indignantly,

"Well, I think they're sweet. I love them."

They were walking slowly back to School House after the final party of the day, which had consumed further refreshment in the ever-open Zoo and Patsy glanced down, amused at her enthusiastic and unnecessary partisanship.

"Do you?" he said. "They're all right, I suppose, for a few minutes at a time. The softening influence of a Good Woman helps, of course." Frances was not immediately ready with a reply and he added in an expressionless voice, "Especially if the Good Woman knocks them out at sight."

"Really, Patsy!" cried Frances. "What's this? A scolding? It couldn't be a compliment."

"Oh, it's not a scolding," said Patsy. "You can't help it. I wouldn't know about compliments."

A faint puzzling darkness threatened the end of Frances' lovely day and she glanced quickly at Patsy strolling easily beside her, his hands in his pockets. He seemed a little remote and there was a note in his teasing which was not quite like his usual reliable friendliness.

"I don't think I like this very much," she said doubtfully. They had reached the door of School House. Patsy had put his hand out to open it, but when she spoke he turned, and seeing her uncertain face he took her hand and smiled.

"My dear girl," he said gently. "I'm sorry. I didn't mean to bother you. There's nothing on earth for you to dislike. You're lovely. In you go. Give a man a chance to keep his head. Good night, Frances."

The door closed quietly, it was never locked, and Frances went slowly upstairs and stood for a long time by her window looking out at the moonlit garden and listening half-consciously to the sound of the river. She had had perhaps the loveliest day of her life but it had left her with a feeling which she could not altogether identify. She did not know where she was.

CHAPTER 17

SPEECH day over, the School settled down, more or less reluctantly, to the hardest part of its year, because examinations public and private were coming so near that they could no longer be ignored as evils belonging to the future.

The Headmaster and Clare looked forward to a period of comparative peace, as routine work and ordinary entertaining seemed easy after the recent pressure, and altogether, as far as they were concerned, there was a welcome slackening of tempo. To Clare this was particularly welcome since Nevill was there for a comfortably long visit and she had leisure to show him all her favourite places, to do all her favourite things and to talk at great length about plans for their future. At the beginning of September Nevill was to begin his job. It was a good one, well known to be a stepping stone for those expected to rise to the heights as surgeons, and he had been able to take on his predecessor's flat so that there was no reason why they should not be married early in October.

"How will you like living in Edinburgh?" asked Frances. "Don't you loathe towns?"

"I like Edinburgh," said Clare. "I'll get a job and we won't stay right in it for long. Surgeons tend to move about for years before they settle. In the end I hope we'll be able to live outside it somewhere, near enough for Nevill's surging, but country."

With the School's return to normal and Clare a good deal

absorbed in her own affairs Frances found herself with time on her hands. She was not bored or idle because Clare was careful not to leave her in solitude very often, and, as Nevill had this time brought his own car, Tishy was at her disposal and she spent a good deal of time playing golf and tennis with various acquaintances, including the cheerful Brownlow girls who were to be in the party for the Leyburn Ball.

She was, however, alone more and less pre-occupied than she had been for some time, and it was now that she came to understand why Ledenham had become so important to her and so dear. Angus, earlier in the term, had realized that here, without any doubts or reserves, was where he wanted to live and work, but by then his passion for Frances was almost over and his desire was not connected with any one person. Frances' ambition was not unlike his. She knew too that she wanted nothing better than to live as part of Ledenham School for the rest of her life, but in her case, as she was beginning to know, the reason lay in one individual. She was a good deal at a loss. It was true that she had been "in love" once or twice before, but this was different. She had no desire whatever to put on her most alluring frocks and place herself in positions where she could be seen and admired, and there was none of the enjoyable excitement which usually accompanied the beginning of an affair. This was solemn, overwhelming and not at all happy, because for the first time in her life she had no idea what the object of this new feeling felt about her, and she sometimes suspected that he took no interest in her at all beyond a mild and kindly friendliness.

Frances, as her counterparts of long ago are said to have done, searched her heart, and she was astonished as well as somewhat awed at what she found there.

Patsy Henderson, large and on the whole untidy, silent and, though not without wit, quite devoid of sparkle, was not at all the type of man whom Frances had imagined to be her cup of tea. But there it was. She loved Ledenham because Patsy was there. She liked boys because they were part of him, and she wanted to live in Ledenham School all her life, but only if she lived there with Patsy.

On the whole she felt inclined to avoid him and was sorrowful because avoiding him was so easy. Beyond one game of golf followed by tea with Miss Perry while Clare was visiting Nevill's family in Edinburgh, she had never been out alone with Patsy and he had never made the slightest effort to be alone with her.

There had been times when she had felt his eyes on her, times when she had been almost sure that there was some-thing between them that they were both feeling, but the less agreeable part of her heart, as she searched it, reminded her tartly that there was such a thing as wishful thinking and advised her to turn it off.

Of all the young men about the School she now saw most of Angus. He was busy enough, but as a newcomer he was, apart from his climbing, not yet involved in many of the out-of-school activities. While Nick and Patsy disappeared with cricket teams and played occasionally themselves for the Ledshire Gentlemen; while they appeared in uniform heavily occupied on "Corps Day"; while they coached earnest swimmers, wrestled with problems of delinquency

227

and sang in the choir now feverishly preparing for the end of term concert, Angus was available. He made up a four for golf or tennis and he and Frances occasionally drifted out to fish or play golf by themselves, and were on terms of easy, even confidential friendship which was comfortable for both of them.

"Frances and Cameron seem to be seeing a good deal of each other," remarked the Headmaster mildly, "but I must say they look very peaceful. 'All passion spent' I dare say."

Clare said to Nevill,

"I wonder if they are falling in love with each other properly after all," and Nevill replied,

"I'm sure they aren't. Angus is wedded to the School, and I imagine Frances' thoughts are elsewhere."

"Yes," said Clare, "I think so. I do hope it goes right."

The Leyburn Ball, which had at one stage of the term been so conspicuous a subject of discussion, took place at the end of June. Nobody knew why its reputation was as high as it was, and most people had forgotten, if they had ever known, why it was held in splendid isolation at the height of summer. It was an ordinary charity ball and had begun its career years ago as one of the many balls held in and around the Christmas season. But there came a year, one of bitter quarrels and widespread feeling when the committee failed to find a date for it and it looked as though the ball was doomed and the charity would have no further support from Leyburn. Nobody remembered who had suggested holding it in mid-summer. It had been agreed that it was just worth a trial and immediately it had become the "ball of the year" and perhaps the most important of Leyburn's social occasions. Girls "came out" at the Leyburn Ball, as Clare had done and Alison would do next year. People had dinner parties and even house-parties for it, and the custom had grown of "having our sherry party" or "hop" or tennis party near the date of the ball, when everybody who could would be at home so that there had come to be something in the nature of a small social season in the district.

The grown-up members of Ledenham School enjoyed this season enormously. It came at a very good time for them, at a comfortable distance both from Speech Day and the end of term, and it was a time too, when they had been seeing a good deal of each other socially and appreciated the mixture of non-school people and the unofficial, irresponsible nature of the parties. They gave as much to the festivities as they received of course, because without the School, its bachelors, its daughters and its phalanx of charming, sociable young marrieds, the season would have been a comparatively thin and tenuous affair.

Clare, Nevill and Frances, with or without Nick, Patsy and Angus motored about the country in the week before the ball itself, attending parties of all kinds, and one of the small, informal "hops" took place in the drawing-room of School House. Frances found that Clare had been right in describing Nick's dancing as a poem. Angus was a gigantic partner, easy and competent and Nevill whisked her about in a casual elder-brotherly fashion. Patsy had been away for most of the week, playing cricket for his home county against the visiting Test team of the year, and though he had told Clare that he hoped to be back in time for her party he had not been sure whether it would be possible. Nothing was heard of him during his absence, apart from the references to him in the Press and broadcast accounts of his match, and it was a bitter blow to Frances when Nick announced in heartlessly cheerful tones,

"Patsy's not back yet, Clare. Hitting it up with the boys I fear."

"Well," said Clare easily, "he knew he could come or not as it suited him."

Frances did not know why his absence from this particular party was such a disappointment to her. She had been able to enjoy the others very well without him. But all the time she had been helping to prepare the house, arranging flowers and setting out Mrs. Higgins' ambrosial buffet supper she had been thinking that Patsy would come in time, and that presently she would be dancing with him. She had thought of him as she dressed, wondering if he would like, or notice, her short frock of shaded pink nylon, and she had thought of him as she rejected the ear-rings and necklace she had bought to go with it and as she ran downstairs looking like a flower.

"I can almost see the dew," said Nick beaming at her, but Patsy was not there to see it and Nick's tribute brought her no comfort. She kept looking at the door for a long time, but she had given it up and the end of the party was not far off when she suddenly saw him dancing with Clare. Clare was dancing with him as she did with Nick, with careless, accustomed ease and a lot of talking, and Patsy, more than a head taller, was looking down with his amused, companionable grin.

Nevill, who was her partner, presently gave her a small shake and said,

"Frances, you have left my last six remarks unanswered and your dancing is missing on three cylinders. What's the matter with you, woman?"

She made an effort to pull herself together and succeeded pretty well, but not before she had caught sight of what she feared was a gleam of understanding in Nevill's eyes. At the end of the dance she caught Patsy's eye across the room and he waved a greeting, but it appeared that this was not her evening. Poor Frances paid the penalty of being the prettiest girl in the room. She was never free of attentive young men, she was swept off to dance the moment the music started, and Patsy himself, who had scarcity value, since this was his first appearance of the season, as well as all the glamour of a brilliant, much-publicized performance in his match, was equally surrounded by admirers and could hardly have reached her even if he wanted to.

They did not exchange a word till the party was over and he came to say good night.

"And also 'hullo'," said Frances.

He smiled down at her.

"Too bad," he said. "I wanted to dance with that frock, but too many chaps had the same idea."

"Did you enjoy the match?"

"So-so. Good fun really. Glad to be back though. I must manage the ball better, Frances. They have programmes. Will you keep the first and the last and supper?"

Frances felt much better, but she said rather anxiously,

"I'm not sure if I'm not supposed to be Nick's partner.

231

What—what happens about 'partners'?"

"Oh, Nick," said Patsy easily. "He's been dancing with you all week. He can sit back and put his feet up."

At lunch on the day of the ball Frances said to Clare,

"Another occasion for a simple little number?"

Clare looked blank for a second and then laughed aloud.

"No, dear," she said in kind tones, "you can be as dazzling as nature will allow tonight," an exchange which baffled the two gentlemen present, but amused the two ladies.

The Leyburn Ball was not the occasion for last winter's dance frock, and the four girls of the party looked very lovely when they met for drinks in Patsy's room before proceeding to dinner at "The Arms", as Leyburn's leading hotel was familiarly called. The Brownlow sisters, who were friends of Nick and Patsy as old and only less intimate than Clare herself, were gay and attractive and very smart Clare's dress had been chosen to match her zircon ring. Its delicate colour was perfect for her as the ring was, and its slim, draped top and wide, full-length skirt made her thin young figure elegant. Frances wore a silver frock, supple and shining, the perfect cut and immense width of the skirt giving full value to the beauty of the material, and the severe simplicity of the style doing nothing to clutter or obscure the beauty of the girl.

"I missed the pink frock," said Patsy beside her, "I'm not going to miss the silver one. Remember—first, last and supper anyway."

Frances turned to him. She was so happy that for a moment she forgot everything else and her face was radiant and without reserve. Patsy looked at her without smiling, his eyes searching and almost stern, and she felt a shock of dismay and humiliation. She coloured and was turning away, when he touched her arm gently and said, "Don't forget now. How are you going? Would you risk the Bentley? It isn't really oily you know, and it's closed up as far as it will."

Frances hesitated, her wits astray and a tightness in her throat, but she nodded and he smiled at her and went away to fill glasses from the jug of cocktail in his hand.

Her self-possession returned to some extent in the easy friendliness of the drive to Leyburn and the hilarity of the dinner party, and when they arrived at the ball Patsy himself brought her her programme with his initials already scribbled opposite the first and last and supper dances. Nick took it from her and exclaimed indignantly, "I must say, Henderson, this is pulling it rather fast. Why the hell should you have all the specials?"

Patsy regarded him with a peaceful grin.

"You've been dancing for practically a solid week. My turn."

Frances' programme was rapidly filled and Patsy, having booked his three dances with her, was filling up his own so that it was clearly not his intention to spend more of the evening with her. He was beside her, however, as the music for their first dance started and took her on to the floor without delay.

Patsy was not an inspired performer as Nick was, but his dancing like all his movements had a smooth athletic grace and his arm, holding his partner firmly and comfortably, conveyed the sense of kind, unfussy friendliness which was characteristic of him.

Frances found nothing to say to him. She did not know where she was with Patsy, and she feared that presently she might have to face great unhappiness. She closed her eyes for a minute and pushed the dread away. They were dancing together now and she would not waste it. The party met for supper and was extremely cheerful and somewhat noisy, but Frances had a heaviness on her which made it almost more than she could do to talk nonsense and be gay, and she was relieved when they left their table.

"Come out for a cigarette," said Patsy. "They won't start again for ages. Will you be cold?"

"No," she said and picking up her silver stole, went out with him.

The ball was held in Leyburn Castle which nowadays houses the town library and museum as well as providing it with a fine set of "Assembly Rooms", and its gardens were on the bank of the river. Patsy and Frances, their cigarettes alight, strolled down towards it and were standing looking at the water before a word was said.

Frances thought, "This is it, I think," and waited.

"When do you go home?" asked Patsy presently.

"My parents are coming back early in August. I'll meet them in London then I expect."

"You've enjoyed Ledenham haven't you?"

"Yes," said Frances, "I've made a hash or two and been a bit miserable sometimes, but—I love it."

"I don't think you've made much of a hash," Patsy said. "You've been lovely and I'm glad you've liked it. You'll be glad, though, to get back to your own world. This would be

234

a dull sort of setting for you for any length of time."

Frances had been leaning on the parapet staring at the river, but at this she straightened and looked at him.

"Oh, Patsy," she said. "You're quite wrong. I don't want to go back." He was serious and his eyes were distressed, and Frances, feeling tears in her own eyes, turned back to the river. Presently he took her hand.

"Frances," he said, I don't think that any man could help loving you, and I believe that I might be able to keep you in Ledenham." Frances moved as if she would speak and he tightened his hold on her hand and said, "Let me finish. I'm not going to try because, though I think you do love Ledenham and—us—now, it isn't your element."

Frances said again, "You're wrong. I think this is my element."

"No," said Patsy. "You think so because you're sorry a good sort of holiday is nearly over. You couldn't live here in this quiet place all your life any more than I could live in London." He paused, but she didn't speak and he went on, "It's hell not to try, Frances, but it's nothing to the hell it would be if we went on with this and found out the mistake later. You're beautiful and—rich. And you're accustomed to—I don't know what sort of life, it's so remote from mine It wouldn't do, Frances."

Frances took her hand away and turned her back on the river.

"It's true you don't know the sort of life I've had," she said. "Patsy—there's no reason why you should—try to keep me in Ledenham. That's your choice. You decide if I'm the girl you want and—trust. But you've no right to make my choice for me. Nobody can do that except myself."

Patsy said, "It isn't that. You don't know what the choice means. This term it's been new to you, but it's a dull place and I'm a dull chap and a comparatively poor one. I have thought about it, Frances."

Frances shook her head. "You've thought about it, but you can't know. I won't have it fobbed off as thoughtfulness for me, Patsy—we'll get it straight. You don't want to marry me because in the end you don't think I'm the sort of girl you can trust. We'll go in now and I'm going to get tidy."

She stayed for a long time up in the cloakroom and when she went down their dance was over, but Patsy was waiting for her at the foot of the stairs.

"What do you want to do?" he asked.

"Oh," said Frances vaguely. "Just carry on. We'll have our last dance and I'll go home in your car if you'll take me. It's arranged."

When the time came they danced almost in silence until near the end Patsy held her closely and said very quietly, "I love you—you know that. But, Frances—it wouldn't do. And I—I couldn't stand it if I had you and then lost you."

"Don't say any more," said Frances. "Let's go home now," and he drove her quickly back to Ledenham and saw her into the School House with hardly another word.

CHAPTER 18

WHEN Clare went upstairs much later she saw that the light was still on in Frances' room and she gave the door a little tap and went in. Frances was still wearing her beautiful silver dress and moving wearily about the room as if she was just beginning to get ready for bed.

"Hullo," said Clare. "Are you just back? I lost you at the end, but I knew you were fixed up all right," and then she saw Frances' face and exclaimed, "Frances—darling, what is it? What's wrong?"

Frances had wept for a long time when she got safely into her room, and then she had decided that with any luck she would be able to keep this misery to herself and nobody need know about it, but Clare's friendly call and friendly voice were too much for her.

Clare said no more but took off the silver frock and helped her to bed, then she disappeared for a few minutes and came back in her dressing gown carrying a hot-water bottle and a steaming cup of milk.

"Here you are, Fran," she said. "Two aspirins. Take them now and drink this up and get warm. You're shivering."

"I'm sorry," said Frances. "I keep on needing you to minister with aspirins and hot milk. Last time though, I hope."

Clare sat on the bed and lit cigarettes for them both.

"What's up? Have you quarrelled with Patsy?"

"Yes," said Frances. "At least—no. Not quarrelled."

"What then? You haven't turned him down have you,

237

Frances?" Her voice was rather stern and sounded less friendly, but Frances laughed a little.

"No fear," she said. "He's turned me down."

"What?" cried Clare. "What can you mean?"

Frances drew a long sobbing breath and told her story, miserably and with a flat minimum of words which left Clare baffled and silent.

"I can't imagine," she said at last. "Patsy of all people going wrong over this. Girls do fall for him, but he's never seemed to see it. And I'd never have thought it possible for him to—to lead anyone on."

"No, no!" said Frances. "It's not a bit like that. He—he does love me. He said so, and I know he does. But I don't suppose he'd have said anything only—it happened that I gave myself away and then, I suppose, he felt he had to—to do something about it."

She explained as well as she could, and in all that she said she was scrupulously fair to Patsy's point of view. Clare sat smoking silently. Nick had said right at the beginning of term that he thought Patsy was in love with Frances. "I believe Patsy's gone in," was his phrase and she had some-times wondered about it. Lately, though Patsy was not one who showed his feelings, she had thought it was so, and for some time she had been fairly sure and Nevill was too, that Frances would marry Patsy if he asked her. They had both thought it would be a very good marriage, and Clare had hoped, as she had once said, that it would "go right" and that the engagement might happen, as many engagements had happened, at the Leyburn Ball. But now it had gone very wrong and she could see no way in which anyone

238

could help. She could easily see Patsy's point. Frances' background could hardly be more different from Ledenham, and there was always some danger of people getting married and then reverting to type with disastrous consequences; but she thought that Patsy was mistaken, perhaps naturally, because he did not realize that Frances now was so different from the Frances who had arrived at the beginning of term. She had not only changed, as any young person might in a new environment, she had, as her uncle said, consolidated the new Frances and to a great extent grown up into the sort of woman she wanted and intended to be.

All this thought took a long time and they sat together in a silence which in Frances' case was very weary. At last Clare got up.

"I think I see it," she said. "It isn't anybody's fault, but it isn't easy. Fran—we can't know all Patsy's feeling. If he said he loves you, he does love you, but he won't give in to it if he thinks it's the wrong thing. I do think that it would be right for you both, but it's his decision. And yours of course, but you have decided. There's nothing anybody can do about it."

"Oh no," said Frances. "Nothing. I'm glad, though, that you think it would have been a good thing It's—soothing."

"Oh, poor Fran," exclaimed Clare, "how dismal this is!"

Frances for the third time in her term at Ledenham pulled herself together and made great efforts to be normal in looks and behaviour. She went about as usual after the ball, but she thought a great deal, thrusting feeling into the background as far as it would go and trying with all her

239

mind and intelligence to face the situation honestly and to see if there was any way in which she could break the circle of unhappiness. It depended on two things she thought. How much Patsy really loved her and wanted her, and if he did want her enough, how to convince him that it would "do". She knew, poor Frances, that men often did fall in love with her in spite of themselves, knowing that it was not the kind of love which would lead to marriage, and there was no way of being sure that this was not Patsy's feeling. She did not think it was, but she would probably never know unless something happened to change his mind about the importance of her different background.

They did not meet for several days, but the climbing expedition which was to take Clare and perhaps Frances up the Needle under Angus' leadership was planned for the Sunday following the ball and on the Saturday Frances rang Patsy up.

"Patsy," she said. "Would you be free any time today? I'd rather like to see you."

"Sure," said Patsy. "Free at 5.30. Will you dine with me somewhere?"

"No. I don't want to do that. Could we play golf?"

Shortly after 5.30 Frances walked out through the gates and met Patsy at the Zoo. Golf lessons had been included in her expensive education and she had always enjoyed it and played a fair game. Given a stroke a hole she was a reasonable opponent for Patsy who was an intermittent golfer, and during this round of the little nine-hole course which had grown so familiar, her concentration was better than his and she finished one hole up.

Patsy grinned.

"Nice work," he said. "You've come on." It had been a companionable round. Frances had spoken of nothing personal and Patsy had been glad to follow her lead, but he thought that there must be something she wanted to say, and he was very reluctant to let this time together come to an end. As they got into the car again he said, "Sure about not dining with me? I—wish you would."

"No," said Frances and smiled at him. "This has been lovely, but I—can't manage dinner though I'd love to, Patsy, really."

"As you say," said Patsy and started the car.

The drive from the Club House to the School took ten minutes and Frances had laid her plans and timed them carefully. Just before they turned into the road which led to the School gates she said,

"Patsy, there's one thing I want to say to you, but I don't want you to say anything. Don't slow down. Go on." Patsy looked at her, but she was looking straight ahead and he drove on.

"It's very likely that we won't be alone together again," said Frances, "so I want just to tell you this. I've grown up in Ledenham. I may have to go back to my other kind of life. I can't see any way out of it just now. But I shall always know that the life I want is here, or somewhere like this."

As Patsy drew up at the door of School House he said, "Frances," but she was already out of the car.

"I must run," she said hurriedly. "Good-bye, Patsy," and was gone.

Once inside the house she showed no haste, but went

slowly up to her room and took a long time over changing for dinner. Clare and Nevill were out and she knew her uncle would be late, but she had been determined that she would have no further discussion or scene with Patsy. She had thought it honest and right to tell him as much as that, and when it was said flatly and briefly, without emotion and, as it were, in isolation, he might believe it, but she would not allow herself to show any feeling again, and she would never plead or seem to plead. The thing was over now and she would not see him alone again unless he came to fetch her.

She smiled at Mr. Fielding when he came to dinner—

"Are we à deux?" he asked. "I'd be in a bad way without you, with no wife and an engaged daughter. What have you been doing?"

"Playing golf—and I beat Patsy. With a stroke a hole, of course."

Her uncle smiled.

"I wouldn't care to take on Patsy with any ball without a handicap. He's one of the people—Cameron's another—whom balls naturally obey. It's a gift and that's that."

"I'm very glad," said Frances, "that Angus is going to be permanent. I know he wanted it terribly."

"Did he? I knew he was pretty keen as time went on. He'll be good—he's getting on terms with the boys, which was the doubtful thing. It's a great help when they like the place and he does that, I know. You like it too don't you—for a while?"

"I love it," said Frances. "And not just for a while. I wish you had a job for me, Uncle Hugh."

"You can come and keep house for me if Aunt Hester goes off for a holiday after Clare's married. It isn't very likely I'm afraid. This is the only time she's done it in twenty-five years. There's only one kind of permanent job for you in the School," he added with a friendly twinkle, "and it isn't my appointment. Anyway, you might not care for it."

"Oh I'd like it all right," she said, "but he won't have me."

The Headmaster looked up quickly.

"Is that so? You surprise me very much, Frances. I'm sorry if there is any pain in this for you, my dear."

Frances shook her head.

"I didn't mean to speak of it."

"I'm afraid my feeble joke rather led to it. I'm sorry."

There was silence for a little and then Mr. Fielding went on quietly,

"These things happen or they don't. That's just got to be accepted, and it's often the case that later on you can see them as part of some kind of pattern. It may be that your knowing Patsy now will help you to recognize the right thing when you meet it."

She had looked startled and he said smiling at her, "It must have been one of those three you know, and obviously, therefore, it must be Patsy."

"Why?" asked Frances.

"Oh," he said vaguely, "his quality, I suppose," and he led her to talk of other things.

Frances had come to regard her uncle with something like hero-worship. His position and authority, his reserve and his wit, and above all perhaps his calm and unfussy manner of dealing with people, she admired and appreciated all the more because she had never found them in her own father. He was able, even brilliantly successful, in his own job and very much richer than her uncle, but she thought now that he had never had real responsibility. His only responsibility was making money for his firm and compared to Uncle Hugh, thought Frances, her father had not begun to grow up. It was going to be very hard to leave her uncle and Clare, the house with its atmosphere of hospitality, the interest and the bustle and the fun, but she knew that she had learned so much that she would never be content with her old, aimless party-going life again, and that somehow she would eventually find what she wanted.

Patsy, when Frances left him so quickly, could do nothing except go away, and he drove round to the Zoo and went up to his study. Presently he ate his dinner, and shaking off all socialities went back to his room and sat down to think.

He was very unhappy indeed. He had been in love with Frances almost as soon as he saw her, ever since the Benenbeck picnic when they had fished together; and he had come very near to losing his head on Speech Day when she was so incredibly lovely and looked at him so sweetly. But he had managed all right and he thought he could have gone on managing and seen her go away without intolerable pain, if only she had not suddenly looked at him with an expression which showed that she could, or even already did, love him. He had had to say something to her then, because he hadn't been able to bear her look of hurt. He thought he was right. She was young, she liked

Ledenham and for the moment she liked him, but she was the kind of girl who ought to marry a duke or a millionaire and wear diamonds and shine in exalted circles. If he let her go now she would do that, or something like it. If he kept her in Ledenham how could she stand it year after year? And yet she had sounded as if she meant it when she said that it was the kind of life she wanted. And the pain of letting her go now was not going to be tolerable.

For the last eight years or so it had been Patsy's custom, as it was the custom of most members of the School, to take any problem that really bogged him to the Beak. The Beak was not only a wise and clear-sighted old bird, he was also completely and absolutely reliable and nothing that a man said to him ever got past him. Patsy now thought automatically that he might have a word with the Beak and was brought up with a start as he remembered that since Frances was the Beak's niece it concerned him personally. But that would be all right, thought Patsy. He would know better than anyone what would be best for Frances and how much she knew her own mind and needs, and he wasn't the man to take offence or read spurious motives into an honest question. Patsy reached for the telephone and a moment later was walking towards the Headmaster's study.

Mr. Fielding was waiting for him thoughtfully. Patsy never gave much away and there was no telling from his voice whether he wanted to discuss an affair of the heart or the examination time-table, but it was a comparatively rare thing for him to ask for a talk late in the evening.

"Sit down," he said when Patsy arrived, "and if time and

245

subject allow, light up. I'm quite leisurely for once in a way."

"Thank you, sir," said Patsy soberly. "It might be longish I'm afraid." He felt for his pipe and the Headmaster said cheerfully,

"All right, go ahead."

"It's a private matter, sir. I wasn't sure if I should bring it to you—I think so." Patsy was not normally a man of many words and he hated the sensation of being "out on a limb" with no way back which assailed him when he had to make anything that might be called a statement. He lit his pipe and pulled himself together, and in response to the Headmaster's patient and encouraging nod plunged in. "The fact is, sir, I am in love with Frances. I think—I almost know—that she likes me a good deal, but I'm—well I'm afraid of it."

"Why?"

Patsy explained; and as he had thought about it and, as it were, discussed it with himself ad nauseam he did it well and the Headmaster thought that his doubts were not unfounded, and were reasonable and manly as he would expect from him. When Patsy had finished he said,

"Have you spoken to Frances herself?"

"A bit. I wasn't going to, but—something happened which made it necessary. I told her that I wasn't going to try to keep her here because it isn't her kind of life."

"And what did she say?"

Patsy grinned faintly.

"Ticked me off. Said I could make my own choice, but had no business to make hers."

Mr. Fielding laughed aloud.

"Good girl. A very good point."

"But she has said," went on Patsy, "that Ledenham is the sort of place and life she wants—only—she's so young. I don't think she really knows. And I'm afraid she'd find later that she couldn't stand it. It's too different."

"Patsy," said the Headmaster who very rarely called his assistant masters by their Christian names, "I don't think I can advise you. If you had asked me earlier in the term I think I'd have agreed with you. Now I'm not sure. Frances has grown up very much. She is a lovely girl—I don't mean pretty—and will be a very valuable woman. I can't see her letting a man down. But whether you're right for her and she's right for you nobody can know except you two."

There was a silence and he went on,

"There are three things open to you, I think. You can let her go, or you can plunge now and damn the risk, or you can postpone it. After all, Frances will be in London—she's not going to another planet or even to Australia. You might very well wait a bit. There will be Clare's wedding for one thing—October. Frances will be here for that."

Patsy's face cleared and he gave a pleasant low laugh of sheer amusement.

"I never thought of it! She came out of the blue and I suppose I expected her to disappear into it again."

"She won't do that," said Mr. Fielding. "At least I hope not. She has become too much one of the family to be allowed to disappear again."

CHAPTER 19

WHILE Patsy went to call on the Headmaster Angus was happily engaged in preparations for the next day's climbing expedition. Not only did he examine ropes and check the gear which he packed into the back of his little car, he also organized the movements of personnel. It was his experience that in parties of this kind much time and not infrequently feeling were saved if somebody made all the plans beforehand and presented the arrangements complete and ready for action, and, as the leader of this expedition, he made the plans.

When he was ready he went round to School House to see Nick and put him in the picture.

"Four cars," he said, "Clare and Nevill can take the food. Patsy can take three boys and some of the gear, your jeep ditto. I've loaded the back of my car, and I'll take Frances in front."

Nick showed signs of rebellion.

"I don't quite see that we can lump everybody about like that. Frances, for example, might prefer to go or come back in another vehicle. You can't just order her into your car."

"Yes I can," said Angus flatly. "I don't know anything about Frances as a climber and I'm not going to take her up the Needle unless I have a talk with her first."

"That applies to Clare too, doesn't it?" asked Nick with a slight grin, but he failed to ruffle Angus' stately calm.

"No," he said, "I know about Clare. She's climbed with you."

248

The next morning was promising, grey and cool, but with no wind to be troublesome and with the look of a day that would probably improve. Twelve people left the chapel after the morning service with an air of haste and purpose, and the "church parade" saw nothing of the School House party which was its usual centre except its backs hurrying homewards.

Angus was proved right about the time-saving of his ready-made arrangements, but whether in this case it prevented feeling is less certain. Clare and Nevill drove off together very happily and Frances got into Angus' little car with agreeable docility, but Nick and Patsy obeyed their orders and loaded up with boys and gear at the door of the Zoo with less enthusiasm. Patsy's talk with the Headmaster had, it seemed to him, cleared things up very satisfactorily. There were no longer only the two alternatives of pledging Frances to Ledenham and him now, with an intolerable risk of future unhappiness, or letting her go with an intolerable certainty of present unhappiness. He would leave it till she had got right away from Ledenham and had had time to think about it from a distance, and in six months or so he would go to see her and then, if she still liked the idea, "O.K." thought Patsy, with a warm glow in his heart. He had told Mr. Fielding that he would do this, and walked back to the Zoo feeling happier than he had done for a long time, but he had miscalculated the effect of the decision on himself. As soon as he admitted that there was a possibility, quite a strong possibility, that presently he would ask Frances to marry him he was almost over-whelmed by the desire to ask her at once. What if he let her go, thinking as she did now that there was no future for them together, and she rushed back to London and married the wrong man? What if she was really unhappy? And what if the thing simply faded out and she forgot him? One way and another Patsy felt that he would say something to Frances which would start her thoughts on the new line, and he hoped that he might manage to get her alone for a bit in the course of the climbing expedition.

He was not therefore altogether delighted when Angus told him briefly that he would take Benson and Carter and Howe and that pile of gear, but he was never ill-natured or a maker of trouble and he thought "Plenty of time" and waved cheerfully to Frances as Angus drove her away. But it proved difficult to find the time.

Frances had got herself well in hand. She had made a real and determined effort to push her unhappiness into the background and prevent it from spoiling what was left of her time at Ledenham both for herself and her friends, and, though she looked more serious and laughed less often than was usual for her, she did not look unhappy and she turned her whole attention to the matter in hand as she always did. She was interested to try climbing again, though it was not a thing which she could altogether enjoy, and she was very much interested in seeing how the Ledenham climbers set about it, especially Angus as the "Leader". The only reserve in her mind about the expedition was that she wanted to avoid Patsy, if she could manage it without its being noticed by the others, or appearing unfriendly to Patsy himself.

Angus' plan was ready. "Benson is going up the Needle,"

he said. "I'll lead him and we'll do it first thing. Clare—you lead Nevill on the West Ridge. Patsy—I want you to go up the Pyke with Howe leading and Carter and Morris. Nick—will you give Frances a trial run? You other two chaps start on the 'Practice'."

This programme went through and they did not meet again till they assembled for a late lunch. Afterwards Clare was to go up the Needle with Angus, and, if time and energy allowed, Frances might do it with him later.

In spite of Angus' scorn the remainder of the party felt a little disinclined to start climbing again immediately after lunch. Their picnic place had a very good view of the Needle, and without anything said or any clear decision being made, they stayed where they were and watched the two who were climbing. The Needle was a rock edge which went up straight and steep to a fair height. It was not a big climb; Angus and Nick could do it easily in half an hour and Angus had taken Benson up that morning in just under an hour, but it was steep and exposed, and without a certain amount of experience and steady concentration it could be dangerous. Clare had been trained by Nick and Patsy and for a time she had been very keen indeed, but she had done no climbing except in this district and she had never tackled the Needle which was the most difficult of the local climbs.

She enjoyed her morning's climbing which was easy since Nevill was a novice, but she did not feel as much enthusiasm as she had expected for the real business of the day. Nevill looked at her with questioning eyes and said,

"No need to do it if you don't feel like it you know," but

251

Nick was grinning with pleasure over this golden opportunity for her, and Angus was getting ready with a calm friendliness and competence which were very reassuring. Clare began to feel better about it and they went off together very cheerfully.

They began very well. Angus was really magnificent, in quite a different class from Nick who had hitherto been the best climber she had known. The first difficulty, half-way up, she tackled with zest and received congratulations when she joined Angus on a ledge.

"That's fine," he said. "Now the long pitch. Hold it, I'm off."

The long pitch too was accomplished successfully, but Clare found herself tiring and at the end of it was not comfortable.

"All right?" asked Angus.

"Bit tired."

"Take it easy for a minute. The next stage is the real test. Do you remember the look of it from below? Watch what I do while you can see me—it's not so difficult after the bend." Angus spoke with complete enjoyment and in a moment was climbing again. "You're O.K. for reach," he said as he started. "Benson's smaller than you and he managed easily."

Clare watched him go, fascinated by his skill and the precision and economy of his movements, but it was when she could no longer see him that her discomfort returned with rising fear and the beginning of nausea. He shouted that he was ready for her and she made an effort to fight down her fear and look at what she had to do. There was a tiny ledge, with bare room for both feet and a handgrip. That was the first objective. She felt a spasm of giddiness and thought fleetingly of Nevill whom she was to marry, and what would happen to both of them if she came off now, but she knew that this was panic and she pushed it away. She would be all right when she started, and she called to Angus that she was coming. Getting up to that ledge needed all her reach and took all her strength. Breathless and trembling she pressed herself against the rock, gripping that uncomfortable hand-hold, and knew that she was done. Nausea and vertigo swept over her in waves and she shut her eyes and held on with all her might.

"Come on!" shouted Angus. "Last lap. You're doing fine." There was a pause before she could lift her head and shriek,

"I can't do it! I'm stuck."

"O.K." called Angus immediately. "Hang on. I'm coming. You're all right."

Several of the watchers below thought that Clare was tiring on the long pitch. Angus paused longer than they expected before he left her, and they saw him after he had disappeared from Clare's view, reach his next stage and heard him shout that he was ready. Clare was being very slow to start. A tension grew in the group watching her. She began to climb, hesitating and fumbling and they thought for a moment that she would fail to reach the ledge. She got there, but before they could release their held breath, they saw her falter and sway and then grip the rock with panic in every line of her.

Frances' face went sheet white and her hand flew to grasp

Nevill's arm as he moved suddenly.

"Keep still—you'll startle her."

Clare pressed herself against the rock. They heard Angus' voice again, but they could not hear her reply though at last they saw her lift her head to call to him.

Patsy and Nick were already on their feet.

"You lead," said Patsy quietly. "Get above them, I'll stay below her. Angus is going to get down—he's fixing the belay. You can get round them, Nick, can't you?" Nick nodded briefly, and Patsy went on as they finished roping, "It's all right, Nevill—the rope'll hold. You chaps get hot water and make tea."

"Yes, sir," said the boys, and everybody went off quietly but very fast. Nevill, his face wooden, went to his car and took out a small case, and Frances beside him said,

"We'll take rugs and brandy and then we can warm her up right away." Nevill nodded and they went to the foot of the Needle.

Nick and Patsy were climbing at great speed, and Angus with the greatest care and delicacy of movement came down towards Clare. Frances saw him stop and, testing a grip far out to his left, change his route with a stride and reach impossible for a smaller man. The boys beside her caught their breath and held it in the few seconds of extreme difficulty which followed, and then he seemed to be hanging at the full stretch of his left arm with only a toe grip to support him as he reached his right arm round Clare. It looked as though she relaxed a little, but it seemed impossible that Angus could stay where he was, and he was not roped now.

Patsy reached the ledge where Angus and Clare had paused and Nick went to the right, up a face which seemed to have neither foot- nor hand-hold, but which took him round the two on the high ledge so that he appeared above them. The pattern of their plan was ready, but it was not easy to carry out. It seemed hours to the watchers before Nick called, "Right" to Angus, and Clare had lost all sense of time when Angus said,

"Clare—Patsy is just below, ready for you. Nick is above looking after the rope. Can you help?"

"I think so," whispered Clare.

"Right. Attend to me and I'll tell you what to do. You're quite safe, but you must think what you're doing." He gave her instructions, move by move till she felt Patsy take hold of her and heard him say,

"I've got you. Good girl—easy going now. Right, Angus."

There was a pause while the attention of both Nick and Patsy was turned to Angus, who now had to manoeuvre himself on to the tiny ledge which Clare had left. Nick could hear but not see him, and Patsy could do both and saw that though the move was not too difficult ordinarily, it was extremely difficult for Angus now, strained and stiff as he was from the position in which he had been holding Clare.

"Take it easy, Angus," he said. "Be ready for him, Nick."

"Right," came Nick's voice.

There was a bad moment while Angus, with his left arm and leg almost useless, got himself on to the ledge, and then Patsy began the task of getting Clare down the rest of the Needle. It was slow but she was much steadier and it was

255

not long before Nevill took her from him. Angus came down without a rope, doggedly and with a tense caution instead of his usual easy neatness. He looked as though he were in a good deal of pain and he stumbled away a little from the others before he sat down.

It was a quiet but busy party for a few minutes. The shivering Clare was wrapped up and the boys with serious sensible faces were bringing cups of hot, very sweet tea. Frances went quickly to Angus with Patsy immediately behind her, and found that he too was shivering and looked exhausted.

"I'm quite all right," he stammered.

"Shut up," said Patsy, "lie down for a minute. Carter—brandy here," and to Frances. "Shove that rug under his head, darling." Frances heard, and some part of her noticed and remembered the word, but her attention was on Angus and she patted him gently.

"Good boy, Angus," she said, "dear good boy."

"So he is," agreed Patsy and Angus grinned faintly.

Nevill was with them then and after a look at Angus said,

"Ten minutes' rest and some tea, and then we'll get them home."

"Is—is—Clare?" began Angus.

"Clare's fine. Patsy—I'll take them both in my car." Angus' stammering protests about clearing up and his own car were swept aside.

"Take him to the house, Nevill," said Frances. "Plenty of room. Be quiet, Angus—do what you're told. I'll bring your car."

In due course she drove Angus' Morris home, with Howe,

a School House Prefect and one of the best of the climbers, as a passenger.

"How much will the School hear of this?" she asked.

"Well," he said grinning a little, "there are six of us. I expect they'll get most of it unless we're told to keep it quiet."

"I don't know about that. There doesn't seem any reason why it should be kept quiet except that Miss Fielding probably feels a bit miserable about it."

"It wasn't her fault," said Howe quickly. "I mean—she didn't make a mistake or do anything silly. It can happen to anybody—to get tired and giddy. But," he added, "we'll never see anything like the way they got her down again."

"No. It was good wasn't it."

"Yes," said Howe. "Mr. Cameron—I didn't think he could get down to her, and then I didn't think he could hang on, and after that he managed to get her down to Mr. Henderson. It looked—a sort of—miracle almost."

When they drew up at School House, the Headmaster came out to meet them.

"Howe," he said. "You and the others have hot baths and you'll find supper laid on for you. I'm very grateful to you all."

"Thank you, sir," said Howe. "We didn't do anything. Good night, Miss Cheriton," and he was gone.

"Frances, dear," said her uncle. "It's time somebody looked after you a little, I think. Nevill is being very firm and medical. They're both in bed. Angus is in worse shape than Clare."

Frances trailed into the drawing-room and sitting down

on the first chair she came to, burst into tears. Her uncle patted her comfortingly and made no attempt to stop her for a few minutes, and then she found that Nevill had taken his place and was commanding her to "drink this".

She sat up and began to dry her eyes.

"I don't know why women always have to cry," she said miserably.

"Shock," said Nevill. "Good way to cope with it really. Go and have a bath, Frances, and then you'll be all right and ready for supper."

"How's Clare?"

"She's fine. Resting nicely. Angus is pretty badly strained. He'll hardly be able to move for a few days, poor chap."

"We owe him a good deal," said Frances.

"We do," agreed Nevill. "I owe him everything."

The door opened and Patsy came into the room still in his climbing clothes.

"Are they all right?" he asked Nevill.

"All right," said Nevill. "I'll try and thank you some time, Patsy—not now. I'll go and see about a drink." And he left the room quickly.

Frances was standing up, still shaken, with untidy hair and a tired, tear-stained face. Patsy went over and took both her hands.

"Frances," he said, "will you marry me?"

Frances was too tired to feel any surprise or any need to consider what she would say or do. With his arms securely round her she cried a little more with great comfort and enjoyment till she was roused by the things which the reserved and normally silent Patsy was saying to her. She looked up and saw in his face the look she had first seen in Nevill's when he looked at Clare, but this was Patsy looking at her and she smiled at him before he kissed her.

"But why now?" she asked a little later. "When we're all shook up and I'm sopping with tears? You're filthy, Patsy darling."

"You're pretty grubby yourself," said Patsy kissing the grubby face. "We'll mop you up."

"No glamour at all," said Frances sadly. "Such a waste of nice frocks and suitable occasions. The silver frock and the garden by the river would have been so much better. What made you think so suddenly that it would—do?"

Patsy said,

"It's not so sudden as all that. I knew I couldn't let you go. But I thought you should go back to London and think about it. I was going to try and say something like that to you and then—" he stopped and caught her close to him. "There was Clare on that bloody ledge and Nevill's face. I knew I'd been a fool to waste time."

"Oh gosh!" said Frances and they were silent for a moment. "How—how dangerous was it, Patsy? Would Clare have been killed?"

"I don't think so. The rope would have held her. But she might have been. She'd certainly have been hurt and there was nothing to stop Angus if he'd come off. Not very nice, but it didn't happen, darling."

"No," said Frances, "but I'm rather off climbing. Cowardly, really, I suppose."

Patsy laughed.

"That'll be quite all right. I'd just as soon you stayed on the floor."

259

CHAPTER 20

WHEN Patsy had gone Frances rushed upstairs to Clare. She went on her knees beside the bed and they clung to each other in silence for a few minutes.

"I was a fool to try it," said Clare at last.

"Why?"

"I can't take risks any more. I was never frightened of climbing and car smashes and things before, but I am now."

"Because of Nevill?" Clare nodded and Frances went on, "I can quite see it. And Clare, Patsy's scared too—of wasting time."

Clare drew back so that she could see her and then hugged her tightly.

"Oh, Frances darling, I'm so glad. I thought it would come right. When you both love each other it had to come right. Well—my stupid fuss has done one good thing. It's given you two a short cut."

On her way down to dinner, clean and fresh and sufficiently glamorous, Frances called on Angus. He was exceedingly well-scrubbed and tidy, and, in bed without his glasses, he looked very young and tired.

"Hullo, Angus," said Frances. "How is Our Hero?"

"I'm fine. A bit stiff," he replied. "Don't make fun of me, please."

"I don't feel like making fun of you," Frances said soberly. "But I don't know how to say what I do feel."

Angus looked offended and spoke severely.

"There's nothing to say. Patsy and Nick and I got Clare

down in a perfectly ordinary way. Nothing to make a fuss about. You just have to be ready for things like that and deal with them. I hope it hasn't spoilt her nerve, that's all, or yours."

Clare and she had both finished with climbing but Frances could not say so. Angus, however, did not wait for a reply.

He looked at her with an expression of friendliness and mischief and said,

"So we're both staying in Ledenham after all."

She was completely taken aback.

"How—how did you know?"

"I heard what Patsy called you when we came down."

Frances burst out laughing.

"He hadn't asked me then," she said. "I don't think he knew he said it."

Angus reached out and took her hand.

"I am pleased about it," he said. "It's grand that we're both staying. And," he added grinning, "I can have Patsy's rooms in the Zoo."

Mr. Fielding, Nevill and Frances had a quiet supper together that Sunday evening. Mr. Fielding's mind was by no means accustomed to dwell on what might have happened, and the young people had minimized rather than exaggerated the danger of Clare's experience, but what they told him combined with their appearance left him in no doubt that both Clare and Angus had had an uncomfortably narrow escape from death or serious injury. He was satisfied that no harm had been done beyond what a day or two of rest would put right, and having seen Clare

261

and Angus relaxed in bed and eating their suppers with good appetites he turned his attention to the two who were at the table with him. Nevill was very controlled, but in some subtle way he looked older and as though it would be a long time before he could be rid of the horror. Frances too was pale and shadowy and very quiet, but behind it she had a look of contented happiness which brought a smile to her uncle's eyes and he was not greatly surprised when Patsy Henderson appeared in the drawing-room after dinner. He greeted him very warmly saying,

"Patsy—when you have a daughter you'll know what I'm feeling now. No man was ever more grateful than I am to you and Nick and Angus."

"I didn't do much, sir," said Patsy. "Angus really did it. He could have managed alone, I think."

"No," said Nevill briefly, "he couldn't."

"Well—between you three it was done, thank God!" said Mr. Fielding and then he smiled and glancing at Frances added, "Have you decided to adopt Course Two after all, Henderson?" Frances and Nevill looked at him, Frances puzzled and Nevill with quick amused enlightenment, and Patsy blushed a little and laughed.

"Course Two it is, sir," he replied. "I couldn't wait."

"Well, I don't think you're taking an undue risk," said the Headmaster. "Frances, my darling, come and give me a hug. You're a very dear child and I'm glad we've managed to place you in Ledenham."

As he finished speaking the door opened and Clare in her dressing-gown came in. She went straight to Patsy and putting her arms round his neck, kissed him. "Dear Patsy," she said. "How lovely to have you for a cousin and—and thank you."

Patsy's arm was round her and he smiled down at her.

"You were a chump, weren't you?" he said. "What came over you?"

"Nevill," Clare answered promptly. "I suddenly thought that if I fell off I'd never be married to him after all, and of course that did it."

Patsy grinned.

"What are you going to do with her, Nevill? D'you want me to take her up again tomorrow to get her nerve back?"

"No," said Nevill firmly. "We'll abandon her nerve. Clare, you may kiss him once more and that will do," and Patsy kissed her very affectionately and they sent her back to her bed.

Unlike Henry Courtney, Patsy was in no hurry to make his engagement known, and the Headmaster pointed out that Frances must have her parents' consent before it could be announced.

"But they won't mind will they, Uncle Hugh?" she asked.

"I shouldn't think so. We'll send a cable if you like. But nobody is to be told till you have their consent."

The cable was sent and next day Frances talked on the telephone to her parents in New York, but before she did so the news of her engagement was all round the School. Nobody knew who was responsible for the leakage. Nick Vincent said that nobody who caught sight of either Patsy or Frances could miss it, but the suspicion that Mrs. Higgins in the School House Kitchen might have had something to do with it was strengthened by Delia's remarks at lunch time on Monday.

"A'weel Mr. Henderson, so you're the lucky one," she remarked cheerfully. "And she's a real lucky lass too. Mr. Cameron can have your rooms then. It fits fine."

Patsy in public was an exceedingly reticent lover. He was never heard to address Frances by any endearing name, and he would not even take her arm, she told Clare, till he had searched the surrounding country with field-glasses and made sure there was nobody to see. He suffered a good deal from the congratulations, jokes and mockery of his friends and said,

"I wish they'd shut up. It's nobody's business but ours."

"I don't believe," said Frances rashly, "that you can be much in love with me. You're not a bit like Henry."

Patsy whirled round and snatching her off her feet kissed her till she begged for mercy.

"And?" he said still holding her.

"All right, all right," said Frances weakly. "Subject closed. You can put me down."

"Just remember your limitations," Patsy said putting her gently on her feet. "You're very small."

The short remainder of the term passed unremarkably. Angus, moving rather stiffly, returned to his sets two days after the Needle adventure, and finding to his intense disgust that he was regarded as a hero, spent a further two days blushing almost continuously.

"He's begun clearing his throat again," said Nick to Clare grinning broadly.

"It'll pass," she said. "He's all right."

"Oh yes," Nick agreed. "He's established, is Angus. Clare,

do you remember our conversation in the copse at the beginning of term?"

Clare laughed.

" 'Patsy's gone in,' you said, and 'it's dogged as does it,' or words to that effect."

"And I was perfectly right as I always am," said Nick complacently. "Quite an eventful term, one way and another."

"You're telling me," said Clare with feeling.

Frances went about looking at Ledenham with new eyes and entirely happy in the knowledge that it was to be her home. She cast off her visitor's detachment and became at once part of the School. Some boys had always greeted her. More had grinned and saluted after she helped with the play, but now they all did. She was, as she remarked grandly to Patsy, one of the School ladies.

The Perrys' gave a dinner party to celebrate the two engagements and Mr. Perry told them with great satisfaction that he had seen that Patsy was doomed.

"I knew how it would be. Saw it from the first, Patsy," he said gleefully.

His sister looked at him surprised.

"I don't see how you could, you know, Humphrey," she said gently. "I never thought of it. But it's delightful," and she added smiling at them all, "Such nice young people."

Mrs. Fielding returned, unfamiliarly tanned, the day before term ended, accompanied again by Alison and Mike. Her husband and Clare were both good letter-writers and she needed to be told very little about the events of the term, but she looked at Nevill with searching eyes before she smiled at him and kissed him and she turned with something of the same look to Frances. Alison was almost overwhelmed by the interest of two engagements and the prospect of two bridesmaid's frocks and presents, but Mike, after a few minutes of embarrassment during which he stared with offended hostility at Nevill, and turned coldly away from his adored Patsy, forgot all about "romance" as he called it contemptuously, and went his usual way.

The last event of the term was the School Concert. Trunks were packed and were being conveyed to the station in relays by Willie, and the School would be empty of boys by 8 o'clock on the following morning. Everywhere were the signs of exodus, and messy tidyings up took place all over the School, but at 8 o'clock in the evening everybody gathered, in an atmosphere of festivity, for the concert. Ledenham had a pleasant, if somewhat embarrassing custom of greeting its masters on this occasion, and as each one entered the hall he was met with cheers.

Frances heard it first when she entered with the School House party and was told by Clare that the uproar of cheering was the School expressing respectful regard for its Headmaster. He made no acknowledgement, she noticed, but looked as calm and bland as usual. She watched and listened with interest as the masters, all of them known to her now, came in, and was almost moved to tears by the pandemonium which arose when Patsy and Nick appeared, climbing to the back of the ramp which held the choir.

But the ovation of the evening was reserved for the unsuspecting Angus when he arrived alone and rather late at the back of the hall and looked round for somewhere to sit. The tales of climbing exploits and particularly that on the Needle had gone round and lost nothing in the telling. Next term would be the Rugger term and the School had suddenly remembered that here was an International forward. The drink and the drugs had been long forgotten. They rose to Angus as one boy with a roar of cheering, and Angus, after one startled glance, rushed from the hall in a panic.

"Angus appears to have left us," said Mrs. Fielding laughing.

"On the contrary," said the Headmaster. "Angus has arrived."

Ledenham School basked in the sunshine of a morning at the end of July, its holiday peace enhanced rather than disturbed by the sounds of the groundsman's distant tractor, the leisurely clankings of cleaners, the lorry unloading tradesmen's equipment, and by the sight of one solitary boy, Michael Fielding, thoughtfully proceeding on his bicycle to an unknown destination.

Also published by Greyladies
Books set in Girls' Schools

LADY OF LETTERS

by Josephine Elder

Lady of Letters explores many of the themes
familiar from Josephine Elder's popular girls' school
stories; friendship, love of learning, being true to
oneself. It tells the story of Hilary Moore, as
scholar, history mistress in a girls' high school,
university lecturer and writer.

Thoroughly at home in her academic life, it is in
Hilary's friendship with an older science teacher
and her romance with a young doctor that tensions
arise and her ideals are tested.

The intriguing disclaimer, 'The characters in this
book are might-have-beens not portraits' invites
speculation on how much of this story is based on
Miss Elder's own life.

SUMMER'S DAY

by Mary Bell

A beautifully written novel set in a girls' boarding school in the late 1940s. The characters – the teaching and domestic staff, their families and a few pupils – are finely drawn with affectionate wit, pithy observation and gentle understatement. The threads of their lives intertwine as the summer term progresses - a perfect school story and an unforgettable gem of a book.

CONVENT ON STYX

by Gladys Mitchell

The nuns of the Order of Companions of the
Poor summon eminent psychiatrist and sleuth
Dame Beatrice Lestrange Bradley to
investigate a series of anonymous letter, but
when she arrives the prime suspect has just
been found drowned in the convent pool
school pond, with, appropriately enough, her
own massive Family Bible.

Dame Beatrice leads a fine cast of eccentric
characters as she gradually unravels the truth
from the sniping gossip of the convent's
paying guests and the rumours of ghosts
among the school children.